A DEAL WITH DEVILS

A DEAL WITH DEVILS

ALL THAT IS HOLY
BOOK 3

JEREMY KNOP

Podium

To Ashley,

for keeping me on track.

Podium

A DEAL WITH DEVILS

PART ONE

CHAPTER 1

Sand from the crest of a low ridge, kicked up by a harsh wind, swept across the cobblestone road. The wind died just as abruptly as it had come, leaving the stale heat of the desert unchallenged beneath a sky of sooty gray clouds hanging low. So low it seemed they might scrape the mountaintops on the eastern horizon as they came rolling slowly over the arid plains of sand and stone.

A small caravan came from the northwest along the old sand-strewn cobblestone highway leading from the Severed Pass to the Darrood River. Three bazaks and eight people wrapped in dark linen. At the head of the trudging column walked a giant made of red clay, taking slow, sure steps. A round-edged humanoid shape the height of nearly two men. As tall as the behemoth stood, the clay man's polearm rose taller still, its crescent blade glinting even in the dim light filtering through the dark clouds above.

The men and women moved wearily, a few of them leaning on spears or quarterstaves as they walked. All of them lowering their heads against the buffeting of another coarse breeze. The bazaks were unfazed, ambling steadily along—their backs loaded high with sacks and bundles, baskets and bladders hanging down their sides.

They were half a day's trek to the next caravansary, little more than a few huts set around a well that was nearly dry. Soon the caravans' paths would be diverted from this section of road, instead taking a smaller southeastern road to avoid the risk of attracting the ire of the devil remnants still harrying the northern roads.

Veering south, the sand began to give way to gravel and bare rock. The land was mostly flat save for the occasional craggy ridge and the wind-carved boulders and spires scattered about the hamada like the weathered monuments of long-dead gods.

A whisper through the stagnant air preceded the fleshy *thwack* of an arrow striking flesh. The rearmost bazak bellowed a reedy, sonorous bleat as it stumbled a step forward and pitched to its side. An arrow, fletched with crow feathers, stuck halfway out of the tumbling bazak's head, just behind a skin-draped eye now bulging and twitching in its socket as the bazak's simple brain sparked and sputtered in bursts of pain and fright.

Shaded beneath an arch of rock weathered in the belly of a narrow fin of sandstone running parallel to the road a few spans away, Odessa crouched, loosing another arrow. One of the linen-clad figures dropped to a knee, clutching the arrow now sticking out above their hip.

The caravan burst into disorder. Shouted commands and cries were muted in the stale desert air. Before the figure at the head of the column could haul their panicking bazak to a run, an arrow punched through their chest and they fell in a heap. The figure was trampled beneath the bazak's wide, rough-padded feet as the beast ambled as fast as its six ungainly legs could manage.

The remaining bazak was hauled off the road away from Odessa as the rest of the caravan scattered, taking up arms or taking cover behind the bazak's corpse. The Red Clay Warrior was already bounding across the barren land toward her, its polearm held across its chest as it charged over the few spans of rough rock between it and its attacker.

Odessa scrabbled beneath the arch and slid behind the fin's far side as an arrow from the caravan struck the arch with a subdued crack. Her entehlo rose from its uneasy rest at her quick movement. Odessa yanked the entehlo's reins free from the stone she had wrapped them about and flicked them over the beast's broad neck. After hoisting herself onto the saddle, she stowed the bow in a scabbard hanging from the saddle horn. The entehlo responded quickly to the light dig of Odessa's heels. She urged the beast toward the arch and snatched her spear from where it leaned by the mouth of the arch. Through the arch's wide mouth she could hear the Warrior's lumbering steps. It was near.

The Red Clay Warrior had nearly reached the mouth of the arch when she and her entehlo burst out from behind the fin of stone at a full gallop, a blur of brindle and iron leading a trail of dust in its wake. A span away along the ridge, the Warrior turned to pursue, charging toward her in graceless, bounding steps. But it was too late. Lying low across the saddle—spear standing flat, the end of its shaft tucked between her side and her iron arm—she charged across the hardpan in a wide arc around the mud-built abomination, moving much too fast for it to catch her.

An arrow glanced off her entehlo's crude armor with a sound like the snap of a harp string. The six caravanners still on the road scrambled into a loose formation, spears and sickle-shaped swords at the ready. Another desperate arrow whistled through the air, streaking past Odessa before the archer dropped their bow and unsheathed a short sword from their belt.

The entehlo's hooves pounded the hard rock and closed the last span of hardpan between Odessa and the caravan in what felt like both an instant and an eternity.

Only a few galloping steps away, Odessa rose in the saddle and steered the entehlo slightly to the right, bearing down upon the center of the hastily formed line bristling with spears and swords. Her heels dug into the entehlo's sides for one final push.

The line quavered then crumbled before the entehlo reached the range of their spears. Some turned to run, others broke off to flank Odessa. But it did not matter what they did. Death came for them whether they fought or ran or surrendered. That was the way of the world.

Her entehlo crashed into those fleeing bodies, trampling two beneath its hooves as it plunged through the caravan. The cries of the trampled were loud and pitiful behind her. Odessa wheeled the beast around and charged again before those still standing could regroup. A man with a spear came to meet her charge as the rest of his companions scattered. Just before her entehlo's hooves were bearing down upon him, he dropped to a knee, the butt of his spear rammed into the stony ground. The point of his spear aimed at the entehlo's chest.

Odessa stood in stirrups and leaned forward in the saddle. With a wooden clatter, she knocked the spearpoint aside. The entehlo's forward motion drove her spear deep into the man's chest.

She let the spear fall from her grip and raced past the man toward the three remaining caravanners in flight. As she charged after them, she slid a long-handled club of devilish design from a saddle loop. The slender iron handle curved up from the grip and flared to a sort of knob with short, stout spikes like the spines of a nopal. She brought the club down upon the backs of the fleeing caravanners, tearing through flesh and crushing bone. The last caravanner fell with her skull caved in, blood and brain leaking into the sand.

As the last caravanner's legs ceased their twitching kicks, Odessa leaped from the saddle and slapped the entehlo's hindquarters, sending it running. The Red Clay Warrior's footsteps shook the earth beneath her feet, and Odessa turned just in time to leap away from the lunging thrust of the polearm.

Balanced on the balls of her feet, Odessa took the club in both hands and waited, standing just outside the clay man's immediate reach. The Warrior's face was a blank sheet of clay sculpted in the vaguest form of a humanoid shape.

In shallow hollows at the center of its head, two stones of polished jade stared, unblinking. The emptiness in those twin bits of jade beheld only enemies and things to be slain. Blind to all else.

Red Clay Warriors gave no indication before their unnaturally long arms snapped into a thrust or a slash. No shift in stance or tension in their hulking clay form. Having no particularly vital areas to guard, they were always in an offensive posture. When the Warrior began to close the distance between them with its usual plodding steps, Odessa knew to be wary. She held the club out across her chest, the head raised near her shoulder. The club was almost too short to be wielded with two hands, so if she had to block there was a good chance she would lose fingers or a hand. The devil she had killed and taken it from had wielded it in one hand with a shield in the other. But she had brought no shield today. Predators such as she were not made to be on the defensive.

When the polearm shot forward, Odessa leaped to the side. Before the thrust had reached its apex, the polearm's crescent blade was swinging toward her, slashing up toward her armpit. Her ironclad arm took the blow, and she elbowed the blade upward. Her accursed arm flared with needles of hot agony that reverberated through her bones like the aftershocks of an earthquake. She ducked beneath the blade before it could come down again and made for the Warrior's legs. With a tremendous swing, the club struck the Warrior's knee like an axe felling a tree. It punched out a chunk of hard clay from the Warrior's leg in a cloud of red dust. Clay crumbled to the ground as the Warrior recoiled, exposing a sliver of bone. The butt of the polearm swung and caught Odessa in the ribs but not before she could swing again. Her club struck its intact leg just above its knee, connecting with a loud crack.

The polearm's shaft pitched her aside and she stumbled backward, clutching her battered side. Her breath hitched as her ribs stabbed her with every inhalation.

The Warrior tottered, huge cracks in its legs growing and widening beneath its weight. Red blood began to seep through the cracks from some spring deep within its clay body. Stolen blood. The blood of tortured innocents. An unsteady step and it collapsed, one leg crumbling to pieces. A cloud of red dust rose around it.

Odessa hefted the club in an iron hand and circled the Warrior as it thrust and swung its polearm ineffectually. When her circling brought her behind the Warrior, it tried to spin and face her, but its remaining leg broke with the twisting motion. It fell to its side with a heavy thud.

Before it could even attempt to crawl or right itself, Odessa brought the hammer down on its featureless head. She left the club embedded in its head and punched her iron fist in the center of its chest until her fist found the curved slope of a human skull. In the mouth of the skull, she found the heart. Clay cracked and crumbled around her arm as she grasped the stony lump of flesh. She jerked the heart free with a snarl and the Warrior slumped onto its face, inert and crumbling.

Still covered in chunks of blood-wet clay, the heart was dark like a bruise. Clenched in her unwieldy iron hand, it looked so small. Whoever the heart had once belonged to was certainly long since forgotten. The victim of a pitiless god.

Odessa crushed the heart in her fist and held it in her grip. Blood dripped from between thick iron fingers, running in channels carved in the metal to the dry dirt. The thrumming throb in her iron-bound arm grew less intense as the blood ran along the runic channels. Whatever life was left in that stolen heart she took for herself. The life pouring from the dead all about her filled the air like a sickly sweet perfume, and her iron-bound arm took it greedily. The carvings covering every facet of the metal fused to her flesh with magic, and rivets drew the essence from the blood and, to a lesser extent, the air to edify her own stolen blood. When she felt she had taken all the energy the heart had to offer, she dropped the pulped lump of meat to the ground.

The caravanner with an arrow in their hip had stumbled to their feet and now ran down the road in a limping lurch. She sighed and wrenched the club from the Warrior's head. The heady intoxication of battle had lost its potency over the few long months since she left Asha-Kalir.

She walked after them languidly. The club swung at her side, its gory head coated in clay and dust.

At the sound of her steadily approaching footsteps, the caravanner glanced back. In the slit of their litham, their eyes grew wide. Odessa could see the hope in their eyes sputter and die in an instant. They turned and sped, but as their injured leg took their full weight, it buckled. Crying out, they spilled onto the road. It took Odessa only a few moments to reach them at her unhurried pace.

They clutched their bleeding hip and writhed. The arrow's shaft had snapped as they fell onto it. Their screaming cries hitched, then intensified as Odessa stopped before them. They were the cries of a woman driven hysterical by pain and abject terror. A human mind helpless in the face of death and its terrible inevitability.

"Please don't do this," the woman sobbed. "Please don't kill me. You don't have to kill me."

The first time Odessa had raided a caravan she had apologized to the caravanners. Told them that she did not want to kill them but she had no choice. But apologies did little to soften the cruelty of murder. There was no avoiding the cold callousness of taking a life.

The woman's shielding hands rose a moment too late. The club struck the top of her skull and her tear-filled eyes spasmed. One eye rolled upward and steadily twitched until Odessa pulled the club free. The woman's body fell in a loose heap, then lay still in the middle of the road. The dark blue linen turned darker still with blood; the gaps between cobblestones became shallow canals of red.

Odessa had cried after raiding that first caravan. Cried until the innocent blood on her hands had dried. But her eyes were dry now. The emptiness inside her that screamed to be sated had taken much from her. Hollowed her out until she was nothing but the hunger that drove her onward. The insatiable hunger and rage smoldering endlessly in the husk of her heart.

Silence again lay heavy in the stagnant desert air. Barren rock stretched toward the east and into plains of sand over the horizon. Lost life evaporated into the air. Air now thick with the stench of spilled blood and voided bowels. And Odessa had to drink it all in. To stew in the gruesome wake of her survival.

The veins of her iron-clad arm throbbed with waves of invigoration as blood splashed across the cobblestones and ran along the channels between them and was drunk by the desert sands. Sand blew across the road and over the corpses littering the ground. The desert's infinite avarice would not allow the bodies to even grow cold before it came to take them.

Moving among the corpses, her runed arm thrummed. Subdued shame, impotent and querulous, shut Odessa's eyes as she soaked in the carnage. Relished the tingling across her skin, life dissipating and seeping into her. She distanced herself from her own treacherous body, finding some faraway place in her mind where there was only quiet and dark. Because she could not leave until she had taken in every bit of stolen life that rose from the lifeblood spilled on the road and from the hot, coppery exhalations of those final breaths. Odessa's rapacious hunger was absolute.

CHAPTER 2

She rode west across spans of bare rock into barren scrubland. Over the rolling hills and low mesas in the distance, the mountains dwarfed the lesser slopes, rising from the murk of the gray-tinged horizon to blot out the setting sun. Two bazaks followed her across the scrub, the first in the short train lashed to the back of her entehlo's saddle. The legs and flanks of the third, felled bazak had been wrapped in some of the caravan's fine silks and loaded on the backs of the two bazaks. Blood soaked the silks, vibrant blues and yellows and oranges all turned a ruddy shade of brown.

It had taken her most of the afternoon to find the two living bazaks, load them with everything the caravan had worth taking, and butcher the dead bazak. Daylight had been nearly strangled from the sky by the time she reached the first low hills. The bazaks' splayed feet crunched over the thin layer of flinty scree at the base of the slope as they plodded along behind her. The entehlo mounted the slope, its almost dainty hooves navigating the craggy terrain with the sort of inborn deftness the bazaks trailing it lacked. They were made for plodding through barren sand and scrub, not scaling slopes. They managed the first hill, cresting it with barely a sonorous grunt but as they drew closer to the mountains, the slopes became steeper and the footing more treacherous. After the first few slopes, the land gave way to sharp, wind-carved cliffs and mesas.

Odessa had come to know these particular hills well in the weeks since she had settled within them, but not well enough to lead two tired bazaks through them at night.

Should have just taken the water and meat, she told herself. *Shouldn't have wasted my time with these two.* But abducting bazaks had been part of the reason she had taken to ambushing caravans in the first place. She knew they were not a waste of time or effort. But as deep night swept over the bare plains behind them and the shadows in the valleys around them deepened, she could not help the denigration. Reproach was one of the only comforts left to her. Like a heavy, lice-ridden blanket wrapped around herself to keep from bitter cold. A rough blanket she pulled tight around herself until it chafed her skin raw.

Her self-reproach did nothing to keep the cold of night at bay. Baking heat evaporated in an instant as darkness bled warmth from the earth. Odessa licked her cracked and bloody lips and readjusted herself in the saddle. There was still a scant bit of light in the western sky above the mountain tops, but it was fading like the flickering wick of a wax-drowned candle.

She urged the entehlo to quicken its pace through a valley that cut through two jagged spurs of rock rising from the ground so abruptly they brought to her mind a massive ship dashed upon some desolate shore, split in two so she could ride the length of its ossified belly. On the other side of the twin buttes, across a few spans of boulder-pocked earth that rose in a sharp grade, a long mesa dominated the land, running from north to south like a wall of sun-bleached stone.

The entehlo trotted at a brisk pace over increasingly unstable ground. Bare earth turned to sharp, shifting scree. Up the slope, scree turned to larger rocks and talus. The bazaks plodded languidly, pulling at the end of their ropes. Their feet were much better suited to the loose rock, but their three pairs of legs were ungainly and ill-suited for a decent trot. They moved north halfway up the slope. The mesa's walls were now only barely outlined in the oppressive dark. Its face was a shadow with crags of pure black. Odessa glanced back and in the dark she could still clearly make out their bulking pale forms, lagging behind and huffing with displeasure. An irritated hiss passed through her teeth, and for a moment she wanted little more than to cut them loose and let them fend for themselves, their backs still burdened with all her ill-gotten spoils.

A sudden jerk and her head snapped forward. The entehlo's hooves scrabbled in the scree, stumbling for a moment before steadying itself. Heart skipping half a beat, Odessa yanked back on the reins without thinking. The entehlo whipped its head and snorted, the bit biting into the corners of its mouth. Scree slid and shifted beneath its hooves.

It took a few moments for both the entehlo and Odessa to calm. *I know better than to hurry on these rocks. Especially in the dark.* She pulled her reproach tight about herself until her entire body was tense with a white-knuckle contempt. *I could have cracked my skull open. And good riddance for it. For all the sense I've got in it, my head should be dashed upon these rocks.*

The bazaks bleated softly behind her, the cold causing their flabs of loose skin to crease and contract. Her clenched jaw was the only thing that kept her from shouting at them. She eased her entehlo to a slow amble, moving north again. She needed to edge closer to the mesa so she didn't accidentally stumble past the mouth of the passage, but after her impatience had nearly caused the whole lot of them to go spilling down a slope of sharp rocks, she did not trust herself.

Her iron hand shifted in her lap, tightening into a loose fist. *We've made enough noise. If there were anyone in this valley they would already be on us.* Her fingers ground together with a low metallic scrape. Even in her mind, the words sounded hollow. A wheedling justification. Her hand was suddenly heavy in her lap. *It's not as if I really have a choice.*

She raised her hand and coaxed the incessant thrum in her blood together. The pounding heat coalesced in her palm and fingertips. In an instant, fire bloomed along the black iron of her hand, tongues of flame coming from a series of vents and joints in the metal. The entehlo shuddered a bit beneath her at the sudden fire, but the bazaks paid it no mind. The flames wreathing her outstretched hand burned bright enough for her to see a man's length ahead of them. It burned bright enough to be a proper signal fire for anyone within a day's ride, she thought.

With the light, she was able to spot the small cairn of flat stones marking the way a half hour later. At the cairn, she turned the entehlo toward the mesa and headed up the slope. The entehlo knew the nuances of the path up the slope. It was steeper here. There were more rocks and larger boulders. A massive rockslide had taken half the mesa's face, and its remains lay spilled over the ground in a wide swath of boulder and stone. Despite the steep grade, the larger rocks shifted less than the scree and made for a safer ascent if one was sure of their footing.

The bazaks were slow moving up the mesa's shattered face, pulling at their ropes as Odessa and her entehlo guided them over uneven stones and around the mouths of crevices hidden between boulders and rocks. Crevices lying in wait to take a passing, inattentive foot. To break ankles or legs. Even trap the poor oblivious walker in its stony grip until exposure withered them to sun-bleached bone. Odessa tried holding her flaming hand behind her in the hopes that a bit of light would embolden the bazaks, but diverting the light from what lay before them slowed the entehlo, its steps tentative and unsure.

Eventually, Odessa conceded and held her hand over her head, the flames lashing more furiously than before, and cast a relatively wide radius of light around the lot of them. Crevices all about them grew wider and deeper with shadow. Holding her hand aloft, Odessa could only imagine how many eyes might be following the light she so brazenly waved about the night. And how far the light of her fire would travel in full darkness. A lump of irritation swelled in her throat. *If these damned beasts could just walk I wouldn't have to do this,* she thought, her teeth grinding.

At the top of the slope, she extinguished her arm with a long sigh and a flick of the wrist. The fire flickered into the dark, the last tongues of flame clinging to the runes carved along the gauntlet before guttering out.

The rockslide had carved a hollow in the middle of the mesa, leaving a shelf of rock hanging above it. Odessa climbed stiffly from the saddle, the muscles of her legs and back tight and sore. The top of the slope was almost solid, and the beasts seemed glad for it. As Odessa walked the entehlo and bazaks toward the back of the hollow, they moved with a steady, unhurried surety even in the pitch black.

Her eyes not yet readjusted to the dark, Odessa felt along the back of the hollow until the side of her hand brushed against a boulder pressed tight against the wall. The boulder was a lump of vaguely rectangular sandstone nearly twice as tall as she. She put the reins between her teeth and slid her fingers into the gap between boulder and wall. With a quiet grunt deep in her throat, she heaved the boulder away from the wall a crack, then slid her arm in the gap. She pressed her shoulder against the stone and shoved the boulder from the wall. The scrape of stone on stone was loud in the silence of night.

Behind the boulder, a wide, almost triangular fissure opened in the wall. A scant bit of light came from deep within the bowels of the fissure. When the boulder was clear of the wall, Odessa took the reins from her mouth and, with a tug, led the entehlo and its train into the cave. The bazaks dragged their many feet and pulled against their leads, but after a few moments of resistance they relented and followed Odessa and the entehlo into the dark stone passageway.

The entrance of the cave was cool. The scent of earth and faint staleness. The dry craggy walls were almost comforting after another day in the open vastness of the desert. A desert seemingly unsuitable for human life. A desert rife with her enemies. The cave was her temporary home, and, as such, just stepping over the threshold loosened something within her, something overwrought and beginning to fray.

The passage descended and twisted around the bulk of some long-buried mass of rock. The foothills were made in the tumult of the World Serpent's death. In its writhing, the Serpent had thrown a cataclysmic spray of dirt and rock into the air and mounded the earth in massive ridges on either side of its twisting body. Shattered rock and dirt piled high had formed the foothills and in their tumultuous formation held within them myriad gaps and crevices made ever wider as dirt was stripped from stone. In these ancient caves, Odessa found a vestige of solace. Of home.

As she rounded a narrowing bend in the passage, the glow of scant firelight was unrestrained. The smell of smoke and entehlo droppings was strong. Odessa led the beasts down the short length of passage into the dim flicker of the firelight. The passage opened into a round cavern almost the same length across as her family's hut in Kalaro.

"You're back!" Poko said, fluttering toward her from their mound of fine cloth by the fire. "I was getting worried."

Odessa brushed past Poko's hovering and hauled the beasts to the corral. She had cordoned off nearly half of the cavern with a rough wall of sandstone rocks and leaned a gate made of stiff hide against the opening. Once the beasts were in their corral and the gate had been replaced and secured with a large rock, Odessa made for the passage again.

"Wait!" Poko called, darting to her side. "You just got back. Where are you going?" Their voice dripped with sickly sweet, desperate worry.

"Closing the entrance," Odessa said flatly, sparing Poko a sidelong glance as she spoke. "Is that all right with you?"

"Oh," Poko said, fluttering back away from her with their hands raised in supplication. "Yeah, that's all right. Sorry."

Odessa left without another word. The vestige of home she found in this cave was the ghost of a bygone life. Haunting her. Mocking her. She lived as an animal. Returning to her filthy den as the sun fell, to sleep and struggle to survive another day.

Using the crude handholds she had chipped from the boulder at the cave's mouth, she dragged it back against the wall and sealed herself inside the makeshift home she so resented.

CHAPTER 3

Odessa sat with her knees to her chest and stared into the fire. Tongues of flame rose from dry dung burned to embers. Bazak legs sizzled above the fire, hanging from the shaft of a short spear set horizontally between two misshapen adobe pillars. The scents of smoke, cooking meat, and dung mingled in the stale air of the cave. Her armor laid beside her, bloody and stinking of sweat. The entehlo and bazaks loudly chewed their small portions of stolen grain and drank tepid water from a trough made of leather stretched over a wood frame. Their loads now lay in a pile with the rest of her ill-gotten gains next to the corral. Half-empty sacks of grain and beans thrown on top of fine cloth and intricately crafted jewelry. The only pieces of jewelry she had found use for were an ivory comb and a bronze hair pin she sometimes used to pick her teeth. Bazak meat was stringy.

Poko sat across from her on their mound of linens and silks, watching her. Firelight danced in their black eyes. Pleading eyes. Pathetic eyes. Odessa turned from them and their incessant gaze, taking her armor onto her lap, along with a strip of leather to which she had glued a layer of coarse sand. She scoured the blood and grime from her armor, working slowly and gently. The glue she had made from entehlo hide was a poor adhesive and the sand came off easily.

"I know what you're doing," Poko said.

"I'm cleaning my armor," Odessa said dismissively.

"You're avoiding conversation."

Odessa focused her attention on scouring bits of scalp, brain, and clotted blood from the scales of iron.

"You can't keep doing this," Poko said.

"I don't have a choice."

"You don't have to do this alone though."

"Fine." Odessa dropped the armor and balled the leather in her fist. "The next caravan is all yours. Get your hands dirty for once. Get some blood beneath your nails."

"You know that's not what I mean."

"Tell me what you mean then."

Poko sighed. "Do you have to be so difficult?"

"Just tell me. Tell me what I should be doing differently. What am I doing wrong? Do you have some issue with the way I keep both of us alive?"

"Of course not," Poko said. "But you shouldn't carry the whole burden by yourself. You have to talk to me. Or that fire in you will burn you up."

Odessa snorted. "I shouldn't carry it by myself. What choice do I have? And what will talking do? Will that keep us fed? Will that keep the Red Clay bastards and the devils from killing us in our sleep?"

Poko looked down at their folded hands. "No."

Odessa took up her armor again and began scouring it roughly. No matter how meticulously she scrubbed, there would always be bloodstains that remained. She had come to terms with that but still she scrubbed and scoured. Futile as it was, she tried and tried.

"I know you're doing what you have to," Poko said quietly as Odessa scoured the gore-spattered hem of the armored skirt. "And I know you've been through a lot. But you can't let it eat you alive like this. There's no light in your eyes anymore. The way you go through the day now, it's like you're sleepwalking all the time."

Odessa didn't look up from her work. Embers of anger smoldered in her chest but did not give way to wrathful flames. There was little inside her to burn. Everything was already burned to cinders and ash. She was hollow save for those embers. And one day even those would be gone.

One of the bazaks folded its many legs beneath its bulk with a deflating sigh. It shifted its weight from side to side as if to burrow into the stony floor. The gentle scrape of tough hide against rock, the grating of Odessa's scouring, and the crackle of the fire were the only sounds in the cavern for a long while.

By the time Odessa finished her scouring, Poko was asleep. The majority of Poko's days were spent sleeping. For a while Odessa had wondered with despondency why Poko had not left her. Why they refused to leave and live their own life. She had been grateful Poko stayed by her side. But over time that gratitude had soured. She resented the fairy's presence. Every day when she returned to the cave, a part of her hoped Poko would not be there to greet her. That Poko had flown away without a word. Sometimes when Odessa left for a day of robbery and murder, she would leave a gap between the passageway and boulder. A gap large enough for a fairy in flight.

There was no reason Poko should suffer alongside her. But they refused to leave. Odessa wondered sometimes if that was the cause of her sour resentment. The guilt that Poko's continued loyalty bred in her. The guilt that Poko's life had become one of blistering heat, buffeting sand, little water, and ample bloodshed. All because of her. She had ruined Poko's life. She had taken scores of lives, but she was taking Poko's slowly. Agonizingly. She would be the death of them, and she knew it. She resented it. She resented herself. Resented her very existence more and more with each passing day.

Scrubbing the armor brought the metal no closer to an unsullied sheen, but she continued for a while longer. Agonizing over dark spots of blood from untold weeks or months past. By the firelight and with the warding runes carved into her iron arm, no spirits could assail her but still the night was not safe. It was then that her own personal ghosts laid claim to her. In her dreams they waited for her. Dreams that may start as warm and comforting. Dreams of home with her family. A home unaffected by plague or punishment. She and Ayana would be running through lush green grass or picking vibrant flowers and bringing them back to their mother and Kimi in heaping armloads. Or perhaps she and her father would be out on a hunt in the placid Arabako Forest. Creeping through the undergrowth, a contented focus on their faces. But at some point, when she had been wholly taken in by the tender dreamscape, it would turn rotten. Sometimes gradually, first with a cruel offhand comment that progressed to her entire family screaming at her. Her family would berate her and call her terrible names. They would blame her for everything, and she would believe them. Then their screams would lose all semblance of word and thought, and they would be nothing but shrieks of rage and terror and agony.

Sometimes the dreams turned without warning. She and her father would be out on a hunt. Her attention would be on a set of tracks cutting through a thicket and some sound would draw her from the reverie of the hunt. She would invariably look to see her father beside her. His throat wide open. Pouring blood down his chest. His gasping breaths spraying hot blood over her face. A wet, guttural cry and he would make to grab her in a desperate embrace. And she would leap away. Because his eyes, glassy and dull, belied a hatred that chilled her to her core. Like a spike of ice driven into her heart. His bloodless face, contorted by hate and condemnation, was too much for her to bear. Sometimes in her dreams, her limbs were paralyzed. Her body rigid as he approached, stumbling as a never-ending flow of blood rushed from his neck. Sometimes she ran. Ran from his cries. Cries like a bellowing godling skewered by spears. But he would always catch her. There was no escaping his bloody embrace.

She paused her scouring to throw another few clods of dry dung onto the fire. Dark had begun to seep in at the edges of the cave. Gathering in niches in the stone. Pouring in from the three cave entrances leading from the cavern like rivers emptying into a lake. Darkness no longer set her skin crawling and her heart racing, but it still unsettled her. Life in a pitch-black cave had not remedied that. The dark was just too suffocating. Too unbelievably immense.

"You should go to sleep," Poko said. Their voice was small even in the quiet of the cave. "It'll be morning before you know it."

Odessa sat with a huff and took the armor on her lap again. "I still have to oil it."

"That can wait until the morning."

"It can't," she said. "I don't want it to rust."

"It won't rust overnight."

Odessa's mouth tightened into a thin line. Her hands holding the armor in her lap sagged a moment. She wanted to resist the fairy's advice. Out of an aversion to her dreams or out of an insidiously gnawing obstinacy, she wanted to snap at Poko. To spit some bitter, acerbic retort as if doing so would eliminate some of the poison in her veins. If only it were so easy. Then her ill temper would have some purpose.

She kept her mouth shut because she knew Poko was right. Her eyelids were heavy. Her entire body was a knot of aching weariness. She had slept especially poorly the last week or so. Their paltry food stores had been steadily creeping toward empty and the roads around them had been quiet. The thought of raiding another innocent caravan kept her up at night. As did the prospect of starvation. Poko would die first. Odessa knew that. Her cursed body could go without food for a while, sustained only by godsblood. That was what had kept her up at night, she thought. The idea of being alone. If Poko died because of her and she were left alone, the massive bulk of guilt she had accumulated would finally crush her.

Poko was watching her with an odd, inquiring expression. She set the armor aside and sighed. "You win." For a moment, she wanted to smile for Poko's sake but was too tired to even try. Stirring her mouth out of its fixed scowl was an increasingly insurmountable labor.

Poko smiled. "She listens to reason! Miracles do exist!" they said, dramatically looking to the bedded beasts for validation.

The smugness in Poko's smile was like a poker digging and stirring in the coals of her anger. She bit the side of her cheek until she tasted blood and lay down on her threadbare bedroll. "Keep the fire going," she said, the taste of blood renewed with every syllable. "And watch the meat too. Don't let it burn."

Poko sat straight and nodded with exaggerated curtness. "I won't let you down."

She put her back to Poko and the fire then curled in on herself like a sick, wounded animal does before it dies. She made herself small, wanting only peace but knowing she would have none.

CHAPTER 4

The cave was dark. The fire's coals were gray and lifeless, only a dim orange glow hidden in its recesses. Between lumps of burnt dung and beneath a layer of ash, there was that faint flicker of life. Poko didn't know how much time had passed since Odessa had fallen asleep. They had only planned to shut their eyes for a moment.

She's going to kill me. Poko clambered out of their bed toward the dying coals. *I had one job. Just one! Keep the fire going. That's it.* Their small hands fumbled in the dark in search of more fuel. The stack of dry dung was only a small jaunt to the right of the fire, but panic and darkness had made the cavern twist and stretch in all sorts of strange ways.

Well, actually she said to watch the meat too. So that's two things. And I can't be expected to do two whole things, right? Poko shook their head in the dark. The beguiling voice of flimsy justification was a sweet one, but they could not afford to listen to it. *If she wakes up and finds the fire's gone out . . .* The thought tapered off as they combed the dark with blind concentration. The strain of survival had stretched Odessa very thin. The constant threat of being found by Asha-Kalir or devils had worn her down to a sharp and jagged edge. It was up to Poko to take some of the strain from her shoulders before she broke entirely.

It was a delicate matter, keeping Odessa from snapping beneath the pressure. Her mood was as the wind: fickle and sometimes frightening. Poko tried their best to keep her from undue upset. Sometimes they found their best to be lacking.

Their hands found the crumbly lumps of dung and Poko smiled. They reck-oned dung had never in all of history elicited such relief and triumph as in that moment.

With an armload of dry dung and a bit of coaxing, the fire was revived. As small flames rose from the stirred coals and embraced the dung, Poko sat and let the tension in their tiny body loosen and fall away. *Letting the fire go out shouldn't work me up this much. I shouldn't have to tiptoe around her.* But the terrible things Odessa had to do to survive—and the terrible things that had been done to her—had stolen something from her. A warmth amidst all the hurt she carried. It had finally been snuffed out. Poko understood why she had grown distant and irritable, but understanding did not make her any easier to live with. Sometimes Poko thought of taking off some day when she was out ranging through the desert or raiding a helpless caravan. But they knew it was foolish. The desert was too vast and their wings too fragile. Already, the thin, rune-marked membrane grew brittle at the edges. They would not withstand the furious winds of the mountains.

The fire crackled greedily in the cave's silence. Poko edged away from the fire as it overtook the dung. Tongues of fire unfurled and lashed at the darkness. Reckless and mindless in its appetite. *I have nowhere to go anyway,* they reminded themself. As if they could forget. *No Court. No home. Odessa's all I have.*

At night, bedding in a dusty cave in the middle of a barren desert, it was hard for Poko to avoid thoughts of home. Of the life they had lost. All because they had met a girl in the jungle. Because they had tried to trick her. Tried to kill her. They had only wanted to help the Court. To fill their bellies. But well-intended mistakes were like bittersweet poison. It was their fault the Court was no more. Nothing but ash at the heart of a dying jungle.

I couldn't leave her anyway. The thought of leaving Odessa left Poko disgusted with themself. *She needs me. Everyone else has abandoned her or stabbed her in the back. I'm the only one she has left.* Poko glanced over the fire at her sleeping form. Her body twitched restlessly. *And she's the only one I have. We're in this together.* A cold despondency wormed its way into their chest. An icy despair seeping into their core. Like a winter's rain soaking them to the bone. *For better or worse, it's me and her.*

Poko stayed awake for as long as they could, keeping time only by the dimming of the flames and the roasting of the meat. After a few hours by Poko's imprecise internal clock, they let the fire recede until it was but a few short tips of flame flickering from fiery orange hollows in the bed of coals. The legs were a deep, crisp brown with bits of black near the bottom where the shoulder joint hung over the coals. With a fine copper torque Odessa had bent into a straight fire poker, Poko spread the coals, momentarily aroused the tongues of flame and sparks before the cold darkness of the cave came to suffocate them. Slowly the coals were smothered, dissipating their warmth and their light and forcing the orange glow back into the recessed hollows between ash and charred dung.

With the poker, Poko swept a few of the hottest coals into a small earthenware pot that had once held wonderful incense. The terracotta incense burner was as tall as Poko's knee and depicted two serpents intertwined, the both of them spiraling up around the pot's belly, intersecting and separating until each formed a handle. Soot tarnished the intricate glaze work that had once made one serpent sparkle with a rainbow's litany of color and the other gleam with jade and ebony. Poko turned the pot upright and the coals rolled to the bottom among crumbled dung. They replaced the vented top that resembled a mountain's peak between the serpents' heads and let the coals smolder, awaiting the next night's fire.

Odessa awoke a few hours later as the way she often did: with a whimper and a jolt. Her body stiff and her breathing fast and shallow, Odessa remained on her bedroll for a few moments. Whatever dreams she had were not the sort to promptly leave when she opened her eyes. They dug their claws in and left something behind upon waking. Some toxin left in the ragged wounds the dreams rent during the night. Or some residue like putrefied grave wax left smeared in the crevices of her raw and wounded mind.

Poko waited, watching Odessa. When the girl's breathing had slowed and her body's stiffness somewhat loosened, they spoke. "You're safe," they said, reciting the morning's mantra in a soft, gentle whisper. "It was just a dream. You're safe now."

A sound between a groan and a grumble came from deep in Odessa's throat as she rose to a sitting position, her back still to Poko and the ashes of the fire.

"Do you want some water?" Poko asked.

Odessa grunted and shook her head. Her grimy, sweat-crusted tunic was newly wet with the cold sweat of her night terrors.

"Can I do anything for you?"

Odessa shook her head again and rose to her feet, joints groaning and popping. A slight yet deep rasp as her iron arm moved, the thick plates occasionally clattering and grinding against one another. Her iron hand was still stained with blood. She never gave the iron-bound arm the same care she gave her armor. Poko did not know how it had not rusted solid with the amount of blood that had dried in its channels and joints. Most assuredly it was the betrayer's magic that kept it free of rust. The same magic that had fused it to her flesh. A foul magic that now could not be undone.

Iron fingers plucked an ashy coal from the dead fire. A spot of orange shone at one end of the small coal like a single star in a sky of pitch black. "Lamp," Odessa said, her voice rough with sleep.

Poko found the lamp, a simple, unadorned disc of clay, not far from their bed and carefully made their way to the speck of ember-orange. Odessa took the lamp and held the coal to the bit of wick protruding from its mouth. She blew on the ember, gently at first. Coaxing the ember until it glowed a fierce yellow. With each puff, her face became vaguely lit in dim, hellish tones. After a while the wick took from the ember a bit of spark and soon took flame. Odessa set the lamp on one of the pillars beside the fire, pillars she had made from sandy dirt and entehlo urine. The rancid oil stank as it burned, but its light was gentle and warm.

Doused in the gentle light of the lamp, Poko returned to their bed. Drowsiness rested heavily in the hollows of their eyes, but they could not sleep until Odessa left for the day. She made them too anxious. Nervous that their sleep may somehow displease her.

The bazaks and entehlo roused from their slumber as Odessa approached the fence. She drank with cupped hands from one of the large goat-hide waterskins taken from the caravan. The entehlo snorted and grumbled for its morning meal.

Poko burrowed halfway into the folds of their fine bedding. *I'm glad she's using the coals to make fire now at least,* Poko thought. *Small victories.*

Odessa's iron hand made it hard for her to control the intensity of her flames. It seemed that throttling the fire's fury could only be done once the infernal floodgates were opened wide. Any time she brought forth her flames, they came in a tremendous rush from her ironclad fingertips to halfway up her bicep. Odessa had tried to light a lamp with her finger after one of her first raids. The flame had incinerated the wick down into the reservoir and caused the whole lamp to burst in a shower of clay and a spray of fiery oil.

Poko remembered how some of the flaming drops of oil had splashed upon their tunic and nearly immolated them. They remembered the stench of burning oil and singing gossamer. They remembered the panic and terror that had overcome them as they swatted at the flames until the fire died. They were glad Odessa had curtailed the loosing of her fire. It was much too volatile. The flames that leaped from Odessa's flesh brought to Poko only memories of the jungle and screaming fairies. It had been easier to forget them in the old man's hollow or in the civilized walls of Asha-Kalir. But in the lonesome wastes of sand, those memories were never far from Poko's mind. Like soot and ash indelibly staining them for the rest of their life.

After Odessa left with the entehlo, Poko slept curled and buried in their bed for a fair few hours. When they awoke, they added a bit of fuel to the coals in the firepot then fluttered to the entrance of the cave for some much-needed sun.

They squeezed through the gap between passage and stone and into a morosely subdued afternoon. From beneath the shelf of the mesa, the slope of talus and scree and the bare stone beyond was all a dull and dreary beige. Like moth-eaten, filth-encrusted sackcloth stretched over the land. *What I wouldn't give to see some green. Not even trees. Just grass. I would kill to see good, green grass again.*

Poko lazily flitted into the air over the talus slope. Thin strips of bazak meat lay on some flat stones near the mesa's overhang, drying into pemmican. Poko paused over the strips of meat arrayed on the rocks. *If that's not a sign that some-one's living here, I don't know what is,* Poko thought with some dismay. Odessa was careful to hide their tracks, but some concessions had to be made to survive. They understood that. But lately it seemed that the concessions were increasing.

But I guess a fairy flying around is a pretty good indication that a certain someone is here too. If Poko had to be trapped inside the cave for the sake of discretion, they would most certainly lose their mind. Concessions had to be made for sanity as well. *So let's not be too overly cautious, yeah?* they told themselves before taking off for the mesa's flat top.

Alighting on the reddish caprock, Poko hoped the view from above would be grander, but beneath the low-hanging pall of gray-brown, everything was drab and lifeless. Even the domineering mountains in all their overbearing splendor appeared lusterless and even dingy in the dim light of a smothered sun.

Poko wandered atop the mesa for a while, sometimes walking and some-times taking flight. They headed north along the mesa's caprock spine, hoping to glimpse something that was not sandstone and dust.

It was a glint of light that finally caught their eye. Just a momentary flash in the distance. Little more than a pinprick of light far to the north. But it was enough. Poko halted their ambling and stiffened, craning their neck and narrow-ing their eyes.

Far to the north, where the ridges gave way to bare stone and swells of sand, there was a shape. A dark shape. And as they stared, another pinprick glint came and went as the shape shifted ever so slightly.

Dessa? Poko fluttered toward the edge of the mesa, squinting. *Did something happen?*

The dark shape was still. Poko plummeted from the mesa's lip, their wings battering the air. They could picture Odessa bleeding into the sand. A fatal wound from which her lifeblood poured out before her affliction could mend it. *It was only a matter of time. Too many out for her head. And we stayed here too long. Got too comfortable. In spite of everything. We were asking for it.*

They swept over the boulder-strewn hillside like a dry leaf riding the crest of a furious gust. Their stomach twisted, squeezing cold bile up into their throat.

A few moments of frenzied flight brought the dark lump on the horizon into shape. A figure lay prone on sand-scraped earth. Cream-colored cloth, scale armor, and a head wrap.

Poko slowed a few spans from the sprawled body. A tall, thick body. Bigger than Odessa.

Tentatively, they edged a bit closer. Their wings flapped tensely, prepared for an expeditious retreat. "Hello?"

Beneath the black scale armor and loose robes, the body was unmoving. Poko skirted around the body to see the wrapped face as it lay, facing the mesa's cliffs. Two horns protruded from the folds of the headwrap, as thick and long as one of Poko's legs. The head wrap was askew, bunched and covering one eye. Dark skin the color of an overripe cherry laid bare in the crooked slit. The exposed eye was half-closed and rolled back in its socket. The eye was a dark copper color.

A devil. What is a devil doing here? Poko hurriedly spun and surveyed the valley for more devils, expecting to see an army of them pouring over the hills, but there was nothing. They looked back to the still body, fear and curiosity mixing and keeping their feet planted to the earth.

"Hello?" Poko asked again, forcing their voice past a whisper. The dry air seemed to have sapped their mouth of any moisture. After another silent moment, Poko took a careful half step forward. "Are you alive?" A stupid question, but Poko couldn't help but ask.

A twitch of the eyelids. A tiny, barely noticeable, spasm. Poko took a step back as the eyelids flitted. The eye swirled, vertical slit contracting in the gloom of day, and fell upon Poko.

Scales clattered and a hand shot out from beneath its robes. But Poko was already in the air, darting out of its grasp. The hand closed around air where the fairy had been but a moment ago, then fell to the ground in a loose, dejected fist.

"What was that for?" Poko shouted, fluttering far out of its reach now.

The eye followed Poko, then began to drift. Losing focus for a moment before regaining it. The body shifted and Poko darted a bit farther still.

"Small one," a hoarse voice said from beneath sand-choked cloth. "Are you truly there? Or are you some phantasm now come as I lie dying?"

Poko cocked their head, an eyebrow raised. "Of course I'm real," they said a bit defensively. They crossed their arms over their chest and slowed the panicked beating of their wings. "Why wouldn't I be real?"

The body slumped a little, tension dissipating with a relieved sigh followed by a coarse and rasping snort of laughter. "Of course I would finally find you when I'm too weak to do anything," it said. "Such is life, I suppose. A cruel bitch to the end."

Poko narrowed their eyes. "You're looking for me?"

"You and the girl, yes," it said. Its voice was becoming hoarser, barely above a whisper now. "I must speak to her."

Poko's mind raced. They needed to find Odessa. Tell her the devils had found them. They had to leave the cave immediately. But Poko couldn't leave. Something kept them from leaving the dying devil. "What do you need to talk to her for?" Poko asked. "More likely you'd put a blade in her belly as soon as you saw her."

The devil raised its head and shook it. "No," they said, more forcefully. "No, I have terms. An offer. I must speak to her."

"I don't believe you," Poko said. "You're trying to trick me. I can tell, I know all about tricks and ruses." But Poko could not tell. They didn't sense any falseness in the devil's words. But devils were half god and wholly wicked. It was impossible to tell what a creature like that was thinking.

"I'm not," the devil said, weaker now. An air of defeat at the fringes of its voice. "You must believe."

"I don't have to do a thing. You're a scout looking to kill her and I'm not going to believe a word you say," Poko said, flitting above the ground. "So if you're going to die, just die."

The devil's head sagged, the tips of its horns touching the dirt. "If I could only just speak to her before dying." The devil turned its head to Poko. Its eye was imploring and desperate. "Would you take with you a message, small one? If I cannot speak with her, take her my message. Please."

Hearing *please* from the mouth of a devil was a strange sensation. It was wrong. Poko hadn't thought devils knew what *please* meant. They took whatever they wanted. By rights of theft and slaughter, what they wanted was theirs. What use would creatures such as that have for *please*?

It was the incongruity of that single desperate *please* that convinced Poko to at least listen to the devil before it died, baked in the desert. "What's your message?"

The devil rolled unsteadily onto its side and propped itself on a shaky elbow. For a long moment it said nothing, only panted and hissed. But when it spoke, it spoke surely, its voice hoarse and pained but clear. "Tell her I offer her freedom. Sak-Tor wants her head. As does Asha-Kalir. Tell her if she agrees to our terms, she can be rid of the both of them. She can be free. She can have anything she wants."

"So what do you want then? In return for freedom and everything?"

"We want what she wants. At least in part," the devil said. "We want Sak-Tor dead."

CHAPTER 5

The devil sat cross-legged and greedily drank the waterskin Poko brought it. Gulping until it coughed, then draining a bit more. "I haven't had a drink in almost two days," the devil said, the skin limp in its hand. Without the headwrap the devil looked almost human. Save for the slitted eyes and the flash of sharp, bestial teeth when it spoke.

Poko sat a good distance away from it, wary. "Take me through this again," Poko said. "Who are you and what do you want?"

The devil set the waterskin down and looked at Poko with earnest conviction. "I am Khara, daughter of Zarin, the mother of some of Sak-Tor's finest warriors. And I come before you, a deserter and an ambassador. We, the Daughters of Ana Yuma, seek to overthrow Sak-Tor and put an end to centuries of subjugation and rape. And I am of the thinking that Odessa could be an integral part of this revolution."

"Why her?" Poko asked. "She and your kind haven't exactly gotten along."

"My kind often doesn't get along with my kind," Khara said with a sharp-toothed smirk. Then she leaned forward as if to confide in Poko some secret. And there was a gleam in her eyes, a fire in the amber. "I saw what she can do. I was there when she felled Pash-Tor. I saw her snuff his magic out. I know she is more than a mere human. She is something altogether new and wondrous. Sak-Tor has fought and killed most every beast and being in this whole world. But she is something he has never and could never anticipate. And I believe that will be his undoing."

"So you want to use her?"

"Use her?" Khara said. "I want to fight alongside her. I want to be her shield sister. Her fighting—it was incredible. Brutal and raw. Like an animal."

Poko scrutinized her. Peering into her intense, almost fervent eyes. They thought she was telling the truth, but just the thought of trusting a devil's words made them uneasy. Poko's wings fluttered as they weighed the devil's words against their own apprehension. "Swear to me that you're telling the truth. Swear to me that you will not hurt her. Directly or indirectly. Swear it."

Khara straightened, the glint in her eyes flaring with surprise. "I swear no harm will come to her at my hand nor at the hands of my Sisters. If she refuses my offer, I leave and you will never see or hear from us again. If she accepts, I will treat her as one of my own flesh and blood. I swear upon my life, it is so."

Poko nodded. "I hope your word is good." They rose to their feet. "Because if it's not, she'll rip your head off."

Khara smiled. "I would expect nothing less." The devil made to rise but her legs quavered and buckled beneath her weight. She caught herself on one knee and remained in that position for a moment.

"Will you be able to walk?" Poko asked, hesitantly approaching.

"Yes." Khara licked her lips and took a deep breath. "Slowly, but I will manage." With a huff, she pushed herself onto her feet, swaying and tottering but staying upright and steadying after a moment.

"I haven't had a thing to eat in a few days," she said to Poko. "I was forced to eat my entehlo when the beast's body finally gave out. They're not built for such dry, dismal places."

"If you can make it to camp, we'll feed you. As long as you act right."

"Thank you." Khara bent slowly at the waist and picked the waterskin from the ground. "But I truly mean neither of you harm."

"We'll see," Poko said, pushing off from the ground and fluttering at the height of the devil's head. "Do you have any weapons?"

"I'm never without them."

"You will be if you want to talk to her," Poko said.

Khara shrugged. Beneath her robes, she drew two long, straight blades. Both of the blades coal-black and vicious looking. Her hands slid down to the guard, shaped like a ram's head with two curling horns, and she flipped the daggers, holding their grips out to Poko. "Take them."

Poko looked at the daggers and then narrowed their eyes at her. "Those things are nearly as big as I am. What am I going to do with them?" They pulled at their thin tunic. "Do you see any pockets?"

Khara smiled. The blades disappeared beneath her robes and were sheathed. "I was only doing as you said."

Poko groaned. "I meant you'll have to leave them outside of camp or some-thing." They turned and gestured for Khara to follow. *Is annoying me a universal pastime around here or something?* they thought as they made for the cave. Poko tried to keep their mind occupied with such inanities to avoid confronting the fact that they were leading a devil to their temporary sanctum. To Odessa. But that confrontation with the reality of their actions was unavoidable.

This is stupid. This is really, really stupid. Poko's dry mouth had turned their tongue to dust and a vicelike pressure squeezed their chest so tight it was hard to breathe. *But if there's a chance of getting her out of this, we have to at least listen. If it means Odessa doesn't have to raid anymore caravans. If it means she can stop running. Because it's only a matter of time before someone catches up with her.* Poko glanced back at the devil, lagging behind. *I suppose someone already has.*

She'd better be telling the truth. Poko scanned the valley again, scrutinizing every crag and boulder. In every shadow could lay an assassin. Khara's plodding footsteps grew closer as she closed the distance between them. *She has to be telling the truth. For Dessa's sake.*

CHAPTER 6

The drab gray of day had darkened. The bloated clouds were now ash-colored and soot-bottomed. Odessa was halfway to the cavern's entrance when she halted and froze. The entehlo she led, not noticing her abrupt stop, bumped into her back with its nose, then stopped a step behind.

The boulder blocking the cavern entrance was not where it should be. A crack, a few hand widths wide, yawned between the rock and the mesa's eroded face. The right side of the boulder had been dragged from the wall. Scrape marks in the dirt were clear even in the dimness.

Odessa's heart lurched. In an instant, her mind conjured up images of Poko's mashed and mutilated body. A figure hiding in the dark, waiting for her to step through the cavern mouth so it could fall upon her and rip her apart. She gritted her teeth as rage and sudden, overwhelmingly solemn, fear swelled inside her.

She let the lead rope drop and gripped her spear with both hands, waiting. A slow, careful step toward the gap and she could make out a low, throaty voice from somewhere in the depths of the cave. A devil's voice. Quiet conversation she could not make out.

Again she thought of Poko. Barely conscious, as devils broke their delicate bones, one by one. Poko trying to scream, their vocal cords raw and ruptured. Only a hoarse squeal escaping.

A faint light shone from deep within the gap. Odessa crept forward. Her entehlo watched from the mouth of the hollow, the end of its lead rope puddled on the stone. It blinked and watched, put on edge by Odessa's sudden nervousness.

Odessa slipped through the gap, spearpoint leading the way. Through the passage, her footsteps were soft but hurried. Half-crouched, her body was tense. Her blood thrummed. The farther into the cave she went, the more her fear receded. Submitting to hate. Whatever devil dared come into her cave and harm Poko would die screaming. Choking on their own blood. Strangled with their own entrails.

Her fingers tightened on the spear shaft. Knuckles white as she neared the cavern. Then she heard Poko's chirruping laugh, quiet but unmistakable. The laugh froze her mid-step. Poko spoke, the words still too quiet to discern but distinct enough to tell that there was no distress in them. Odessa's brow furrowed and the tension in her body worsened, twisting her until she might break. *What is this?* She swallowed a dry lump in her throat. Her chest tightened around her tremulous heart. An ugly realization pushed through muddling confusion. *Poko's betrayed me.*

The devil spoke, its voice a sonorous purr. "We are really not so different, small one. The bonds of blood and tribe are strong. But the act of breaking them. Breaking them in pursuit of a higher purpose. That is an act of immeasurable strength."

Odessa inhaled slowly, urging her feet to move. Slowly creeping toward the cavern entrance. A devil in her cave. Speaking of loyalty. A sensation akin to purest revulsion squirmed in her belly. Blood pounded in her ears, nearly drowning out the cavern's conversation.

Through the cavern entrance the devil's shadow flickered against the far wall. Its hulking frame, topped with crude, barbarous horns, was on the far side of the fire, facing the cavern entrance. *Waiting for me,* Odessa thought. *Sitting in ambush.*

So far she had only heard one devil's voice and saw but one shadow silhouetted against the wall, but there could be more. That gave her momentary pause, but its grasp was weak upon her. Indignation and hate had their talons sunk deep into her flesh and would not free her any time soon.

"It's hard leaving what you know behind. You just feel lost," Poko said.

"You need purpose," the devil said. "Your purpose is your guiding star."

They spoke like two old friends reunited. Two apostates reminiscing on bygone treacheries. Odessa could take it no longer. Before Poko replied, she burst from the dark into the cavern.

Poko and the devil sat opposite one another across the fire. They were alone. Poko gave a cry as Odessa charged across the cavern. The devil dropped their dripping piece of bazak and jumped to their feet, empty palms held aloft.

The devil hissed in alarm as Odessa's spear rocketed toward its chest. Its raised hand snapped with incredible speed, taking hold of the spear behind its head and yanking it off course.

"Odessa!" Poko shouted. "Stop!"

Odessa tugged the spear, trying to rip it free from the devil's grip and submerge the point in the devil's guts. But the devil's grip was firm, two hands now clamped tight on the shaft.

"Please, stop this," the devil said hurriedly. "I don't wish to fight."

As the devil woman spoke, all Odessa could see was the flashing of razor teeth behind its lips. Odessa roared, reversed her grip, and charged forward, twisting the spear upward and using it as a battering ram, forcing the devil back to the far wall.

The devil, backpedaling, struck the wall with a gasp. The spear laid across the devil's chest, pressed against its ribs. As the devil struggled, pushing against the shaft, Odessa lifted her iron hand from the spear and cocked her fist back. But before she could plow her fist into the devil's skull, Poko alighted onto it, taking hold and clinging to the punching surface of her fist like seaweed stuck to a boulder.

"Stop!" Poko screamed. "It's not what you think! She's not your enemy!"

For a split second, Odessa's fist made to lurch forward. To mash the fairy between iron and shattered skull. To kill both of them in a single, savage blow. Pressure built up inside her. The pounding in her ears like the boom of thunder reverberating all the way down her spine.

She stayed her killing hand and, not taking her eyes off the devil pinned to the wall, said to Poko in a hiss, "Start talking. Now."

Poko explained to her in a spluttering hurry the devil's proposition. "She's not with Sak-Tor or anyone of those devils hunting you down. She's a deserter. She and her Sisters, they're—they want to help you if you will help them." At this, Odessa began shaking her head. "They'll protect you from Sak-Tor and Asha-Kalir! You'll be safe!"

"You're a damned fool, Poko," she said, no kindness in her words. "These things lie and murder as easily as they breathe."

"You should at least hear her out."

"I should cave her head in and be done with this," Odessa said. "Now get off my hand."

Poko squeezed themself tighter against her iron fingers and glared at her intensely but said nothing more. A certain strain built in Odessa's arm. She wanted to drive her fist through the devil into the wall behind it. She needed to kill it. But she couldn't. All because of the damned fairy.

Odessa lowered her fist a bit and eased some of her weight from behind the spear across the devil's chest.

The devil took in a wheezing breath. "You are all the fighter I had hoped you to be," she said with a pained grin. "That spear thrust was remarkably fast yet still quite solid. In my current state I could only just stop it."

Odessa's weight bore down on the shaft again, but the devil had reaffirmed her grip and kept it from crushing against her ribs. Odessa scowled. "Shut your mouth." Then she yanked the spear from the devil's grip and, shaking Poko from her iron fist, took it up in both hands again. "Sit down against the wall. And keep your hands out of that robe." Odessa kept the spearpoint trained upon the devil's center as it slid down the wall and sat on the stony ground.

"Odessa, this isn't necessary," Poko cried, darting about her shoulders.

"It is fine," the devil said, a placid, almost beatific look upon its face. "One can never be too cautious in this world of ours."

"Shut up!" Odessa shouted. "Both of you!" The abrupt roar echoed in the cave, giving the illusion of many of her, all equally incensed and gruff.

Poko was quiet but still fluttered around Odessa, watching her nervously. Odessa ignored the fairy, focused singularly on the devil before her.

"Who are you?" Odessa asked.

"Khara, daughter of Zarin, the mother of—"

"Why are you here?" Odessa interrupted.

"To offer you terms of alliance," Khara said. "Of friendship even."

Odessa glared harder. "Devils have no concept of friendship. Or alliance. All you know is slaughter and slavery."

"You are no stranger to slaughter yourself," Khara said. "I saw you on the battlefield, when you killed Pash-Tor. He was not one of the most adept when it came to magics, but he was no novice either. He was still a force of destruction on the battlefield. And you killed him. You slew one of Sak-Tor's generals. I tell you, it was a wonderous sight. Even in the midst of battle, I was awe-stricken."

"When did you supposedly desert then?"

"As soon as I heard you had fled Asha-Kalir," Khara said. "I had to find you. I knew I needed to speak to you." A glimmer of something Odessa thought was fanaticism glinted in her eyes as she spoke.

"How did you find me?"

"I followed the bloodshed," Khara said. "You leave behind you quite the wake."

"Liar," Odessa spat. "You had other devils to help you. Other scouts watching the roads."

The glimmer in the devil's eyes flickered. Khara shook her head, almost affronted. "No, that is not true at all. I combed the desert for you. I continued finding signs of bloodshed—looted caravans and destroyed clay men—in this western edge of the plains. So I rode for days, searching for you. Finding tracks and losing them with the winds. I followed you until my entehlo could go no farther. And still I searched. Then last night I saw your fire all the way across the plains. A dot of fire moving across the valley, but I knew it had to be you. It was your arm, wasn't it? Your immolated arm." Khara smiled, a sharp-toothed grin that set the hairs on the back of Odessa's neck on end. "I could not sleep last night, I so looked forward to this moment."

Odessa smiled piteously, her eyes devoid of humor. "Is it everything you'd hoped it would be?"

Khara's smile did not so much as falter. "It is an honor. To be so near Pash-Tor's slayer . . . I am undeserving."

"You're out of your mind," Odessa said.

"May I offer you our terms now?" Khara asked.

Odessa stared at her for a moment, face impassive as she turned the devil's words over in her mind. After a few seconds, something shifted in her face. A coldness that came with the narrowing of her eyes.

The spear shot forward just as Poko lit the cavern with a burst of spectacular light.

"Run!" Poko shouted as Odessa blinked, amorphous blobs of light dancing in and totally obscuring her vision.

A shuffling sound. Scrambling limbs. Odessa swung the spear, hoping to slash or clout the devil, but she was disoriented. The shaft struck flesh but it was a glancing blow. Footsteps passed her toward the passage.

Shit! Odessa turned to follow, running into the white that dominated her vision. Then her shin struck the adobe pillar beside the fire and she spilled to the ground.

"Godsdamn it!" she screamed, scrambling to her feet and scrubbing at her eyes as if she could scrape the blindness from them. "Poko, you treacherous little shit! What do you think you're doing?" She had no idea if Poko was still in the cavern with her but still she screamed and cursed at them. She spun in slow circles, gesturing wildly as something at the periphery of her vision began to take vague form. "You let a devil into our home and you expect me to let it live? Not even that, you want me to *listen* to it. Are you out of your godsdamned mind too? Or are you just that stupid? Are you so incapable of taking care of yourself, you'd let your kill in and invite them to dinner?"

She thought she heard a scuffling and turned, swinging the spear through empty air. "Oh no, that's not it. That's not it at all. You didn't just let it in. You let it escape! You *blinded* me and let it escape. You're not just stupid. You're a back-stabbing little insect I should have crushed the first time I saw your smug, deceitful face." The fire's heat interrupted her tottering revolutions, and she turned away. "But why am I surprised? You tried to have me killed the first time we ever met. This isn't new for you, is it?"

She waited for a reply, shadows beginning to bleed into her vision. When there was no reply, she screamed, "Poko! Poko, I know you're there! Answer me, Poko!" She screamed until her voice was hoarse. Until her voice gave out completely. "Poko!"

By the time her voice was gone, her vision had long since returned. She was collapsed on her knees in the empty cavern. Her eyes misted but she felt no sadness. There was too much rage in her to leave room for sadness.

CHAPTER 7

The blood was cold and thick. The surface of the pool had begun to clot and scab at the edges. But against Ayana's skin, it was like an exquisite oil seeping into her every pore, cleansing her inside and out.

She lay nude in the pool of blood, totally submerged and breathing through a reed clenched between her teeth. Small, muted drips came to her from the channels feeding the pool, the sound muddled in the viscous medium. The blood muddled everything. Sound. Thought. Time. Everything lost definition in the pool. Beneath the surface lay a wholly different world. An infinite void where she could be alone with the goddess. She was never closer to Talara than when in the bloody womb of the pool.

She found strength in the blood and her skin prickled and buzzed. Enervated by the sum of many lives. A pulsing thrum beat deep within her, growing steadily louder. She was at peace at the bottom of the stone pool. Contented. Fully and totally satisfied. The same feeling she might have had after a large meal with those she loved.

A whisper rippled through the pool. "The mists draw near," Talara said. Beneath her eyelids, Ayana could almost see the goddess's form. Massive and imposing. Like the shadow of a mountain had fallen over her, she could feel the immensity of Talara's presence so tangibly. "Today shall be the day, my Ayana. You must be the bulwark against the mists. Against this corruption. Lest this world be barren and lifeless. No life and no death. The end of this cycle. The perversion of all that is true and holy."

Whistling through the reed, Ayana's breaths quickened, becoming deeper as something like a warm, dank ecstasy unfurled inside her chest.

"You cannot fail, Ayana. You stand at the precipice of a new age, but you must not fear. For I am with you. You are mine in perpetuity. Not only are you the bulwark, you are the gateway. The gateway between god and man. Life and death. You are rot incarnate. Death begets life. Life begets death. And you are the interstice."

The blood around her grew heavy and dense. Yet comforting. Safe.

"When you face those that dwell in the mists and those Gray-stricken, you must destroy them totally and indiscriminately. Reduce them to offal for the maggots and worms. Destroy them so completely that these aberrant corruptions of the Gray become little more than sustenance for my lowliest. Kill them all. Eradicate the plague they carry with them. Then let them rot."

Ayana emerged, her face rising from the clotted surface. Blood splattered the air as she spit the reed from her mouth and took a deep, unhindered breath. The iron taste of blood filled the sanctum and it was sweet. She rose to her feet, blood pouring from her ashen body. Bits and gobs of coagulated blood clung to her skin. Her face tilted to the ceiling, she listened to the rhythmic drip and plop echo in the cold stone room.

"How do you feel?" Kunza's voice came from outside the pool, a crack in the placid stillness of the sanctum.

Ayana wiped the blood from her eyes and opened them to the dimness of the sanctum. Kunza stood at the edge of the pool with a linen towel draped over one arm and Ayana's kaftan over the other. The brazier behind him cast a corona of sickly orange around him. His cape of vulture feathers caught the light in its plumage and his shoulders bristled with fiery feathers. His features were obscured by shadow save for his eyes. They glowed a dim, restrained red.

"I feel perfect," she said with no exaggeration. She felt like a leaf carried on the wind. Carried higher and higher. Past clouds of matte gray into a clean, pure sky of moon and stars. She waded through the pool, tacky blood clinging to her shins. There was a grace to her movements she quite liked. Like a stalking lioness, she moved with surety and lithe tension.

Kunza held out the linen towel and Ayana took it as she mounted the steps leading out of the pool. Blood dripped from short, tight dreadlocks that came down to her neck. A thick mixture of fat and ash had been added to her hair when the locks had been twisted so that the drying blood did not form mats. Instead, the blood gave the dreadlocks a ruddy ochre tint. Against her dark, ash-stained skin, it made quite the striking contrast. Ayana liked how she looked. She looked how she pictured Ogé's first people had looked. The first men and women made of godsblood and earth. The closest humanity had come to divinity. Until now.

She dried herself as best she could, patting and scrunching her dreadlocks so they did not dry in clumps. Blood dried fast in the open. She scrubbed tacky smears of blood from her ankles and from between her toes. The towel was so thoroughly soaked when she was done that it looked as if it had been dyed red from the beginning.

"That was just what I needed," Ayana said. It had been nearly two weeks since she had taken her last bath in the sanctum's pool. She and Kunza had been in Noyo for too long. Discussions with envoys from Asha-Kalir and quashing dissidence from those still loyal to the dead Sovereign took much of their time. But time for such banalities was thinning. The Gray's encroachment had forced them into action before preparations were finished.

She gave Kunza the sodden towel, took her kaftan, and slipped into it. It was long and black with thin strips of red running down it and red embroidery about the wrists and neck. Some small drops of blood still dripped from her hair onto her shoulders, but the kaftan hid them well.

Kunza held out the thin kidskin gloves she was made to wear. She took them, careful not to brush against her fingers against his, and pulled them on. The black of the gloves hid the stains of ash and blood.

"Do you have any . . ." Kunza started then paused, his words lingering in the vaulted sanctum. "Doubts?"

"No," Ayana said, stepping away from the pool. Her bare feet on the cold stone never touched the blood still running in channels throughout the floor. At the edge of the sanctum, hidden in shadowy alcoves, were the exsanguinated corpses and the few unseemly bleeders they had gotten from Asha-Kalir. "I know what I have to do. And Talara says I can do it."

Kunza followed behind her. "Are you afraid at all?"

Ayana furrowed her brow and slowed a step, allowing Kunza to catch up. "Of course not. I have Talara's blessing. She's chosen me. I have nothing to fear." She resumed her pace, irritated now at Kunza's low estimation of her.

Kunza nodded. They left the sanctum, trailed by four Shadows, and entered the long hall. Work was still being done in the hall: tiling and statuary work. The delicate *tink* of small hammers and chisels against stone filled the hall. Ayana and Kunza walked carefully on the untiled floor as to not disturb the substrate of pebble and thick mortar.

"The Goddess has been speaking to you quite often now, no?"

Ayana nodded. Just walking beside him, she could feel Kunza's feverish jealousy.

"What does she say?"

"She tells me what to do. And makes sure I know I can do it."

Kunza nodded again. "Of course."

As they neared the middle of the hall where the mosaic floor was being set, they moved to the side where a strip of walkway allowed them to walk freely. As they passed the men and women laying the mosaic, the *tink* of hammers and the scrape of stone stopped. Each man and woman kneeled and bowed their head until Ayana and Kunza had passed.

"Are you sure you are ready?" Kunza asked. "If you aren't, we have more Shadows in the city. We can mobilize all of them if needed."

"Without those Shadows, we won't have the city," Ayana said. " Anyway, I'm ready so it doesn't matter. My whole life has led up to this moment." She smiled, rousing atrophied muscles in her face to life. "I'm on the edge of a precipice."

They reached the stairs twisting upward into daylight. "Do not be too eager to jump off," Kunza said. "You may not like where you land."

Ayana's smile faded to a frown. "Why are you doubting me?"

"I'm not doubting you," Kunza said, taking the first few steps up the stairs. "I worry about you."

"You should be worrying about our people and our future and our *Goddess*," Ayana said then began taking the stairs two at a time, leaving Kunza behind. His faith could fluctuate from fervent and fiery to weak and tepid at a moment's notice. She could not be around him when his faith wavered. It could be contagious. She knew that. Like a foul miasma. A plague easily contracted and spread. She could not lose heart nor faith. Too much lay on her shoulders.

Dark gray morning was giving way to sallow day when Ayana crested the last few steps of the winding staircase into the circular building set atop the temple like a barrow. Its domed ceiling towered high above her, painted a dark violet. Tiny bits of polished silver glittered in constellations set about the dome's interior. Flickering above the braziers set in niches around the room was a sky full of stars. The stolen night sky made manifest.

She exited the temple's vestibule through two heavy wooden doors that bore Talara's serpentine visage carved in painted relief. Her bat-nosed face was split by the seam of the doors and her body, looped like entrails, made an endless spiral that seemed to continue past the threshold. Within those loops of her body were images of men and gods alike telling the story of Talara's ascension and the creation of man. But the story did not end there. The doors were a history and a premonition.

Two ash-faced guards in black quilted cotton were standing outside the vestibule and quickly took the doors as she passed through them. With a deep bow, the guards closed the doors behind her as she took the few stone steps from the vestibule to the dirt road leading to town. Kalaro spread out before her, bustling. More mudbrick buildings rose in various stages of completion on the outskirts of the village. Homes and barracks and the sorts of buildings that produced the means of war. The sound of hammers against bronze rang out from the other side of Kalaro. A steady clanging rhythm. Spearheads being straightened or mounted. Swords and daggers reworked or reforged entirely. War was fast approaching. Like nothing ever experienced by mankind nor by any living god of this age.

The vestibule doors opened behind her and she knew Kunza would be at her side at any moment. She started down the road before the doors closed again, hurrying toward town. When Kunza caught up with her, he said nothing. They were both beginning to grasp the nuances of the hierarchy Talara was assembling. It chafed them both still, but they would fulfill the roles the Goddess had made from them. And a Priest served his soon-to-be Sacred Queen as well as his Goddess.

It was Ayana who spoke first. The silence between them had begun to irritate her more than Kunza's weak faith. Silence was to her like an itch sometimes. A nagging itch that she could not relieve herself.

"Did Ajatunde speak to you about the new huts on the river's edge?" she asked as if she and Kunza had been speaking the whole walk to town. With the influx in residents, huts were sprouting up in Kalaro at an alarming speed, and as such, huts were drawing closer and closer to the riverbank. As mild as the wet season was in the mountains, the rising of the river was sure to flood at least a few of them.

Kunza cleared his throat. "She did," he said. "And I asked her why she hadn't stopped them from building there before they were already thatching the roofs."

Ayana snorted softly. "I find it strange that all life may end if we fail and she's worrying about wet feet."

"If she would just listen to Kufu about all this construction, I doubt she would have to worry at all. But if she had nothing to worry about, I doubt she would know what to do with herself." They were passing the wattle huts of the enslaved, nearing the town proper. "But her worries do have some precedent. Kalaro grows too quickly."

"It cannot be helped," Ayana said. Slaves prostrated themselves in doorways as she passed. "When the rest of the world falls to ruin, Kalaro has to be able to stand on its own. It has to grow, and grow fast because that time is fast approaching."

"If Kalaro collapses in onto itself before the world falls into ruination, then it's all moot, no?"

Ayana frowned. "Talara won't let Kalaro collapse."

Kunza nodded but Ayana knew he was unconvinced.

The plaza was packed with ashen figures. Some wore kaftans and tunics while others wore quilted cotton. And they all waited for her.

As she approached, the mass of people—her people—knelt and bowed their heads. Ajatunde, standing by the fire in the center of the plaza, kneeled but did not take her eyes off Ayana and Kunza. Her gaze was resolute and reverent. At the edge of the plaza, Ayana stopped and raised her arms, lifting her people to their feet as she did so. It still confounded her how they did as she bade. The sensation of a crowd's eyes all trained upon her still made her skin tingle, but she was no longer scared of it. Ministering to her people was rote now.

She did not have to say anything. Serenely, with an air of beatific grace, she stepped into the plaza and the ritual began. The mass took a more orderly shape. The men and women in quilted cotton took their places. Kneeling in a line before the crackling fire. Their heads bowed low, foreheads nearly brushing the dirt. There were nearly one hundred of them in rows before the fire. Ayana stood facing them. Kunza and Ajatunde took their places behind her, each on either side of the copper pot sitting a few paces from the fire.

One by one, she went to them and, with a gloved hand against their cheek, whispered in their ear the words Talara had told her to say. Words she had spoken nearly hundreds of times now. "Your sins are heavy burdens upon the soul. Lay them bare and be absolved by Talara's mercy and kindness." After she said these words, the warrior she said them to would whisper in her ear, telling her of all the death they had wrought and all the curses they had uttered and all the perversions and hate that lay in their heart. And Ayana listened, her face gentle and impassive.

When each sinner confessed, they stood and took with them an effigy made of plantain leaves or corn husks to the copper pot. As Ayana went to take the confession of the next warrior, Ajatunde would take the effigy from the sinner and Kunza would draw a bit of blood from the sinner by pricking the bottom of their tongue with his obsidian blade. The blood and saliva would be let to drip upon the effigy before the effigy was dropped into the pot and the sinner could take their place among the other warriors again, their mouth still filling with blood.

After the last effigy was placed in the pot, Kunza scooped coals from the fire with a soot-stained clay bowl and dropped the coal into the pot. The effigies took to flame quickly. Dry leaves curling and twisting as they turned to ash. Layers of leaves peeling away from the effigies as flames licked them away to reveal the offering at the center: a piece of cacao. A ceremonial bribe for the Goddess. Ayana stood over the pot, breathing in the smoke as it curled out of the mouth of the pot. The sweet, redolent scent of plantain and maize and cacao was lost to her. All she could sense was the filth of their sins. It filled her nostrils and choked her throat. Clung to her skin and clogged her pores. First it tingled and then it stung as it sank deeper into her body and soul. The blood of the pool had invigorated her, making her strong enough to bear the sins of her people, but it did not make it any less unpleasant.

She swallowed her disgust and sucked in another deep breath. The effigies were nearly reduced to ashes, but the smoke still poured out of the pot in a thick ribbon of filth. Her eyes stung and watered.

"The burden of a sinner's heart, I take unto my flesh," Ayana whispered under her breath. "My Goddess, give me strength."

Just as the last few tongues of flame flickered, she reached into the pot and scooped up the hot ashes between cupped hands. Embers and ashes scalding her hands, she turned and spoke to the warriors. "The sins and transgressions of your past now lie in my hands." Flakes of ash and tiny embers drifted as a light breeze wafted through the valley. She raised the mound of ash above her head. "And from my hands, I offer them unto Talara for only through her can we be redeemed. Only through her will we find salvation."

She swallowed again, her mouth already drying. Her tongue already beginning to stick against the inside of her mouth. She lowered her cupped hands before her breasts. Her face upturned, she closed her eyes. The ash in her hands was not so much hot as corrosive. The filth of sin held within these ashes was a concentrated poison. "Through me, Talara's love is made manifest. I take these sins unto my own flesh so that Talara's mercy be upon you."

She paused, letting the words settle in the air. Then she lowered her face and shoved the ash into her open mouth. The ash became a tacky paste in her mouth, and it tasted like death and excrement. Caustic heat filled her mouth and began forcing its way down her throat. That acid pain melted through her mouth to the bones, making her jaw and teeth ache. Her hands tightened into fists and she swallowed half of the ash. Her throat contracted and convulsed, trying to reject it. But she swallowed it all and without complaint. Because for Talara's people— her people—she would do anything.

The urge to vomit wracked her insides. Scratching and battering at her ribs. Tearing at her throat. Her throat constricted and her jaw clenched in spasms. Her hands trembled and strength drained from her legs, but she repressed the urge to release the molten heap searing through her insides.

When she opened her eyes she saw her people through a sheen of tears. Ajatunde was at her side, supporting her should her legs fail. Ayana rested a hand on her shoulder, steadied herself, then stepped toward the warriors still kneeling before her.

"Your sins are Talara's," Ayana said. Her voice was little more than a croaking whisper. "Through her everlasting mercy, you are purified. Thank the Goddess, for her love is eternal." The searing pain in her belly was spreading, bleeding into her legs, but she continued undeterred. Channeling Talara's words, she continued, "Calamity nears and with it the end of all that we know. But it is through Talara's mercy that we are able to face it with our souls unblemished and pure. And it is by Talara's might that we will prevail." Sweat dappled her forehead and a terrible, white- hot ache pounded behind her eyes. "Praise to our Goddess, Talara, who eats the sins of the world so that we may live and love for as long as the world turns."

A chorus of praises followed her words, but to Ayana they were muffled. As if she still laid at the bottom of the pool. Her head felt light and airy and when she lifted her arms in exalted repose, she thought she would tip over. But she remained upright. Nearly panting with the effort but upright nonetheless. She shouted to the ash-gray sky, yelling in a crackling, reed-thin voice, "Praise be to Talara!"

More shouts of praise joined hers. The caustic agony in her core eased a bit. Softening and becoming almost pleasant. It was pain surging to the verge of pleasure. Pushing her to the boundary between torture and ecstasy.

The sins of her people, while pernicious and malignant, were a wonderful poison. Making her both more human and more than human. The blood mixed with the ashes of sin made a cement that filled the cracks within herself. Hardening her soul and steeping her body in that which made the Goddess Talara what she was now. With the blood's edification and the burden of her people's sin, she could be made into Talara's image. She could be made into a martyr. The foundation of a utopia that lay on the horizon, just beyond her sight.

Ecstatic, she and her people reveled in the pure splendor of Talara's love.

CHAPTER 8

The devil had left a pair of daggers on the floor at the mouth of the cavern. In the fury that had come in erratic tides after Poko and the devil's departure, Odessa had kicked the daggers and sent them skittering across the cave floor. Now, leading her train of entehlo and bazaks, Odessa kept them tucked in her belt, a hilt at either of her kidneys. She meant to return the daggers. To sheath them in the devil's throat and chest. Or perhaps only return one dagger to the devil. The other could be for Poko. Since they wanted to take the devil's side, they could share her fate. It was only fair.

For two days of continuous plodding, these thoughts were Odessa's only comfort. But she could hardly think beyond these vague fantasies of revenge. She would kill Poko and the devil. And then? Yakun. Tarik. And then? Kunza. Kalaro as a whole. There was nothing stopping her now. And there was much to be done. A ladder of vengeance to be climbed. Rung by bloody rung she would climb.

Tracking the devil proved difficult. Odessa had torn down their camp and left the cavern with the arrival of dawn, but in that time, Poko and the devil had disappeared. Melted into the night and evaporated by dawn. She had found some signs of the devil in flight to the north, past the talus and scree. Footprints left scuffed into the hardpan. But the ground was resistant to such traces. Or Odessa's eyes were not suited for such meticulous scrutinizing. Either way, she had not seen any sign of the devil since yesterday. But she had to continue. If she stopped, they would escape. The ladder of vengeance would be pulled up out of her reach. And she would be left adrift in a vast, barren desert. Alone and aimlessly wandering. Until she finally collapsed and was buried beneath the dunes. Another set of sun-bleached bones swallowed up by the endless hunger of the desert.

"I kill them or I die," she muttered to herself through dry, cracked lips. She was leading her train over a slight ridge of sand-dusted rock. The mesa was far behind her, and now cracked hardpan stretched in all directions. Nothing to be seen between her and the horizon. But she continued north, head down, leaning forward, and dragging the train behind her. "Nobody betrays me ever again. Never trust a soul again. Can't trust anyone." Tarik came to her mind. Standing by as Yakun and Azdava bound her and pumped her full of innocent blood. She licked her bleeding lips, thinking of furtive kisses stolen in the halls of Asha-Kalir. A sour taste in her mouth now. Like something dead. "I was stupid. Stupid to think I could ever trust anyone. Forsaken are forsaken by everyone. Everyone is against me. The whole world is my enemy."

Intermittently throughout the day, she mumbled such things to herself. Whenever she grew tired of the huff and stomp of the animals behind her. Whenever the crush of her revolving thoughts became too much. And always she spoke of betrayal and revenge. Circling these points in what was, by now, a well-trod path of thought.

The entehlo puffed and panted behind her. Spots of foam built at the corners of its mouth. The train occasionally stopped only long enough for Odessa to catch her breath. That constant exertion and the stifling heat of midday was burning the poor beast to cinders but she couldn't slow down.

"I don't need them," she whispered. "I don't need anyone."

She wandered the desert, drifting east and west as she plodded northward. Her boots were heavy. Her shoulder ached from the weight of her iron arm. Beneath her scale, she was drenched in sweat that constantly stung the chafed skin around her shoulders and armpits. Black spots danced at the periphery of her vision, growing larger when the erratic rush of her thoughts receded and her mumbling quieted.

"Poko." A twinge of pain spasmed in her chest. A sharp aching like the agony of a phantom limb. "Poko, I'll make you regret ever crossing my path. You won't ever fool me again. I swear it. I swear it on my tainted heart. You won't ever hurt me again."

Poko and the devil were out there somewhere, hiding in the vast emptiness of the desert. And she would find them. Even if she had to scour the entire desert to do it. If she had to scorch the entire earth to flush them from their hiding she would do it. Her mind set unerringly upon this single thing, she felt there was nothing she would not do to find Poko and the devil that had taken them away from her.

CHAPTER 9

K hara emerged from the cavern's entrance with a waterskin filled from what remained of the chaff-littered trough. "The ashes are cold. She must have left not long after we ourselves fled."

Poko sat cross-legged on the boulder pushed aside from the gap, chin cupped in their hand. "Of course she's gone. You know where our hideout is. You could bring all your devil friends in and slaughter us in our sleep."

"I suppose I will have to track her again."

"I just hope she's cooled down by now," Poko said, frowning. Odessa's screams as they fled still echoed in their mind. By doubling back, Poko and Khara had hoped they could regroup with Odessa when she was in a better state of mind. But in the back of Poko's mind, they wondered if she would ever be in a better state of mind again. *She's finally broke. Worn too thin, she finally couldn't take it anymore. We pushed her too far and she snapped.* Poko shook their head and tried to dismiss their pessimism, but it would not leave them entirely. A thin residue of foreboding remained.

"She very nearly killed me, didn't she?" Khara asked, an odd reverence in her tone. Like she were recounting a stroke of good luck she still could not be sure was real.

Poko stood and took flight, gliding from the boulder to flutter in front of Khara. "Yes, she did. And I would prefer next time we see her, nothing like that happened again so let's maybe get a plan together beforehand, yeah?"

Khara scoffed. "A plan? The plan is to find her and talk to her." She smiled and started toward the talus slope leading into the valley. "I think you will find that I can be quite persuasive."

Poko followed her down the slope. "Huh, I didn't really get that at all the other night."

"I admit, her surprise entrance put me on my back foot a bit. But do not worry. I will wear her down eventually."

"We're going to die," Poko said. As soon as they said the words, they regretted them. Their stomach tightened and their skin prickled with unease. Meant as a joke, once those words spilled into the air they became real. Ominous portents jokingly spoken into existence.

"Have heart, small one," Khara said, laughing. Oblivious to the ill omen now loosed upon them. "This soon will be but another tale to tell around the fire." Khara paused, attention focused on bazak dung lying on the scree. Then she continued down the slope. "I suppose it won't be but another tale, no. A brawl preceding the alliance that brought down Sak-Tor. That has the makings of legend."

"I envy your confidence," Poko said flatly.

They continued for a while, following the footprints left by the bazaks in the shifting scree. They were slight, shallow depressions appearing here and there where the scree was particularly loose. Khara was quiet, intently following the tracks northward.

After a long while, Poko had to let loose a thought that had been nagging them since the night they had been forced to flee. "I really didn't think she would react like that." Khara had paused, eyes searching for the next footprint, but now she glanced at Poko, waiting for more. "I mean, I expected it wouldn't go smoothly, but I thought I would be able to talk her down. I didn't think she would explode like she did."

"I am the enemy in her mind," Khara said, divining Odessa's course by some track or trace unseen by Poko's eyes. "She has spent many months fighting my people. That is not something that can be easily overlooked. Especially when your enemy has invited herself to your fire."

"Then why did you go? We could have waited! We could have figured something out to avoid all this."

"I was parched and nearly out of mind with exhaustion," Khara said. "But most of all, I was impatient. I wanted to see her up close. To see that I had not imagined her or merely built her up in my mind."

"All this because you saw her once in the middle of a battlefield?" Poko asked.

"She did what I could only dream of. A human woman. Alone." Khara was quiet a moment, her gaze on the horizon ahead before it fell to the scree again. "I had always dreamed of rebellion. In the same way a child dreams of growing wings and flying with the birds. It was just fanciful delusion whispered in secret among Sisters. But when I saw her kill Pash-Tor, I felt a hope I had never felt before. I saw my dream materialize in front of my eyes and I had hope for the first time in my entire life. So yes. All of this because I saw her in battle."

They continued until night fell and a few hours after that. Khara's eyes could plumb the dark quite well, and she could have traveled all night had she not been so terribly exhausted. Since Poko found her half-dead, she had barely been able to get any sleep. The night they fled, she ran through the night over the valley floor until scaling the eastern ridges at dawn, and the day after she only slept a few hours before rising to head back to the cavern in the vain hope of finding Odessa there. Exhausted as she was, Khara had resisted Poko's demands that she rest, but after a few hours of pained trudging she finally relented.

Khara lay down on the bare hardpan beneath a boulder jutting from the ground and fell asleep almost immediately. Poko had only just barely landed when they heard the thin, rhythmic hiss of Khara's sleeping breath.

The next day they awoke and set about Odessa's trail again. Her tracks becoming distant and hard to discern in the hard-packed soil and bare stone. While Khara did her best to stay on course, Poko ranged about the desert, making wide looping arcs around Khara in search of any sign of Odessa or her train. But the desert was too vast. There were too many vague shapes on the horizon that could have been her but were in fact just boulders or dry shrubbery. Weak mirages shimmered atop the sand and hardpan, playing with their eyes so they trusted nothing but what was directly in front of them.

More days passed yet there was no sign they were drawing closer to Odessa. Their water was depleted, the little pemmican they had found still laying out on the rocks by the cavern was nearly gone and only worsened their thirst, and lack of decent sleep weighed heavily upon their beleaguered bodies.

Three days since they left the cavern a second time, Khara abruptly stopped. Poko, their mind wandering elsewhere, continued fluttering a few moments longer, then stopped and turned back. "What is it?"

Khara was on one knee, fingers pressed into the stony soil. "Hoofprints," she said quietly. "Six or seven entehlos. Maybe more." She rose and followed the path of the entehlos as they took a sharp right turn, following for a few steps and then spun in a slow circle, eyes scouring the ground. "Odessa's trail turns with them." She back-tracked a few paces, where the other entehlos joined the trail, and sank to her knees. Bent over, her fingers ran across the ground, tracing hoofprints. "There hasn't been bazak tracks since the day before yesterday. I thought the ground here was too hard for them to leave tracks but . . . " Khara swallowed hard and did not continue.

"What do you mean?" Poko asked, darting close. "What are you saying."

"These aren't her tracks."

"What do you mean they're not her tracks?" Poko asked, a shrill edge rising in their words. But Khara didn't reply. Her eyes narrowed and flitted back and forth across the horizon. She rose and scanned the horizon in all directions. Her circular survey stopped suddenly and she froze, staring to the northeast.

"You should go," Khara said flatly. "Go now."

On a ridge far to the northeast was a single figure. After a moment there was another figure beside it. And another. At this distance they were ants crawling upon the horizon. Almost a dozen of them rising above the ridge.

Khara kneeled and drew a small, stout knife from her boot. "Go, Poko," she said. "Go back the way we came as fast as you can."

Before Poko could reply, Khara was gone, running full tilt to the west. Running towards nothing in particular but more barren desert and the mountains looming far in the distance.

"Wait!" Poko cried, fluttering in place, uncertain. "What are you doing? Where are you going?"

There was no answer save for the pounding of hooves coming down from the northeastern ridge.

As dehydrated and exhausted as Khara was, she sped across the hardpan in a breakneck sprint. The riders coming off the ridge were fast.

After a moment's hesitation, head whipping from Khara's flight to the approaching riders, Poko did as they were told. They flew away from the rumbling of hooves and shouting devils.

When they glanced back, they could see the riders bearing down on Khara. Entehlos snorting and bellowing. Khara wheeled around as the first riders drew close. Her dagger whipped wildly through the air, then she half-crouched, weight balanced on the balls of her feet. The riders surrounded her. Circling slowly around her. She spun slowly, head swiveling as they trotted.

When a rider drew near, she charged, dagger raised. She ducked beneath a swinging sword and plunged her dagger into the rider's side. Dagger still plunged into the rider, she pulled the rider off the saddle. The entehlo began to buck and kick as Khara jumped to slide into the unoccupied saddle. Before she could clamber up, the circle had closed, collapsing in an instant with the pounding of hooves. A club whipped through the air and struck Khara in the middle of the back just as she slid into the saddle. She pitched forward and a hand dragged her down. She tumbled in a cloud of dust kicked up by the torrent of hooves.

Eyes misted with tears, Poko could watch no more. They flew hard back the way they'd come.

CHAPTER 10

Her mother was still asleep when Ayana came to say goodbye. On a mat of dirty rush in the corner of the room, curled like an infant. Lip twitching, dreaming of words unspoken. Ayana stood in the doorway and watched her sleep for a while, knowing that she could not tarry long. Only when she slept did her mother look at peace. The respite of dreams was all she had left.

"Mama?" Ayana said quietly, taking a step inside her mother's dingy room. The astringent odor of sweat and sloth was almost palpable, but Ayana pushed through it to the mat where her mother lay, softly wheezing. "Mama, it's Ayana. I'm leaving."

Her mother's eyes fluttered open. There was a light in them that immediately died when she realized where her waking had brought her. To a world bereft of so many of the things she had loved the most. Things all stolen from her.

Ayana bent down beside her mother's turned back, trying to avert her eyes from the angry reddish-purple spots at her elbow and the back of her head. Bedsores becoming darker and more inflamed with every passing day. "Mama," Ayana said. "How do you feel?"

Her mother shifted her bone-thin frame but did not turn to face her. "I don't know yet," she said, her voice dry and brittle. "I just woke."

Ayana mustered a wan smile and a warm tone of voice. "I suppose you're right." Her eyes drifted to the bony protrusions that were her mother's vertebrae. Even through her dingy bedclothes, they jutted. Her arms were stick-thin and flared at the elbows where her sores were the most irritated. Although Talara had banished the plague from Kalaro, still her mother wasted away. Stricken by a disease of the heart and the mind. A disease Talara had no dominion over. "I came to say goodbye, Mama. We're leaving for Noyo today. Do you remember?"

"Going to war," her mother said. "My remaining daughter goes to war."

"War isn't quite right. It's more of an extermination. Like taking up arms against locusts."

Her mother was quiet for a long while. Then her back began to spasm and her ribs rose and fell in jerks, and Ayana realized she was crying. She laid a hand on her mother's back, the ribs so clearly defined against her fingers. "It will be fine, Mama. Don't cry, I will be fine. Kunza won't let anything happen to me."

A whining sob escaped from deep within her mother's throat and the spasmatic rise and fall of her ribs grew deeper and faster. "You used to be my little girl," her mother said, her words husky and pained. "You were my little girl."

"I still am," Ayana said.

Her mother shook her head weakly, her matted curls barely moving. "No, you're not. Not anymore."

A lump swelled in Ayana's throat and her eyes stung. "I grew up, Mama."

Another long pause. Only hushed sobs from her mother. Ayana blinked her tears away but the bulwark that held them at bay was crumbling. Then her mother spoke. "You didn't grow up. You changed. He changed you." Her sobs were loud now, rattling from her chest. Ayana's eyes misted. "He's taken everything from me. You and your father and your sister. And he made you a monster just like her."

Ayana drew her hand back and held it balled within her other as if burned. Now her own tears came. She could barely take a breath. Like her mother had punched her in the chest and caved in her ribs. And her heart ached. With every quivering beat, it ached and agonized. "I'm not a monster." Her words were pleading and weak and she hated the sound of them. For the first time in a long while she thought of her older sister. Both she and her mother had seen her screaming and aflame. Had seen the corpses she had wrought come back from the Night Jungle in bloody shrouds. Both she and her mother had felt the same shame like a cold rain upon them. "I'm not like her." The quavering in her voice steadied a bit. "I'm nothing like her."

"You're a monster," her mother whispered hoarsely, still sobbing. "A tainted monster."

"She's Forsaken and I'm the Goddess's Chosen." Ayana rose to her feet, feeling a scream rising in her chest. "I am nothing like her!"

Her mother mumbled and muttered but Ayana could not make out the words, if there were any to discern at all. Ayana wiped the tears from her eyes, looked down at the muttering skeleton that was her mother, and marched out of the room, restraining hurt and anger in equal measure.

An army of two hundred left Kalaro that morning, comprised almost entirely of warriors and slaves. The majority of Kalaro's Shadows and beastfolk were already camped north of Noyo. Waiting to meet the Gray in its steady southern sweep. Massing to meet destruction head-on.

CHAPTER 11

Khara was jerked forward by the rope around her wrists. In the murk of walking unconsciousness, she stumbled, barely able to catch herself before tumbling face-first in the sand.

"Hurry up," the soldier holding the opposite end of the rope snapped before giving the rope another yank. Khara lurched forward and tried to keep pace with the soldier's entehlo, hastening her leaden feet to a slow, clumsy trot.

Her skin was peeling and her bare feet were blistered and burned. Sand and dirt packed the oozing wounds on the soles of her feet and the claws of her toes were all chipped and broken to the quick. She had been stripped of everything but her loincloth. Harsh wind had abraded her skin raw, and it continued still to lash at her.

When her pace began to slow, the soldier yanked the rope again. The yank hauled Khara's arms forward and pulled the muscles of her back taut. She hissed with pain. A massive bruise spread across her back, shades of mottled yellow and purple and brown radiating from around a gash between her shoulder blades.

"Walk, damn you," the soldier hissed from behind her headwrap. "Or I will drag you across this godsforsaken desert."

Khara licked her cracked and bleeding lips and forced herself onward. She was beyond exhaustion. Every muscle in her body was overwrought and screaming but her mind was elsewhere. Lost in a liminal place of kaleidoscope darkness. Far removed from the desert sands that tore at her body. She found herself drifting continually from this interstice and back again, leaving herself whenever the corporeal pain became too much for her mind to bare. Each time the rope about her wrists was yanked, she too was yanked from that place. But each time she came from that place she drifted back to it sooner than the time before. She knew there would come a time when she would not return. And that thought both relieved and terrified her.

As she oscillated between consciousness and fugue, time became a vague notion barely registered at the periphery of her mind. She thought they had been marching three or four days. But beneath the ash-gray sky that glowered with the same gloomy disposition morning, midday, and evening, it was hard for her to tell. Night was the only true measure of time's passing. By the time day turned to night, Khara was beyond exhausted. A tremulous grasp upon consciousness, each night was as easily recalled as her dreams come morning. With soft blackness slowly winnowing her vision to a pinprick and her exhausted mind sloshing in her skull like melted wax, trying to remember her nights was like trying to grasp a handful of fog.

Some indeterminate length of time later, one of the riders farther up the train raised a horn to their lips. A lowing bellow rose to fill the desert's quiet. It dragged on, first cracking that quiet then pulverizing it with its continued thunder. Even when it had stopped, it rang in Khara's ears a few moments longer.

Again pulled from the interstice, Khara blinked wind-whipped tears from her eyes and forced the darkness winnowing her vision back just a bit. The train was making its way down a slight, stony ridge along a path worn through the harsh rock over centuries. The path cut down the ridge into a wide valley of dust and scrub brush. Hints of green hid among the scrub like flecks of mica in a drab stone.

In the near distance, nearly a half hour's march, was a sprawl of adobe huts. Outside that sprawl were dozens of domed tents. The placid bellowing of entehlos came softly in the distance. At the horn's call, riders mounted entehlos and rode out in a line of five to meet the train as it approached.

The closer they marched to the village, the heavier Khara's feet became. The more she pulled against the rope that dragged her onward. She could no longer fade away to that liminal place. Dense dread seeped into her every pore. The compounding dread that anchored her to the mortal world weighed so heavily upon her she thought she would collapse beneath it at any moment.

A gruesome end awaited her in the village. As exhausted and muddled as her mind was, her fear was sharp and well-defined like a long shard of glass rammed up from beneath her ribcage through her heart and into her brain. With the riders approaching and the familiar sounds of Sak-Tor's encamped armies coming from across the valley, there was no avoiding that dread and fear.

When the riders drew near, she could feel their eyes upon her. In their fixed gazes, she withered and cast her eyes down to watch her bare, bloody feet moving step after step closer to her demise.

"You've not come back empty-handed this time, I see," one of the village's riders said, her voice needling and a bit curious. "Another deserter?"

"Not just any deserter," the head of the train said. She was broad-shouldered and spoke with a voice like coarse sand ground against bits of glass. "I present to you *the* deserter." She motioned forward the soldier holding Khara's rope, and the soldier yanked her toward the head of the train. "Khara, daughter of Zarin and one of Sak-Tor's finest. The Deserter Princess herself." The contempt in her voice was cold and harsh like a blustery gust of wind.

One of the riders leaned on her entehlo and squinted as Khara was hauled before them. "That cannot be Khara. She's so . . ."

"Pathetic?" the head of the train said. "Yes, after months of hunting I too was a bit underwhelmed. I had expected a decent fight at the very least. But no matter. We have the bitch now and we can finally cut the head off this Sisterhood nonsense."

Cut the head off the Sisterhood? Khara thought. Despite the grim certainty before her, she felt the ghost of a smile brush against her cracked lips. A bitter, humorless smile. *I'm nothing but a Sister with a paltry bit of battle fame to my name. Killing me will amount to nothing. Your Conqueror King will still die.*

The rope was jerked again, and the train continued its march. Close to the village now, the silence that had hung over the train was broken and chatter replaced it. Khara ignored it all, thinking only of Sak-Tor. Of Sak-Tor screaming and bleeding. Clutching his entrails as they came spilling out from his belly. And Odessa was there, watching as he died. Killing his impotent magic as she had Pash-Tor's.

As they brought her through the outskirts of the village and past the jeers and insults of her fellow warriors, Khara's thoughts turned to her what lay before her. And then she found herself plummeting back into the interstice. Whatever ground her dread had anchored her to had fallen out from beneath her feet like a sinkhole. Now the weight of dread only quickened her descent.

Past tents and huts still spattered with the blood of their former occupants, she was taken to a courtyard in the center of the village. In the courtyard, thick iron posts had been driven deep into the ground. Five of Khara's Sisters hung by the wrists from shackles positioned high on the posts. They sagged against their shackles, nude and bloody from old wounds and new. Their horns were broken at the base. Only blood-crusted stumps remained. None of her Sisters so much as glanced in her direction as she was brought to a post of her own.

The soldiers ripped the loincloth from her hips and twisted her arms over her head. The manacles closed around her wrists and bit into her raw skin. Khara's head hung and she stared down at her feet.

A speech was made to thunderous approval, but Khara could not hear it. Her eyes had begun to roll back in her skull as she fell deeper into merciful unconsciousness.

It wasn't until hands gripped her horns that she jerked back awake. She whipped her head back and forth, trying to pull free but their grip was solid and unrelenting. The thought of having her horns snapped was suddenly too much to bear. Dying was one thing, but to have her horns broken—that was a humiliation too grave for her to take without a fight. She was surprised to find she had any fight left. Khara pulled her body up, shackles digging deep into her wrists as she did so. She pressed her back against the post, drew her knees up as far as the body in front of her would allow, then sent them pistoning forward. Both her feet struck the soldier's left knee, and she heard a wet crack as they stumbled backward. The soldier tottered, hands still clinging to her horns, but as they began to topple, Khara twisted her head down and away. She ripped free of the soldier's grip as they fell.

More soldiers rushed forward as the fallen soldier moaned and cursed. She stood, arms bent awkwardly above her head, and bared her fangs. "You can kill me and you can torture me," she said, the cry crackling in her raspy voice giving her words a fraught yet savage tone. "But nobody touches my horns."

The fallen soldier was helped up and taken away. Three other soldiers came to fill her place. Two soldiers to hold her legs and one to break her horns. Two of the soldiers looked young and as soft as wet clay, but the third was tall and broad with the demeanor of a storm on the horizon. Khara remained totally still as they approached, a snarl etched on her stony face. Her eyes never left the storm-faced soldier. Her muscles twitched with flagging vigor, and she could already feel the vast ocean of her fatigue turning and flowing back into her legs and arms.

When the soldiers came within arm's reach, she kicked and bucked. Her foot struck one of the young soldiers in the stomach but as she drew it back another soldier caught her by the ankle. She kicked at their arms, but the third soldier caught that leg and, with it, shoved her back against the post.

"Take this leg," the veteran shouted. The soldier Khara had kicked in the stomach shuffled forward and for a moment all three of them held her legs. Khara thrashed and spat. Her strength was failing. Her limbs slowly turning soft and unresponsive even as she fought.

The storm-faced veteran let go of her leg and stepped in close. Khara whipped her head back and snapped as the veteran's hands reached for her horns. But the hands were too quick. Before her mouth had closed, they gripped her horns and yanked her head straight.

"Traitorous bitch."

The veteran wrenched her horns downward. In that moment, Khara jerked her head down as well, vainly hoping to pull free at the last moment. The veteran's hands slipped up her horns a bit, but a second later Khara's head was jerked down and two cracks reverberated in her skull. A skull filled with white pain that blossomed in her eyes as they widened. More cracks as the two broken horn tips were loosened and then ripped off like hangnails.

Blood ran down her horns and spread in wide red ribbons across her forehead. The pain pulsed, worsening with every beat of her pounding heart. She blinked wildly, tears spilling down her cheeks. Her brain was addled by pain and shock. The veteran tossed the horn tips to the ground, then took Khara's hair by the roots and held her gaze. Her eyes were narrow and the color of burnished bronze. "I'm ashamed to share the same blood as you," she said. "You're a disgrace to our father's name. Cowards such as you should die in the womb and spare the rest of us the indignity of your weakness." She spat in Khara's face, the spray striking her blood-streaked forehead. "I pray you live long enough to watch as the rest of your prudish bitch Sisters are brought here. I will have you watch each and every one of them flayed and gutted before you."

Khara's head began to loll, her bleary eyes growing distant and unfocused as pain swept her further away. The veteran tugged Khara's hair and scalp. She blinked a few times, her eyes remaining dazed and distant. The fingers in her hair tightened, pulling her scalp taut, and then the veteran slammed the back of Khara's head into the post and left her reeling.

Head full of reverberating pain and eyes awash in blood, Khara followed the veteran's departure. Her vision blurred and occasionally doubled as she watched her push through the crowd, a pack of soldiers trailing behind her as she made her way toward a large hut. She watched the crowd break apart in knots and clusters. Following soldiers like her as they left to rest or go on patrol.

Head swaying and mouth hanging slightly open, her eyelids grew heavy. Any remaining strength soon left and she sagged from her manacles, totally and entirely unconscious. In that unconsciousness she found no dreams or solace. Only hot, pulsing pain.

CHAPTER 12

As Odessa's store of water dwindled, she began abstaining from water and instead rationed what was left to the beasts. The entehlo, its eyes glazing and its mouth agape, was only given enough water to wet its mouth. For Odessa's thirst, she had begun leeching blood from the poor entehlo. A small incision through the entehlo's tough hide near its artery gave Odessa enough to quench her thirst and reinvigorate herself in a few lapping sips. She did not want to do any of this to the entehlo. It had served her well. It was a fine beast. But its time was drawing to an end.

She had made camp in the wind-carved hills nearer the mountains. A canyon had been carved between two mesas, and she and her train nestled in an alcove of striated sandstone. She had lost the devil's trail days ago. Now she sat listening to the occasional breeze gently moan and howl down the canyon as she debated whether to turn back and see if she could find the trail again or let the beasts loose and let starvation and exposure take her.

All her wrath had burned her hollow and now she was collapsing in upon herself. A flame-gnawed scaffolding falling with a puff of cinders and smoke as its final, ineffectual retort. Sitting against the canyon wall, she closed her eyes and banged the back of her head against the stone in a slow, steady rhythm.

There's nothing to do now. Her head struck the wall again. *Not enough water to do anything but sit.* Another gentle burst of white blossomed behind her eyelids. *Sit and wait.*

The entehlo still panted, though they'd been resting nearly an hour. The bazaks were dull and docile, their legs curled beneath their fleshy bulks. They had thinned a bit, their wrinkled skin hanging a bit looser than before. There was little roughage for them to supplement the diminishing stores of grain and beans.

When hitting her head became too much effort for what little solace from her thoughts it provided, she let her head hang. A thin strip of half-dried bazak in her hand went uneaten. Most of the meat that had not been sun-dried had begun to spoil. And in her hasty retreat from the cavern she had left the majority of her pemmican behind. She had done what she could to salvage the meat she had. The last few days, the bazaks had walked with thin strips of meat hanging from a string along their sides so they could dry out. But it was too late. A sourness had already seeped into the meat. The kind of sour tang that caused the stomach to convulse as soon as it washed over the tongue.

This is how the Forsaken really die. Not by the mob or anything so grand. We die quietly, and we die alone.

She felt little sadness about her fate. She was too tired. Too empty for such feelings. An ember of discontent that she should die in such a stale and barren place. A place devoid of both life and color. In the end it did not really matter. She knew to where she was destined. Where she left life was of little import.

With my body the way it is, I wonder how long it will really take. Will I last a week? Two weeks? Maybe even a month feeding off all the life I've taken. She clenched her iron fist and with her other hand tossed the meat away. It struck the opposite canyon wall and landed in dust and dirt. *This cursed blood of mine won't let me die easily. I'm not even allowed that much.*

She wiped the grease from her fingers and drew one of the devil's daggers from her belt. Its iron was a matte black, but its edges gleamed in a silver corona. She stared at its razor's edge. Tried to imagine bringing that edge to the side of her throat and dragging it across her neck. But she couldn't. All she could see was her father's throat being opened in front of her. The gaping hole in his neck that had yawned wide, splitting skin and muscle, as he fell.

Her finger picked at the leather wrapped around the handle before she turned the knife's point toward her chest. Her armor was piled near the bazaks. Their weight and the desert heat had made her strip free of them a day ago. Only a sweat-stained tunic lay between the knife's point and her chest. It wouldn't take much force to plunge the sharp blade between her ribs and into her heart. The point wavered a hand's width above her breastbone. Her iron hand wrapped around the other and steadied it. *I should just do it,* she told herself. *Get it over with.* She took a deep breath, her chest expanding so the point was, for a moment, just a bit closer. *Just one little thrust and that's it.*

But she couldn't do it. She let the dagger fall into her lap. In that small space between the dagger's point and her chest, there was something in the way. A barrier she couldn't pierce. She did not have a name for that wall keeping her from suicide's release, but to her it felt like cowardice. It was a craven sort of hope that had stayed the dagger. A pitiful delusion. In that gap between blade and heart was a potential future in which she could live and die peacefully.

It was a feeble, spineless lie. But some timid part of herself wanted to believe. If only as an excuse to avoid having to make such a definite decision. To hold her own life in her hands and snuff it out would take a fortitude she found she did not have. At least not now.

But she knew there was little she could do now to salvage her current situation. The desert would have her eventually.

When the soreness in her legs and back had receded to a dim agony, she forced herself onto her feet and set about unloading the beasts of their burdens. She stripped them of everything, leaving them naked and free, and then dumped the rest of the fodder on the ground beside their nearly empty water trough. There was no reason they should die with her. Whether they lived or died would not be up to her.

By nightfall, she had gathered everything that would burn from her looted and piled it on a high ridge east of the canyon. It had taken all day, but the pile of wicker baskets and fine cloth doused with perfumes and oils was waist high and would burn brilliantly.

The land to the east was broken up by mesas and hills, but on the ridge she could see for quite a distance. And be seen.

When night was just beginning to swell to full dark, she lit the pile with a gout of fire from her iron hand. The oils erupted with a *whoosh* of flame. The pile burned foully. With an acrid, pungent stench, it belched black smoke and sent it roiling up into the night. Lengths of rope and a stack of wicker baskets burned with furious vigor. The fire rose taller than she stood and singed the air itself.

Odessa sat hunched on a boulder beside the fire, her spear leaning against her and her bow across her lap. Two devilish daggers in her belt. Firelight glinted in her eyes beneath furrowed brows as she kept her vigil on the eastern horizon now lost in darkness.

I'll die fighting, she told herself. *That's the only way I'll go.*

And so she awaited her death all through the night. The fire sputtered and soon receded to a dark red smolder. And when it did not come with the arrival of dawn, she waited still.

But death would not come so easily.

CHAPTER 13

Putrid smoke drifted from the pile of cinder and ash, charred leather and cloth. At the center of the pile, cloth remained barely singed. The remains of her entehlo's saddle, hollowed by flame, now looked like the blackened carapace of some massive crustacean. In the dingy pale light of morning, the smoldering pile seemed pathetic. All the death Odessa had wrought in the accumulation of these things, and this is what they amounted to. They had not even burned well. Worthless even in their own destruction. But in a way, Odessa was not surprised. The spoils of her slaughtering were as tainted as her bloody body. No good would come from them, just as she would do no good to anyone or anything. She was a parasite. A hardy parasite doomed to live another day.

She stayed hunched on her rock as the dim slate of morning turned a milky, tepid shade of gray with the coming of day. The land stretching far east was still, yet she kept her vigil. Waiting for movement from the shadows of mesas or from behind hills or ridges. But no riders charged over the sand and stone, nor did any Red Clay Warriors lumber into view, their Shadows trailing behind unseen. The ribbon of smoke beside her continued to unfurl into the lifeless expanse of cloud above, twirling and billowing like a streamer of silk caught aloft.

Her red-rimmed eyes soon tired of their vain survey and fell to her iron hand. The damned gauntlet now as much a part of her as the godsblood. Both of them foisted upon her without her consent. She had affected little agency in the course of her damnation. Her only fault, apart from taking part in the murder of a god, was the stubborn way with which she clung to life. But she had not known any of this would happen. She just didn't want to die. If she had known her father was going to pour Egende's lifeblood into her, she would have let the boar god gore her to shreds. If she had known in Kalaro what future awaited her, she would have let Kunza carve her heart out in an instant. But she hadn't. She had only reacted and continued reacting to every tragedy that lay before her. And in doing so had damned herself further. Absolution and redemption now so far out of reach they seemed to exist in a world beyond her own. She now lived in a world of blood and ash and iron.

She had been tracing the blood-stained lines of runes carved in her iron arm when she heard the flutter of paper wings. Her body tensed and in her chest something strained like an overwrought muscle.

"Odessa!" Poko's voice came like the trilling of a songbird. A stark anachronism in such barren, lifeless desert. "I can't believe I found you! That fire was risky but it sure saved me a lot of time looking."

Odessa did not lift her head. The soft susurrus flutter of Poko's wings seemed to come from but a few steps in front of her, where the ridge began to fall off toward the east.

"What are you doing?" Poko asked, the fluttering drawing closer and lilting to the right.

The iron plates of Odessa's hand ground against each other as her fist clenched. *What am I doing?* Her arm throbbed, radiating up through her shoulder to her collarbone and jaw. Her grinding teeth ached with the pulsing heat. A fire bloomed in her chest, burning hot and oily. Her breath was slow and deep as she deliberately worked the bellows of her rage. *You back-stabbing bug should be on your knees begging my mercy. And you ask what* I'm *doing?* The conflagration in her chest roared with the pounding of blood in her ears. Her eyes rose, looking out from beneath knitted brows. When Poko caught her gaze, their bright expression fell, crestfallen and suddenly fearful.

"What— " Poko started, darting backward as Odessa sprang onto her feet.

Odessa held the fire inside her, letting it rise and roil. But she did not let the fire free. Instead she let the pressure burst loose in a gust of hot air. Poko cried out, wings beating the air, as their wings failed them and they fell to the ground in a heap. Lying spilled onto the sand and rock, Poko watched as Odessa took up her spear. Their dark eyes were wide and wet. "Dessa?"

The air around Odessa was still but carried an inescapable electricity like static brushing against her skin. It was a strangely stagnant atmosphere. Any magic in the air dead, save for her own nullifying force. There was a strange clarity in her mind. Looking down on Poko, their tiny body scrabbling away from her as she slowly made her way toward them, she felt like she was walking on air. Every particle of her being intensely vibrating in unison. "Where's the devil?" she asked in a toneless hiss.

"Sh-she got captured." Poko's gaze fell from Odessa's glowering stare to the spearhead pointed at them. "Dessa, I'm sorry I brought her into the cave, but you have to know that I didn't do it to hurt you. You know that right?"

"You betrayed me." Odessa took another slow step, the spearpoint never wavering from its target: Poko's chest. "I thought I could trust you. I thought you were different."

"You can trust me," Poko said. "You can always trust me! I've had nothing but your best interests in mind this whole time."

"Liar."

"I'm not lying!"

"You're a liar!" Odessa shouted, towering over Poko. "Just like everybody else!" She thrust the spear. Its point stopped and hovered a hairsbreadth from Poko's heaving chest. Poko lay frozen beneath the spear. "You sold me out to save your own hide."

Poko shrank back from the spearpoint. "No, I didn't!"

"Stop lying!" Odessa's hand shook and the spearhead wavered. The vibration of her cells was weakening, replaced by the ever-persistent pounding in her ears. The throbbing now filling her entire body yearned to thrust the spear forward. Only her need for understanding staying that killing stroke. "I thought you cared about me. You were all I had left. How could you do this to me?"

"I was trying to help you! I still am trying to help you!"

Liar. The pounding in her head grew louder, beginning to reverberate through her skull. Her patience was an eroded nub of raw flesh. She could take no more lies.

"Just put the spear down. We can talk about this," Poko whined.

"There's nothing to talk about anymore," Odessa said through gritted teeth.

Poko stiffened. "Yes there is. There's lots to talk about." Poko's words rattled from their mouth in a quick, quavering staccato. "They caught her. She was trying to help you. To help us. And they captured her. The other devils captured her. That proves it wasn't a trick, right?"

"No. It doesn't. Because I don't believe a word that comes out of your mouth."

"Why? Why don't you believe me?" Poko leaned forward, chest nearly pressing against the spear tip. "I've been with you, by your side through all of this. Everything that's happened to you since the jungle, I've been there. In the desert when everything got real bad, I was there. And now you don't believe me? So what happened, huh?"

"You left me!" Odessa shouted, jerking the spear back. Hot, angry tears filled her eyes. The rage inside her collapsed like the scaffolded fuel of a dying fire. The air lost its electric luster. "You took that devil's side and left me all alone!"

"I thought you were going to kill me! I was letting you cool off, but you were gone by the time I came back."

The spear was raised again but there was little strength in Odessa's grip now. "You took its side. You turned against me."

"There are no sides!" Poko rose slowly now that there was some space between them and the spear. Hands raised. Watching the spear. "Just us and those who want to kill us. And she isn't one of them who want us dead. She wants to fight with you! Alongside you."

The spear sagged in her grip. "You chose a devil over me."

"You know that's not true," Poko said.

The spear jerked upward. "You blinded me and ran off with it!"

"You were going to kill her! What was I supposed to do?" Poko sighed.

"You were supposed to let me kill it," she said flatly. "I kill devils. It's what I do."

"That would have been a big mistake."

"Everything I've ever done has been one mistake after another," Odessa said. The tension had begun to drain from her body. "What's one more mistake?"

Poko took a tentative step toward her. Odessa turned her head and looked out over the desert below. She bit her quivering lip. Shame and sadness had come to douse the embers of her rage.

"Don't," Odessa said. "Don't come near me."

"It's okay." Poko continued toward her at a slow, measured pace. Talking as they would to a panicked animal. "Everything is okay. And I'm sorry, Dessa. I'm sorry I made you think I betrayed you. I would never ever betray you. We're in this together. Forever. Right?"

A choked sob came from Odessa's throat and she pressed her eyes shut for a moment. Tears spilled from her lashes. Such a torrent of tears was unfamiliar to her now—they stung and scalded her unaccustomed eyes. "I was going to kill you." Her iron fist loosened and the butt of the spear fell to the ground. "I almost killed you."

"It's okay," Poko said, only a handful of steps away. "I know you wouldn't have done that."

But I would have, Odessa thought. The spear slid from her left hand and fell with a clatter to the ground. Her hand went to her quivering frown, holding back a sob. *I wanted to kill you so bad.*

Poko stepped close and laid a hand on her calf. "I forgive you."

Odessa turned and stepped away from Poko's gentle touch. The tears were streaming down her cheeks. "I'm sorry," she said in a shaky, husky tone. "I'm sorry for everything." She kicked at the embers of the fire, knocking a clump of charred cloth across the ridge. A trail of ash and sparks followed it.

"I can't control myself anymore, she said, wiping at her tears with the back of her hand. "I just get so angry. So godsdamned angry all the time."

"It's not your fault," Poko said quietly. "You didn't want any of this."

Odessa shook her head. "Just because I didn't want it doesn't mean I'm free to hurt everybody around me." She sniffled, then blotted a drop of snot from her nose. "I thought I'd be rid of this by now. I really thought he was going to cure me."

Poko was quiet a moment, taken aback by her sudden candor. "I did too. I don't know how I didn't see it. I didn't sense it."

"He was a good liar," Odessa said, taking a seat on the boulder she had spent the night on. "He had to be. A blasphemer without cunning dies quick."

Poko said nothing, perhaps waiting for Odessa to say more, but she didn't. Her watery eyes had drifted back over the desert. It was quiet for a long while.

It was Poko who broke the silence. "She got captured, Dessa. We were trying to find you again and Sak-Tor's devils got her."

The wind rose and whipped coarse sand into the air. Plumes of sand from the faraway dunes of the east obscured the line of the horizon. "And?" Odessa asked.

"She got captured looking for you. Trying to help you."

"She was trying to recruit me to be her pawn," Odessa said curtly. "She was just trying to use me."

"I really don't think she was," Poko said.

"Well, pardon me if I don't immediately trust your judgment." Odessa turned from the ridge's edge, an ember of irritation stoked to life in her chest. "Yakun was as rotten as they come and he got past you, didn't he?"

"If you would just hear her out— "

"Save it," Odessa said, rising from the boulder. "None of it matters anyway. Even if I agreed with you and wanted to rescue her or whatever you've got planned, I can't." Ash and sparks stirred by another gust of wind twirled above them. "The bazaks are gone. The entehlo was on its last legs when I cut it loose." She waved a hand toward the remains of her signal fire. Her funeral pyre. "And I burned everything I could."

Poko looked between her and the fire then took a step toward it, finally taking the time to parse through the half-charred remnants hidden beneath the ash. "Why?"

As the wind settled, Odessa took her bow from the boulder. "I didn't set it to get your attention." She took the quiver from its place against the boulder and lashed it to her belt. Then she met Poko's eyes again. Poko's eyes were filled with confusion, concern, and a fair bit of pity. But Odessa's were dark and grave. Odessa nodded toward the eastern horizon. "I was trying to get theirs."

On the horizon, in the wisp of sand spraying over the crest of dunes, figures scattered about the ridge were in motion. The shapes of rider and mount spilling down the dunes and disappearing again behind slopes and ridges.

CHAPTER 14

Y ou should go." Odessa tightened the strap of the devilish helmet beneath her chin. "I left what food I had in the canyon back there. There might be some water in the trough too."

Poko fluttered to her side and began darting frantically around her head. "You don't have to do this. Just run."

The riders were spread out across the distant plains, darting through valleys and skirting around ridges to encircle her. They were still quite far away but the circle would close soon enough. And when it closed it would tighten fast around her. "I'm not running anymore." Odessa's finger tapped the grip of the club in her belt. Two devilish daggers sheathed at her back and wearing a devil's armor, she thought it somewhat fitting that it was devils that had found her first. She had taken much from them. Although she could not help feeling a bit disappointed that she would not die hacking apart Shadows and Red Clay Warriors. To have been afforded one final revenge would have been a proper and satisfying death, but the Forsaken could not be too particular. "I'm tired. I'm not doing this anymore."

"You don't have to do this anymore!" Poko hovered in front of her face, less than a hand's width away. "If you take Khara's deal, you can be free! You can go anywhere! Do anything!"

Odessa watched the fairy soberly. The fairy, so impassioned, could barely contain their distress. Their words came in a chittering cascade, and they gesticulated with wild, fevered abandon. But there was nowhere in the world she could go where she would be allowed even a modicum of happiness. If the devils or

Khymanir's soldiers or Kunza's Shadows did not get her, the Gray would. Even in the event of some miracle that allowed her a peaceful, natural death of old age, there awaited an endless, pitiless void. "You've been a good friend to me," she said. "Despite my ill temper, you've been good to me. And I'm thankful. Truly."

A choked moan escaped Poko's mouth. "Stop. Don't do this."

"It's too late," Odessa said. "Now go."

"You don't have to get Khara out. You don't have to do anything. Just please run away. I'll do anything. Just go."

"You've done enough for me, Poko." A trembling spasm brushed Odessa's lower lip. "I owe you more than you could ever realize." *You kept me human,* she thought but could not say. A lump had swelled in her throat and strangled off any further saccharine words.

"So, what?" Poko's voice was shrill and warbling. "You're just going to lie down and die?"

"No," Odessa said in a low, choked tone. "I'm going to take as many as I can with me."

"And what if you kill them all? You've been in worse fights before. A few devils is nothing to you."

Odessa nodded, not wanting to tell Poko she had seen nearly two dozen figures spread throughout the desert plain before them. All of them atop lamellar-armored entehlos. "You're right," she said huskily. "I've been through worse." Poko's dark, pleading eyes bored into her, suddenly full of hope rimmed with purest despondency. A soft part in Odessa's fire-hardened, battle-scourged heart ached looking at those eyes. That weak part of herself, the girl she once had been, could not bring herself to betray that naive hope. "If I kill them all then I'll think about rescuing your devil. Happy?"

Poko sniffled. "If you're alive, I'll be happy no matter what."

"You should really go now." The words barely came out from Odessa's choked throat.

"At least go to the canyon. You can hold them off there."

Odessa nodded dismissively and waved them off. She had no plans of leaving the ridge. The decision had been made and there would be no shrinking from it. The ridge was as fine a place to die as any.

Poko left, fluttering down the ridge toward the canyon. Odessa stood solitary on the barren ridge, a thin wisp of smoke rising from the ashes still. Her spear, rammed into the earth beside her, was like a flagpole with no standard to fly.

It was a strange feeling to stand before her own death. Toes hanging over the crumbling edge of a precipice down which there would be no return. Even in the baking desert heat, she was cold. Chilled. Abyssal cold licking at her feet and legs before it could swallow her whole.

Terror so pure it threatened to freeze her solid. Crushed by the dread of what awaited her after death. Amid these pure and toxic emotions, Odessa felt just the slightest tinge of relief. After she was gone, her family might not have to bear the shame and dishonor of sharing the same blood. Poko could move on. Perhaps find another court of fairies and regale them with stories of the Forsaken girl and her pitiful end. There might have even been a bit of contemptuous and sardonic mirth in the churning of her suicidal emotions. Whatever plans Yakun and Talara had for her would die with her. And that thought was enough to carry her through to the end if nothing else would. Spite was a sufficient motivator when nothing else remained.

The devils riding up the ridge across from her own made no further pains to conceal their presence. Odessa wondered if they had her encircled now. A semi-circle of around two dozen riders was arrayed from the top of the opposite ridge and down into the valley. Close enough now for her to make out their features. Shadowed eyes and sharp, dark-colored horns curling out from beneath their helmets.

Before the semicircle could collapse and fall upon her, Odessa had an arrow nocked and the bowstring drawn.

"Bloodsucker! You are caught!" a devil with long horns curling out from her head called out from across the valley. Her voice was as clear as a pealing bell in the fragile stillness. "Lay down your arms now and you may yet have a quick death!"

Odessa's iron fingers pinching the arrow's nock tightened. Beneath the metal, her knotted muscles throbbed with strain and the anticipatory tingle of blood-lust. She licked her lips and tried to work some spit into her mouth. Her stomach had become cold and sank in her belly. The precipice crumbled beneath her feet.

The arrow flew with a hiss.

The devil that had shouted raised her shield the instant the arrow took flight. The arrow punched through the entehlo's armored skull and the beast dropped, its front legs giving out and making it tumble forward and slide down the ridge. The devil was leaping off her mount when Odessa loosed her second arrow. The arrow caught her in the throat.

"You will have me dead or you won't have me at all!" Odessa shouted, near hysterically. The other riders, at the entehlo's felling, tore through the valley toward her. Hooves churning up clouds of dust. She let fly two more arrows, downing another entehlo, before the first riders began their charge up her ridge.

The rushing roar of her pumping blood was loud. Louder than it had ever been before. Louder even than the pounding of hooves up the ridge. Any thought she may have had was drowned in that thunderous thrum.

Arrows shot toward her, but she was already in motion. She dropped the bow, ripped the spear from the ground, and took careful steps backward down the slope's opposite side until she could only barely see above the crest of the ridge. Arrows were still streaking through the air or skittering and snapping upon the ridge. Her weight balanced on the balls of her feet, she felt light. Almost weightless. The heavy dread was lifted with the racing of her heart. *This is it,* she thought in a momentary flash before the thrum overtook the thought. Her breathing was quick. Her palm was clammy against the smooth spear shaft. As the first devil horns began to rise above the ridge, a thought struck her through the rush. *In this moment, I'm free.*

The first riders were upon her in an instant. Cresting the ridge and racing toward her. Entehlos in iron-paneled armor charging over the ridge. All she could see were hooves and legs and clattering armor. The earth shook beneath her at the impetus of furious hooves. Rattling through her bones. Odessa leaped out from the entehlo's path as the rider's polearm flashed toward her. She ducked, knocked the blade aside, then rammed her spear up. The entehlo's rush brought the rider slamming in to the spear. The spearhead punched through the devil's armored middle and stuck there.

Before Odessa could rip the spear free, another rider was bearing down upon her. The impaled rider's entehlo continued its headlong dash. The spear was ripped from her grip as another rider's club hurtled toward her head.

Her iron arm caught the club's gnarled head with a loud crash. The impact pushed her back, staggering her. Barely staying upright, she lurched down the rest of the slope. Jolts of pain coursed up and down her arm. The rider passed her and turned to double back as four more riders charged down the hill.

Spittle flew as she let loose a scream of primal frustration. The pounding in her ears crescendoed. She drew the booming thrum into her arm. Flames burst from the myriad channels along her arm, wreathing its length in furious gold fire. Fire that swelled until her entire right side seemed to be ablaze. The flames were hotter and more intense than anything she had conjured before.

At the sudden, fiery eruption, entehlos barreling toward her veered away. Their riders' swings and thrusts were made ineffectual. A polearm's hooked blade glanced off her shoulder.

More riders were making their way downhill, slowing and circling her. Sweat dripped from her brow and her skin was scorching beneath her arm, but she did not let the crescendo fade. She clung to it, pouring more of that thrumming energy into the flames.

More than a dozen riders surrounded her and more were coming. One of the riders, a weighted net slung across her saddle, slowed outside the revolving circle of riders. "You seem to misunderstand, bloodsucker," the net-wielding rider said. "You are not to die here, quickly or otherwise. You are to die at the hands of

Sak-Tor, King of Conquerors." Her tone was flat with ill humor. "Your crimes against the Torva are many. Surrender now and you may lessen your agony in the coming judgment."

Odessa's flames snapped and roared, rising over her helmet in their fury. Her gaze met the devil's even as circling riders passed between them. "No one's going to capture me. Ever." The flames flared, racing along iron scales across her chest. "Not while I'm still breathing."

"Your fire burns bright, but it will not burn indefinitely," the devil said. "We have hunted you long enough to know that much. And when your fire dies, what will you do then?"

Odessa's iron hand fell to the club in her belt. Sliding it free, the flames leaped to the leather belt and began to consume it. "I'll rip your heart from your chest." Her other hand whipped one of the devilish daggers from its sheath. The fire was spreading across her oil-seasoned scales. The laces and leather backing of her armor had begun to catch flame as well. There came a soft tinkling of falling scales when she moved. But she continued pouring her all into the fire. *If you won't kill me, I'll kill you. I'll kill you all. You can all die here and I'll drink up your blood until you're skin and bones.* A few of the circling riders made weak jabs and swings in her direction. Keeping her at bay.

Die. Die. Die. The words came like a mantra. In rhythm with the pounding drumbeat of her racing heart. The riders continued circling her. Almost thirty riders. Circling around and around. "It's kill or be killed, you horned bitch!" Odessa shouted. Months and months of accumulated rage and hate bolstered her words to the point they barely seemed like language at all. She hated these devils as she hated Kunza and Yakun and Khymanir and Tarik. She pointed her club at the devil. More scales fell clattering to the ground. "Now which will it be?"

The devil sat astride her entehlo, unmoved. The circle continued its spinning, so many sets of eyes trained upon her. Spears, polearms, and clubs trying the air in front of her.

They're playing with me. Just playing with me. The flames had spread across her chest and torso. Even stretching in a thin layer down her left arm. Flames wasted if they were not scorching devils. But she could not quash their avaricious abandon. The fire was ecstasy. She felt truly alive. This was her true self. She could not restrain it any longer. *But they're playing with me like a cornered animal.*

A thrusting spear glanced off her helmet with a clang. Odessa's fire-wreathed hand snapped forward and snatched the withdrawing spear. The shaft charred and cracked as she yanked. The rider holding the spear came toppling off her entehlo. She struck the dirt with a crash and a wheeze.

No, they're not playing with me. Odessa stood over the rider as she clambered to her hands and knees. Odessa's flame no longer flared and raged. A dawning thought came to gently smother them. *They're poking and prodding me to keep me at bay.* Breaking the burning spear in her grip, she was reminded of snapping spears in the Arabako Forest. The jabbing of hunters' spears as Egende gored and terrorized. *They're right to fear me.* Odessa drew the flames back into her pounding blood. Holding them until her veins bulged and her heart ached so deeply she thought it would burst. *I'll show them what I am. What a monster I've become.* The flames had settled to a few thin lines of orange in the channels of her arm. The pressure built inside her.

The devil was struggling to her feet when Odessa brought the club down on her helmet. The metal crumpled with a crunch and squeal. The devil's amber eyes bulged and blood poured from their nose. Shouts surrounded her. As did the snorts of spurred entehlos. The thunder of myriad hooves in sudden motion. The devil with the net was shouting, but her voice was lost in the din.

She held the flames inside for a fraction of a second. Letting them build inside her arm just a moment longer. Building toward an ultimate climax.

Just as the first polearm swung to take her head, she let go. She let go of everything. And forced the flames out of her like she never had before.

CHAPTER 15

The explosion's concussive blast tore through the canyon where Poko hid, sending rocks tumbling from the walls and dust drifting down in wisps. Poko was curled beneath a shelf of rock, their hands clamped over their ears to block out Odessa's shouts. But the rush of hot air through the canyon made them open their screwed-shut eyes. They blinked and wiped their away their cowardly tears as the blast echoed in their head. For a moment that was all they could do. Then the screaming came.

Dazed, Poko scrambled out from beneath the shelf and took flight. Racing out of the canyon toward the blast. All the while, their mind was a jumble of confusion and fear and worst- case scenarios. The harsh, agonized braying of entehlos and the guttural cries of devils. Shouts and curses drowned out by wails of pain.

The thought that soon stuck in their mind like searing hot shrapnel was that it had to be a cannon or blast powder. In their flight, Odessa's body, charred and mangled by shot and shrapnel, refused to leave their mind. Limbs blown asunder. Ribbons of flesh and entrails strewn about.

Near the mouth of the canyon, they could smell the acrid stink of burned flesh. They emerged from the canyon's mouth to see bodies aflame. A pile of burned bodies. A black mass of limbs and trunks, twisting and thrashing. Entehlos writhed and kicked in heaps on the ground, their flesh charred. Some of the beasts, those only partially scorched, ran panicked. Bellowing as they fled. Devils pinned beneath their dead or dying mounts screamed and coughed.

Those with scorched lungs lay gasping and wheezing. Those who could move did so slowly and with great effort.

Poko stopped when they saw Odessa rise from the center of the heap. For a moment, Odessa stood, hunched over and swaying like a drunkard. Blood streamed from a deep gash across her forehead. A flap of skin flopping as her head slowly canted back and forth. Assessing the gruesome scene.

Shock and relief had just begun to dawn in Poko's stupefied brain when Odessa lurched to life. She brought up her club and bludgeoned a gasping devil. Like a harvester in a field of blackened limbs, she picked her way through the heap and set about her work. Moving like a wraith among them and caving their heads in with wild, frenzied swings. The devils who could move hurried to gather their arms or perhaps try to flee, but before they could, Odessa was upon them. Her movements quick with manic agility, the devils were too dazed and in pain to resist. One devil had gotten to her knees and had leveled a spear at Odessa. Even feinted and thrusted. But Odessa batted the spear away as if it were a buzzing fly, closed the distance, and bashed the devil's helmet until its peaked top was a misshapen bowl.

Poko's fluttering slowed and they landed and watched as Odessa slaughtered the devils. This had been what Poko had wanted. Odessa was alive. But watching the detached ferocity of the slaughter made Poko's heart rise to their throat.

Poko knew they should say or do something. But shock had affixed their feet solidly to the ground and their risen heart lodged in their throat. All they could do was watch and listen. The crash and crunch of the club caving in helmets and skulls was savagely loud.

When the last devil was dead many times over, Odessa's swings began to slow. Then she stopped and stood like she had fallen asleep standing upright. The club slipped from her hand and she fell to her knees amid the burned corpses.

Poko moved without thought, racing across the valley toward her. When they drew close, their shock all but dissipated, a spike of worry jabbed inside their chest. Odessa's gaze was vacant. Her eyes blank and empty.

The grooves carved in Odessa's iron fist glowed the color of hot coals. A shimmering haze coalesced around her arm. Wisps like threads of mirage drifted lazily from the corpses, rising from ribbons of putrid smoke to gather about Odessa.

Poko stopped a dozen steps away from her. The air around the heap was thin, and there was a sort of pulling sensation at the edge of their perception. Like something tugging at their soul.

Poko opened their mouth to speak then shut it again. The haze around Odessa's arm was thinning. It was seeping into her. So Poko waited, uncertainly, for it to disappear. Waiting to see what would happen once it was gone.

It took only a few seconds for the rest of the haze to have sunk into the glowing channels and disappear entirely. Still Poko hesitated.

"Odessa?" they said, barely more than a whisper.

Odessa was quiet. Blinking and staring at her iron hand. Blankness still in her gaze.

Poko took a step closer. "Dessa?"

"They wouldn't kill me," Odessa said lifelessly, still staring vacantly at her fist. "And I'm too scared to kill myself."

It felt like someone had punched Poko in the chest. For a moment, they were speechless. "You poor thing," they said finally.

"I'm scared to die. That's why I killed them, I think. Why I made the firestorm."

Poko looked at the charred bodies piled around them. A few entehlos were still kicking and writhing pitifully. "I didn't know you could do that."

"Me neither." Odessa blinked and there was a glimmer of light in her eyes. Faded but there. "I just wanted to burn a few before they cut me down."

The stink of burnt flesh and the horror around them was making Poko sick to their stomach, but they strained to smile. "Always the overachiever, huh?"

Odessa did not answer. She only swayed, blinking slowly, then turned to Poko. "Looks like I have to save your devil now, huh?"

Before Poko could say anything, Odessa fell forward and landed atop a devil with a pulped face. Poko rushed forward, panicking for a moment before they realized Odessa was asleep and not dead.

While Odessa slept, Poko was left with the smoking corpses and bellowing entehlos. Left with time to think. *The poor girl's falling apart,* Poko thought. *I don't know what to do.*

CHAPTER 16

Gray fog blanketed the land. From the sprawling camp set in a barren field a few days north of Noyo, Ayana and Kunza waited for the last scouts' report. They sat beneath the awning of Kunza's tent, which had been placed on a slight rise in the field so they could look over the camp, neither of them speaking. The totality of the gray gloom around them was devastating to the morale of the troops and it was not any easier on them. All throughout the camp, thick waves of fog drifted. The sky above was dark, day and night. An hour's walk north of the camp, a wall of milky gray rose. A wall of mist so thick it looked to be impenetrable. But within it lay untold horrors. Within it hid pure annihilation.

Their last party of Shadows were due back from the mist within the hour, but Ayana was becoming impatient. After a few more painful moments of seated waiting, she rose and paced the length of the sparse tent.

"Sit down," Kunza said sharply. His voice was dry and brittle. "Pray if you must busy yourself with something."

Ayana stopped her pacing. "What good is prayer here? This damnable mist muffles everything. I could not hear the Goddess if she was screaming in my ear." She began her pacing again.

Kunza was about to say something curt and biting when the Shadows emerged from the near mists, slinking past the trenches at the far edge of camp. He rose to his feet. "They're back."

It took a few minutes for the Shadows to make their way through the camp. Once they reached Kunza's tent, eight Shadows filed inside.

"What is your report?" Kunza asked.

One of the Shadows stepped forward. One of the few blessed with a voice. "Target position is confirmed. Path around the largest concentration of Blighted was found."

Kunza gestured to the table filling the back half of the tent. A sheaf of parchment bearing a map of Noyo and its surrounding areas was stretched upon it. Symbols and figures had been scribbled all over its face. "Show me," Kunza said.

Ayana watched and listened as best she could, but too many nervous thoughts chattered in her mind. Up until this point she had been able to stay composed and detached. But now that the day was upon her, she could not calm the nervous energy coursing through her like static. If their plan failed—if she failed— Noyo would be totally engulfed in Gray within a cycle. And then it would be Kalaro next swallowed in Gray.

After the Shadow scouts' report, things moved quickly. Kunza and the scouts led her through the tangle of tents and campfires at a near trot. They had amassed nearly five thousand soldiers, human and otherwise, at this camp at the edge of the mist. With the fog and the bustle of so many bodies, traversing the huge camp was not easy. Ayana stayed close behind Kunza. Her beastfolk entourage was following at a distance behind them she knew, but she could not see them no matter how hard she looked. The mist had doubled in thickness in the week since she and Kunza had arrived.

When they reached the edge of camp, Kunza stopped and faced her, his ember eyes muted in the mist. "You are sure you can do this, yes?"

"Yes," Ayana said, pulling off her gloves and tucking them in the belt of her kaftan. On the cusp of battle, she was deaf even to Kunza's lack of confidence in her. Now his words were like the mutterings of people in a neighboring hut. Inconsequential and irrelevant. She knelt, plucked a blade of dry brown grass, and straightened with the blade pinched between her fingers. The grass had died weeks ago with the coming of the Gray. But it did not rot. Nothing rotted in the Gray. It was a perversion of all that was natural.

She took a breath, held it, then let it out through her nostrils. Between her fingertips, she felt the tingling and focused on it. Clung to it. In a few seconds, the blade of grass began to brown, then blacken and crumble away. Tiny pieces of detritus scattered on the dead grasses below.

"I can do this," Ayana said, brushing the rotted grass from her fingertips.

"I only wish you could have been given more time to hone your gift," Kunza said. Ayana had only begun to truly harness the rot within the last few months. But she knew it was not a skill that needed practice. It was Talara's doing. Talara's might made manifest through her body. She was but a vessel for the Goddess's glory. There was no honing a Goddess's gift. She knew that, but Kunza's words had truth in them, and she too wished she had been allowed more time to more thoroughly grasp Talara's power.

"Have faith, Kunza," Ayana said, a bit solemnly. "Not just in the Goddess. Have faith in me as well."

"I do." Kunza raised his hand as if to reach out and reassuringly touch her shoulder but stopped himself. "You have become everything required of you and more. And I am so proud of you, Ayana. I know you are capable of this and so much more. But still I worry."

A warmth touched Ayana's heart. The damp gloom of the camp had only worsened the sullen cloud that had hung over her since leaving Kalaro. Since speaking with her mother. But Kunza's kindness was like a warm drink on a cold day. It permeated her frigid insides, filling her chest and thawing that which had lost sensation.

"Thank you," Ayana said. "For everything. If you hadn't brought me into Talara's embrace I don't know what would have become of me." But in a vague sense she did know. She would have become like her mother. A withering husk of a person.

Kunza smiled as much as his perpetually solemn demeanor would allow. His wizened face seemed unfit for such expressions but the slight smile was warm and kind nonetheless. "You should go now," he said.

Ayana nodded but did not move. She looked around to see nearly one hundred Shadows now lined in rows behind her. But there was no one else. She turned back to Kunza. "I know I'm supposed to act like Talara's divinely appointed. And this may be improper, but . . ." Her gaze drifted to the wall of Gray, then back to Kunza. "I am scared. I am full of doubt. I know I shouldn't—Talara tells me I shouldn't be—but I am. Now that I'm here, I'm scared, Kunza. Our fate rests entirely with me in this very moment and I don't know if I'm enough."

Kunza's hands rose and this time did not fall away. He took her by the shoulders and fixed her with his hearth-glow gaze. "You are enough. Talara chose you for a reason." His fingers squeezed her shoulders through the cotton of her kaftan. The warmth in her chest blossomed further. No one had touched her since she had taken godsblood for fear that Talara's rot would consume their unworthy flesh. Even through fabric, they thought it sacrilege. Trying to act as she thought Talara's Sacred Queen would, she had taken the burden of loneliness and isolation without complaint, but now she realized how much her heart yearned for the kind touch of another human. "I know you are capable of things far beyond what today entails. Today is but the first step. So do not worry about our fate or what is or is not proper. Just do your part and we shall do ours. And by the day's end, we will be celebrating the first victory of many."

Ayana nodded, her heart close to bursting. Since her treacherous father died, she had not felt such compassion from anyone. For most of her life, she had thought Kunza a miserably irritable old ka-man. She had never known such kindness resided within him. He had never taken a wife nor had children, yet she saw him now very much like a father. A father to all of Kalaro. Perhaps all of future humanity even.

She relished his kindness for a moment longer. It was like lingering at a fire before returning to the cold outside. Then she said, "Thank you, Kunza. I appreciate that. Truly."

"Of course, my Queen," he said kindly, giving her shoulders a squeeze, then releasing her. "Now go. Let the Shadows lead the way. Do not take any unnecessary risks. I will let the ritual commence by the time you reach the spore column."

Ayana nodded, wanting to say more but knowing there was no more time. Instead she turned to the Shadows and her three beastfolk companions standing before the rows of Shadows. "To the spore column," she ordered them.

The Shadows formed four groups and situated themselves around her. Her beastfolk, two goat-headed men, and a jackal-headed woman stayed close at her side, spears in hand. Ayana wrapped a vinegar-soaked cloth around her nose and mouth before they entered the Gray. The first few breaths she drew through the cloth stung her nostrils and made her cough, but she soon grew more accustomed to it.

Entering the wall of Gray was like wading through water. The air was so thick and heavy. Ayana could barely see her beastfolk s' backs at arm's length in front of her. It was suffocating. Devoid of any wind. Any sound. It was like walking into another world. As she walked, following her beastfolk s' brisk pace, she began to notice a chill in her fingertips. But it was not exactly a physical sensation. The Gray was sapping her strength. Leeching life from her exposed skin. When she put her mind to it, the draining chill receded, but it would return if she let her guard slacken.

It was impossible to tell how far they had traveled or for how long. Everything was milky and opaque. The grade of the ground beneath their feet would sometimes fluctuate but not often. Ayana had no idea how the Shadows could find their way through the mist.

Occasionally she heard wheezing moans in the near distance. Sound was muffled in the suffocating fog. Ayana could barely hear the tromping of her beastfolk s' bare, bony feet. After a while, she began hearing moans much more clearly. Some turned to garbled cries or gurgling whines as a Shadow killed the Blighted. In the fog, she never caught sight of a Blighted. None of them reached the center of their formation. The Shadows were an impenetrable bulwark.

When the wet sounds of the Blighted being cut down came more frequently, she knew they were getting close. The ground beneath their feet had grown somewhat spongey. Like walking on a layer of dead leaves without the crunching and crackling. Suddenly the formation stopped. She could hear nearby hacking and stabbing. The thud of bodies falling on soft soil. Her head swiveled back and forth trying to make out anything in the soupy grayness. Her goat-headed companions pressed close to her, their spears pointed out in opposite directions.

She took a few deep breaths, drawing the tingling feeling to her fingertips again. Making it spread up her fingers, to her knuckles, and then her wrists. A comforting cold like a wet rag on feverish skin surrounded her trembling hands.

The jackal-headed woman made a grunt and gestured to Ayana to follow. Ayana walked behind her, her feet sinking slightly more with every step. She nearly tripped and fell over a soft lump the size of a log that struck her shin. The jackal-headed woman steadied her and then guided her the rest of the way. She soon noticed Shadows in the mist around her. Their black robes little more than lumps of black lost in the tangles of fog.

The ground began to slope. That was when she knew she was at the column. She could not see it yet for the Gray all about her, but she could feel it. The draining sensation intensified. A few steps up the soft slope and she could feel a constant outward rush of air. The only breeze she had felt in the stagnant mire of mist. But it was somehow wrong. Its caressing touch was sickening. It felt as if it left some sort of residue behind to seep into her pores.

There was rhythm to the breeze's fluctuating gusts. Like a series of bellows working in tandem, alternating between filling and emptying a hundred times per minute. Or like a palpitating, many-chambered heart.

She came within arm's reach of the spore column before she could make it out through the mist. She could only see a portion of it, but she knew it had to be many times taller than she was. She could feel its towering presence. It was thicker around than any tree in the Arabako Forest. Its uneven surface was lichenous, the pale off-white color of unbleached bone. From between the myriad lichenous ridges stretched across the column's surface were what looked to be fungal gills but made of flesh. Tiny feathery fingers rose from these gills, and they quivered with every exhalation the column took. The gills took turns exhaling. Thousands of them alternating breaths. The entire fleshy column trembling and pulsing with its constant sighs.

Hesitantly, her hand trembling despite the reassuring tingle, she pressed her palm against the column. As soon as her skin touched its spongey surface, she could feel the life being drained from her. Like arctic cold sapping a bare body's warmth, the column absorbed her strength. She pressed her other hand against the column and forced the tingling to her palms. Her blood began to pulse as she concentrated, pouring all she had into her palms.

The column's leeching began to lessen, but still it was too much for her to bear for long. She drew her right hand back, balled it into a fist, and sent it rocketing forward. Her fist sank wrist-deep into the column's quivering flesh. It was like punching through stringy gut. She plunged her fist deep, to the elbow. All the while concentrating the electric cold of rot in her hands and then her arms. She plunged her second fist into the column just as she had done the first. The entire mass spasmed.

Behind her came the sounds of battle. Blades striking bodies. Bodies striking bodies. Flesh ripped apart by blade or by jaws and claws. She poured herself into the chill energy coursing through her arms. Soon the lichenous gills around her submerged arms began to blacken and peel away, the flesh rotting and sloughing off. Her arms began to tremble but she did not let up. Her decomposition began carving two massive holes in the column, gnawing a blackened crater around each of her arms. When her arms became visible after sections of dark, oozing column came falling off, she could see a shimmering dark aura radiating from around her forearms and fists. She rammed her fists deeper into the column and spread the rot further. The quivering of the column's gills became irregular and fluttery. Almost pained.

The more she rotted, the faster it spread. Like a tidal wave gaining speed, the wave of blackening sludge and slime wormed its way through the column's center. Great pieces of fungal flesh sheared from its sides and fell to decompose on the lichen-covered ground, which in turn would begin to rot.

Whatever the Gray was, it was not alive. It drained all life from the living and then corrupted and commandeered their flesh. Using the living to spread its spores. The Gray was so powerful it even drained the life from those fungi and bacteria that caused rot. But the Gray column of stolen flesh was powerless against the Goddess's pure might. It would rot like anything else and so, too, would its proliferating spores. Ayana smiled, but it was much more akin to a snarl. She began punching into the column, pulverizing huge chunks of column and leaving cancerous craters behind.

Soon the column began to collapse, massive pieces of rotting flesh falling all around her. As her decay began to spread around the column's base, the mist thinned just the tiniest bit. Allowing her to see the bedlam around her.

Gangly, fleshy white figures, some bipedal and some on all fours, darted through the fog at the Shadows, snarling and howling in guttural tones. She noticed scattered along the slope the corpses of many such figures, buried and melting beneath the lichen-like flesh that covered the entire slope.

Fleeing from the collapsing column, she leaped over a half-buried Blighted corpse to meet the jackal-headed woman as she skewered a four-legged lump of sloughing flesh through its disjointed mouth of fangs. As she neared the jackal-headed woman, a great force struck her, knocking her to the ground. She spun onto her back to find a giant-sized figure hulking over her, its face pale and misshapen. Lumps of lichenous ridges marred half its doughy body. Its crooked mouth opened disturbingly wide, loose skin pulling taut and even tearing, to reveal black gums and a mouth packed with disordered rows of fangs. The roof of its mouth and its sinewy tongue were covered in sharp teeth.

Massive clammy hands gripped her wrists as she reached out to stop the lunging jaws. The loose, doughy skin on her wrists began to blister and peel away as lesions quickly gnawed away the flesh. Ayana pulled free of the figure's decaying grip and caught its neck in both hands before its jaws could close over the bottom of her face. Her fingers dug into its neck and bored blackening holes into it until her hands were curled into fists inside its throat. Yet the jaws continued snapping, the figure's weight bearing down on her. Her arms were trembling terribly as she pushed its slavering face aside. Before her arms gave out, a spear pierced its skull and one of the goat-headed men was heaving the massive body off her.

The jackal-headed woman helped her to her feet. Ayana ripped the vinegar-soaked cloth from around her face and threw it to the ground. It was covered in the figure's slobber and gobs of its clotted blood. Her beastfolk ushered her toward the circle of retreating Shadows, and the Blighted surged from the mists. Bronze blades flashed in the mist, and black, congealed blood spread across flesh as the Blighted fell in heaps.

She joined their ranks and they retreated. As they fled, the mist became thinner and thinner. Kunza's ritual had begun. Talara's decay was spreading across the land. Without the column's constant tide of spores, it would overcome the Gray here. Once the Gray had thinned enough for their human and giant troops, the Blighted extermination would begin in earnest. And Ayana would have more columns to find and destroy. And they would begin chipping away at the tide of annihilation.

The dark aura around Ayana's hands had dissipated; now her hands spasmed and ached. Light-headedness clouded her thoughts and her vision became blurred. But she felt happier than she ever had been. A victory against the end times had been won by her hand.

The seeds of a new world had been planted in the humus of the damnable column. And she had planted them. Ayana, Sacred Queen of Talara's People, had done it.

CHAPTER 17

The entrails of her Sisters that had been draped over the stumps of Khara's horns had begun to rot. As they had disemboweled the Sisters shackled alongside her, the camp had cheered. The entrails had been hot as they fell upon her head and shoulders like garlands. Her gutted Sister was still writhing as they had done this. Someone in the camp had called this the Princess's coronation and it had spread throughout the jeering masses. All the while they hollowed out her Sisters and covered her in their slick, blood-slimed guts, she did not cry out or utter a sound.

But now, three days later, she quietly cried. She only allowed herself to cry at night, when but a few guards stayed in the plaza. Every night she cried, but rarely did she have enough moisture in her body to produce tears. Her choked sobs were little more than raspy gasps.

Morning was fast approaching. And with morning's arrival would come one of Sak-Tor's sons, Pon-Tor. Pon-Tor would either bring her to his father for her punishment or he would dispense the King's justice himself. She had heard of Pon-Tor and his proclivities; she knew, either way, she was going to experience pain and humiliation she had never before thought possible.

All of Sak-Tor's sons were sadistic rapists with a penchant for wanton slaughter, but Pon-Tor was especially cruel. From what little Khara had heard of him, whenever it was his turn to go from village to village and inseminate those unlucky Torva due for breeding, it was not uncommon for one of his compulsory bedmates to end up dead. Knowing that he would be here in the morning, Khara seriously considered biting off her tongue and choking to death on her own blood. But she thought the guards would see her and staunch the bleeding before she was able to die. But as morning drew closer, the thought became more tempting.

After a while and without meaning to, she fell asleep and was awoken by the clarion ring of horns. Khara felt sick. Her body already so weak from days and days upon the post, she knew she could not take much more. And it was only going to get worse.

She could not lift her head as Pon-Tor's procession entered the plaza. Shouts and exaltations came from the most loyal among the camp. Heavy footsteps crunched across the plaza. Coming closer. Then thick fingers were wrapping themselves in her hair. They jerked her hanging head up. The half-dried entrails hanging from her stumps swung in erratic arcs.

Pon-Tor had a wide face. His skin was pitted and dark as a ripe olive. He scowled and his narrow, wide-set eyes held a glint of malice. Her head was thrown back down as Pon-Tor stepped away to speak with his audience.

"Sak-Tor, our King of Conquerors, has decreed that Khara, daughter of Zarin, will be brought before him and be punished for the crimes of desertion, dereliction of duty, theft, and sedition. For this she will be flayed and broken upon the wheel at the hands of Sak-Tor himself," Pon-Tor announced, his voice booming. Khara's heart sank. "I am to bring her to the main army's camp along the Darrood so he may mete out her punishment. But before that, I have been tasked with extracting some answers from her treacherous lips."

He turned to face her again. Taking a step toward her, he pulled a pair of short-handled pincers with wide jaws. "Where are your fellow traitors?" he asked, shouting so the audience might still hear him. When she said nothing, did not lift her gaze, he swung the pincers hard across the side of her head.

Her skull rang, loud and bright. Hot blood poured down the side of her head and dripped onto the dirt below her. "I know your fellow cunts are somewhere here in the western plains. Now tell me where they are."

She said nothing again, and this time he punched her in the stomach. Her body curled, back pressing against the post as she wheezed and hacked.

"Where were you with them last? Where were they going?" he continued, standing beside her, a hand on her shackles. He shook her arms, as if she might have fallen asleep and needed to be roused. When she still did not respond, he set the blunt jaws of the pincers around the small finger of her right hand. "If you don't start talking I will break every bone in every finger you have. Then I start cutting them off. Do you understand?"

Khara nodded but still didn't talk. Her small finger snapped with a tiny crack. The pain was tremendous. She stifled her screams for the breaking of her first two fingers, but after that she could not restrain her cries anymore.

When Pon-Tor had broken all her fingers and still not gotten the information he wanted, he slid a dagger from a sheath on his belt and touched the blade to her crooked small finger. His inquiries were as distant as the jeers and shouts of the crowd. Her eyes rolled back behind twitching, half-open eyelids.

Pon-Tor twisted her already broken little finger over the blade. Broken bones and ruptured tendons ground against one another. Khara's eyes widened and she sucked in a quick, harsh gasp. "Tell me one thing," Pon-Tor said. "One thing and you keep your fingers." He leaned close, almost conspiratorially. The stink of sweat and spices was cloyingly redolent. "Is the old crone with you?"

Khara panted. Both her hands were aflame with fiery agony that throbbed and pulsed down her arms. White hot agony filled her mind, but still Pon-Tor's question permeated the pall of explosive pain. The old crone was Remaka, one of Sak-Tor's eldest daughters and the Sisters' Matron. To Pon-Tor and the rest of Sak-Tor's Torva, Remaka was dead. Thought to have been lost in the sack of Malbrogdva in the far northeast. When the siege was almost at its end, the Malbrogdvans, in a final desperate act, regained the dikes north of the city and destroyed them, flooding everything outside the city walls. Remaka and her soldiers were lost among the flood. By the providence of war, she and her most loyal soldiers fled among those rising waters. Leaving thousands of her own floating dead in those brackish, debris-choked waters.

To hear Remaka's name come from Pon-Tor's mouth, Khara's stomach sank. Word of Remaka's involvement would reclassify the Sisters from a ragtag band of deserters to an insurrection let fester too long.

Pon-Tor leaned close to her face. "Yes or no. One word and you'll be spared any more pain."

Kiara struggled to meet his dark, intensely virulent gaze. Looking into his eyes was like standing before a great conflagration. Waves of intense heat poured off them and battered her eyes away.

A moment passed. Pon-Tor did not even blink as he sawed through her little finger, slicing through skin and cartilage in a few strokes. Before he tore the severed half of her finger from the bleeding stump of tendon and bone, Khara's scream tapered away and her eyes rolled back into her skull.

A few of Pon-Tor's heavy-handed slaps brought her back to consciousness. Her cheeks stung and her jaw ached. Her bleeding stump burned more intensely than she had ever thought possible. Blood like molten metal poured down her hands and flowed in thin rivers of fire down her arms.

Pon-Tor was holding the severed digit before her unfocused eyes. "Yes or no."

Khara's vision was a narrowing hole that shifted and shook with the pulses of molten pain. Unconsciousness pulled at her—the fugue come to rescue her—only for a sobering throb of agony to bring her back to the conscious world and the severed finger held before her eyes. Her mouth soundlessly opened and closed like a speared fish pulled from the water. Speech was beyond her. Too much pain addled her mind. All she knew was that she did not want to hurt anymore.

The finger fell to the ground at her feet and rolled a bit before Pon-Tor's boot stamped on it. He ground the toe of his boot into the dirt and took her by the hair again, yanking her head up to meet his gaze. "One word. All I want is one word." The dagger's point dug into her cheek, just hard enough to draw blood. "Or I stop cutting and start skinning." The dagger left her cheek to gently prod at her belly. Her abdominal muscles contracted with a jerk at the blade's touch. Pon-Tor leaned close, grinning with a darkly mischievous glimmer in his eyes. "Our king wants the privilege but he won't begrudge me taking a small piece for myself." The flat of the blade slid up her belly. Her skin prickled and twitched beneath the blade's caress. "Just a strip down your back." His breath was hot and wet against her ear. "I'll make a belt from your hide."

A choked groan escaped her. A low, plaintive moan was the best she could muster. The closest thing to an affirmative she could draw from a throat torn raw by dry air and constant wailing. She wanted to tell him Remaka was alive. She wanted to tell him everything. About Remaka and the Sisters. Anything to make the pain stop. She had never felt such cowardice, and it revolted her like nothing in her life ever had. No battlefield had reduced to her such a quivering craven. Not even as a child spear-bearer had she felt such a coward. And perhaps that hurt more deeply than anything she could be subjected to.

At her moan, Pon-Tor looked at her. A sick satisfaction had sharpened his grin. The dagger withdrew from her belly. "Did you want to say something?"

She licked her lips and tasted dried blood. Her hands were trembling and felt both hot and cold at the same time. The fugue beckoned from the back of her mind, but she resisted it. She searched within herself and found the only thing that remained unyielding and immutable inside her exhausted mind. And she grasped it with all the strength of spirit she had left.

It took considerable effort to raise her head and look into Pon-Tor's sadistically enraptured eyes, but she did it. She had to. She had to remind herself of the face of her enemy. Her true enemy. It was hate that she held within herself. The hate of a young girl in an unjust world. The hate of a woman—a warrior— dreading the day when someone like Pon-Tor would come and steal away what little agency she had.

She cleared her throat. It felt raw and inflamed. "Blight take you all," she said hoarsely. "I hope you all die screaming."

Pon-Tor's smile faded, and his brow knit to cast a dark shadow over his cruel eyes. Without another word, he took her bleeding hand roughly and began slicing and sawing again. A spurt of blood and an explosion of pain and another finger fell to the dirt. Khara screamed her lungs empty. Thrashing against the post. Kicking at his legs. Her screams and resistance weakening with each finger severed. After the third finger, unconsciousness took her in its merciful embrace.

CHAPTER 18

It was pain that had submerged Khara in the black mire of unconsciousness and it was that same pain that pulled her from its soft and nebulous grasp. She was groaning before she realized she was awake. Pulsing agony like waves of heat radiated from her hands. Her hands were covered with dry blood cut through by myriad streams of scarlet. Rivulets of blood had flowed down her arms and chest to pool in the dirt around her feet.

Her head was hanging, her blood-matted, dirt-caked hair and her Sisters' desiccated entrails hung down before her eyes. Twilight's muted tones were giving way to pure, unadulterated night. It was dark but her eyes could plumb the night's depths well enough to make out the shapes of the tents around the plaza in the pitch black of the darkest desert nights. A part of her wished her eyes were less attuned to such dark so she would not have to see what had been done to her. But the constant white-hot throbbing would not let her avert her eyes for long. She had to see. She had to know. Reluctantly, she twisted her head upwards to survey her mutilated hands. Not wanting to see but knowing she must.

All the fingers of her right hand had been cut off at the middle joint, leaving four bloody stumps to twitch and spasm.

I'll never hold a spear again, she thought, overcome for a moment by a wave of wistful melancholy. Then she snorted with derisive, almost delirious bitterness. There were a great many things she would never do again, fingers or no fingers.

He left me the thumb at least. The thumb of her right hand remained twisted askew but intact. That was a small consolation. She wiggled the lone digit back and forth. Next to her bleeding stumps, it looked tall and somehow sadly proud. *How very kind of him.*

Light-headedness gave her thoughts an airy, half-formed quality. She was unsure whether she was lightheaded due to pain, exhaustion, or blood loss but, in the end, she reckoned it did not matter. Death was on the horizon and coming fast. She could only hope she died before Sak-Tor could put his many hands on her. Mutilated fingers would be the gentlest of Sak-Tor's torments. She had seen captives hung by their feet and flayed alive. Heard the wet rip of skin pulled loose of living, bleeding flesh. If it came to that, she would bite her tongue off. If a more peaceful death did not take her before that day came, she would bite her tongue off and choke on it.

Slowly her head began to hang once again, the strength ebbing from her, until her chin was nestled against her collarbone.

What is stopping me from doing it now? Her eyelids were beginning to grow heavy as the interstice swelled to take her again. *I could just bite down on my tongue and be done with it. Compared to my fingers, I doubt it would hurt all that much.* Her jaw clenched and unclenched as if in anticipation. Her tongue pressed against her front teeth, rubbing dryly against them. *I could do it. Imagine the look on Pon-Tor's face when he comes to take more of my fingers and he finds me dead and smiling. Wouldn't that be a fine sight.*

She was drifting back into unconsciousness, contented by visions of suicide, when a soft sound like rustling leaves drew near. Then a gasp.

Khara lifted her sagging head and blinked. The fairy was a few paces in front of her, hovering at chest level. A pale figure floating in the growing darkness, almost lambent in the twilight's dimness. A small pouch hung from a cord around their neck. Their fingers covered their mouth as they fluttered closer, eyes wide.

"Oh my goodness," the fairy whispered. "What did they do to you?"

Khara ignored their question and instead asked her own in a voice cracked and rising barely above a whisper. "What are you doing here?"

Poko's attention had wandered to Khara's mangled hands and it took a moment for them to draw their eyes from her bloody stumps. "We're going to get you out of here."

Khara shook her head. "You cannot. There are too many warriors. And one of Sak-Tor's generals. There is no leaving this place for me." Poko opened their mouth to respond but Khara continued. "Leave me. I doubt I could walk as I am right now."

"I can't just leave you like this," Poko said. "You got caught trying to help Odessa. I can't let them cut you to pieces after that."

"Yes, you can. You have to," Khara said, hating the words as they came. She wanted to be rescued. To be saved. To see Odessa charging through the tents, arm ablaze. Putting a spear through Pon-Tor's guts and then carrying Khara away to safety. It was a wonderful fantasy but fantasy it would have to remain. Odessa was too important. To risk her life for Khara, that would be suicidally foolish. Odessa was to serve a much greater purpose, Khara knew. And perhaps this had always been Khara's purpose. "I require one thing of you, small one. Please. Take Odessa north, a week's walk north of the Severed Pass. There is a town built atop a mesa, Laliksha. Find Remaka. Tell her Khara sent you. Tell her Sak-Tor knows she still lives, and he knows she is a Sister."

An uneasy look came upon the fairy's face and their eyes fell away from Khara's. "I'm afraid it's too late for all that."

Before Khara could respond, a crash rose from somewhere in the camp, followed by bellowing and bawling. Next came shouts and hurried footsteps. The twilight's calm shattered into fractured pieces of commotion.

"She was supposed to give me more time," Poko said, fluttering to Khara's shackles.

Khara jerked her wrists to and fro in the shackle's grip. "Leave me! Get her out of here!"

"Stop moving!" Poko snapped as they took the pouch from around their neck and undid the tiny drawstrings. "This is delicate stuff."

Khara twisted her head up and watched as the fairy poured a fine black powder into the keyhole of the lock securing the iron bands that pinned her wrists. "Have you lost your mind?" Khara asked. "Where did you even get that?"

Poko stuffed something in their mouth and chewed as they slid a thin piece of rope into the hole, so it stuck out above the rim. They spat the wad they had been chewing into their hands and plugged the hole around the rope and then said, "From some friends of yours. We're lucky Odessa's fire didn't get it all." From the pouch, they took a curved strip of rough iron affixed to a carved wood hand and an oblong piece of knapped rock. The pouch fell to the ground as the fairy took the iron and stone in each hand, holding them clumsily. Cumbersome and unwieldy, they had to hold the iron in the crook of their elbow as they raised the rock. The rock struck the iron and shower of sparks filled the air in front of the fairy, then dissipated just as quickly as they had come. Afterimages were singed into Khara's eyes.

Another shower of sparks and the short twist of rope caught flame with a sizzling hiss. It turned red and then turned to ash as the flame moved down, past the spit-wet plug. Khara twisted her head away from the sizzle of stray grains of powder on the face of the lock. Poko darted into the dark.

A concentrated boom shook the post. New bouts of pain burst along the inside of her hands and wrists. Smoke issued forth from the ruptured keyhole.

Poko returned and yanked with their whole body against the bands of iron still set in the lock's blasted innards.

It was Khara who popped the shackles loose, leaning with her whole weight away from the post and pulling with all the meager strength she had left to her. The shouts were growing louder and nearer. Fires were being lit all around camp. The plaza was coming to life. Soon guards would be upon them.

She fell to her knees, scraping the skin against rocky dirt. Her muscles were limp and lifeless. Poko was yelling for her to get up. To run. But her legs, curled beneath her, were deadened.

Get up! she screamed in her head. But her quivering muscles were unmoved. The roar of a camp in turmoil grew more furious around them. The din of chaos and the cover of darkness their only advantage.

CHAPTER 19

Odessa felt weak. Drained. Hungrier than she had ever been. The corpses of the devils that had tried to capture her had done little to replenish what she had burned in her conflagration. Their blood had only barely slaked her thirst. She had begun to shake. Wracked with chills despite the desert heat. There was an aching fatigue in her muscles and a heaviness in her bones. She needed more blood. She needed to drink it in. To bathe in its invigorating splendor.

The crowded corral was filled with panic and bedlam. Plumes of smoke rose with the bellowing of terrified beasts. Frenzied entehlos bolted back and forth in the staked corral as flames rose along the fence. Entehlos charged through the open gate out toward the outskirts of the camp while others, eyes bulging with terror, rammed through sections of fence and ran through the center of camp. Careening around tents or trampling over them, eliciting screams as devils fell beneath canvas and hoof.

Odessa ran from the corral, cutting between two tents. She reached out as she passed the tents, her hand still aflame. Her fingers brushed against coarse canvas and fire leaped to gnaw into the tent. Shouts of alarm came from inside the burning tents. Similar shouts were coming from all about the camp. The smell of smoke mixed with the chaotic din of shock and terror was to Odessa a familiar and comforting embrace. The heat of battle was the hearth at which she found solace now. It was the altar to which she prayed. Her head pounded with a yearning so deep it nearly consumed her entirely. An inescapable need like a sinkhole yawned in her belly, pulling her inside out in its insatiable hunger. Her teeth bared, she ran to the center of the camp, setting fires as she did.

Long, flickering shadows were soon dancing along canvas walls and over the flame-lit ground as devils made way for the intruder. Shouts of alarm followed Odessa. She darted between tents around old adobe buildings, buildings becoming more prevalent the farther she ventured into the camp. Rounding a corner, she suddenly found herself face-to-face with a devil dressed in only a calf-length tunic, a spear held across her chest. Before the devil could react, Odessa had the devil's face in her iron hand. She let loose a flare of flame, consuming the devil's screaming head. Bits of charred skin and flesh came off in Odessa's hand as she shoved the flailing devil into the wall of a nearby tent.

More devils were appearing all around her, charging through the wide alleyways between tents and buildings. She could hear lowing entehlos tearing and tromping through canvas and could hear screaming devils nearby. She ran even though she wanted nothing more than to stop. To stop and kill every devil that came at her. To open them up. To sink her iron arm into their chests and take all that they had within them. Her skin itched with the need to sate her hunger. But she had promised Poko. She would save the devil first. After that, she could kill until the incessant knot of pain in her belly, the pain that had kept her up at night all throughout their journey to this camp, was gone and forgotten. Until she was contented in a river of blood.

Through a gap between huts, she could make out the plaza's bare dirt. She darted into the corridor between the buildings, running at a headlong dash. Then the gap was blocked by a group of devils, all of them in full armor. Spearpoints filled the opening. But she was too near to stop. And she would not have stopped even if she could have.

In the few steps between her and the wall of spears at the mouth of the gap, Odessa had drawn two clubs from her belt. Spearheads flashed toward her as she came within two paces of the devils. Her nerves were raw and attuned to everything around her. Like an obfuscating layer had been peeled from the surface of the world and she could perceive it all in perfect clarity.

The club in her flaming fist, already reddening at the bare iron handle, struck the shaft of an incoming spear and snapped it. Another spearhead glanced off her armor as she knocked a third spearhead away. Then she leaped. And then she was in the mass of devils. Snarling as she swung the clubs with reckless abandon. Iron crashed against iron. Bones cracked and snapped. One of her clubs found the gap between helmet and facemask, and a devil's brow and eyes erupted in a burst of red. Odessa pummeled the devils until they were ground. Burying her clubs in helmet and skull.

When the devils in the gap were dead or dying, Odessa took an instant to breathe in the coppery odor of spilled blood. The stench of voided bowels sullied the metallic tang that would usually set her teeth on edge, but her arm nonetheless thrummed with stolen life.

She ran into the plaza as it began to fill with shouts and hisses. Silhouetted in torchlight, devils were running across the plaza, all of them congregating in the center where the devil lay. Poko was darting above the naked devil as she tried to rise, then fell back to the dirt. The fire wreathing Odessa's arm flared brilliantly as she sped toward them. Sprinting as fast as she could. But no matter how fast she ran, the devils would reach them first. There was no avoiding it.

She skidded to a halt halfway across the plaza, dropped her clubs, smothered the fire in her arm, and then slid the bow from its place across her shoulders. As fast as her hands could move, she began nocking arrows and firing. She dropped the first devil as it came within a few paces, now on its knees, braced against one of the upright posts in the center of the plaza.

In the dark, all she could do was launch arrows into the indistinct shapes of charging figures. Striking devils as they fled in clusters toward the posts, their bodies dropping and stumbling over one another. But they continued to come. All manner of weapons raised. Weapons poised to cut, stab, and bludgeon the devils' bare flesh. Poko would be stomped into the dirt.

Odessa launched an arrow almost every five seconds. Most of them found purchase somewhere in a devil's body. When she had loosed almost half of her quiver, she heard footsteps quickly approaching. She whirled, dropping her bow and deflecting a sword with her iron arm. The arm flared to life as she lunged the devil with the sword and planted a burning fist in their stomach. The sword came down on her arm and pain reverberated up to her shoulder. She kicked the devil away and started back toward the center of the plaza.

Poko and the devil were making their way to her now, the devil lurching clumsily forward. Odessa rushed to meet them.

"Poko, get out of here!" Odessa shouted as she took the devil's arm and hastened her unsteady pace with a jerk. Dragging the dazed devil, Odessa looked at her and snapped, "Move faster, damn you!"

The devil's pace remained unchanged. She could barely keep her head upright. Odessa could hear devils behind them, drawing near. Boots scrabbling. Armor clinking. Sucking in ragged breaths through bared fangs.

"There!" Poko shouted, fluttering before them and pointed to the right. Two entehlos had charged into the plaza, trampling the devils clustered there. Odessa yanked the devil towards the gap opened by the entehlo and the devil stumbled, nearly taking Odessa down with her.

Odessa cursed under her breath and slowed just long enough to take the devil around the waist and throw her tall body over her shoulder like a sack of meat.

Her knees buckled a bit as she set the weight on her shoulder and then she began to run, rushing toward the gap as fast as her pumping legs would take her.

Halfway to the gap, an explosive gale of wind struck her like an oncoming entehlo. The gust lifted her into the air and threw her to the ground, where she skidded a distance before coming to a stop. The devil rolled, softly moaning with each jouncing impact.

"The bitch is mine!" a low, grating voice like shifting earth boomed over the din. Across the plaza stood a male devil nearly as tall as two men, lit by two female devils holding torches beside him. Two horns twisted and curled over the sharp crown of his helmet. Even at a distance and in the dim light of torches, Odessa could see his fangs exposed by a callous sneer. He took a step forward. Another devil rushed to his side with a sheathed sword held out to him. He took the curved hilt and pulled a long and vicious saber free from the sheath. "And I will not abide those who try to take what is mine!"

The air around him began to swirl, kicking up wisps of dust. The torches guttered and the devils holding them shrank away from the whipping wind. All the devils now standing at attention around the plaza seemed to shrink back from the rising tempest around him.

Odessa was scrambling to her feet, reaching for the devilish dagger on her belt. Fire sprouted along her fingers up to her wrist. Her heart was racing much too fast. Her blood felt thin and lifeless in her veins. She felt depleted.

The devil general started slowly toward her, the saber's tip grazing the dirt. "I'm surprised to see a creature such as you in league with these cunts." As he drew near, Odessa could feel the static of magic radiating from him and his weak tempest. "Or perhaps you merely wanted a post next to her. Is that it, blood-sucker? You wish to experience my knifework firsthand? In the flesh?" He swung the saber in a quick, vertical arc. Even from across the plaza, the rushing gust of wind that struck Odessa was strong enough to nearly knock her over despite her half-crouch.

This is bad. She glanced back at the devil. Poko was ministering to her as she struggled onto her hands and knees, her limbs trembling as she did so. Behind them, devils had filled the gap to their escape. Outside the camp, a saddled entehlo awaited them. No doubt snorting and pawing at the dirt anxiously during all this fire and bedlam. But the entehlo was far beyond their reach now. *We're not getting out of this.*

"Poko!" she shouted. "You have wings! Leave!" She could not allow Poko to die here. The devil was already half-dead. Odessa had died the day she and the other hunters had killed Egende. Their deaths would be no great loss. In fact, Odessa felt, in an anxious, jittering sort of way, great relief in dying here. If she could die killing a brutish devil general—slain in the throes of battle against a creature of pure hate and cruelty—she would die satisfied, she thought. At peace before she was dragged into the endless and unrelenting abyss.

A distant boom cut through the tumult like a crack of lightning splitting a pitch-black sky. The devil general stopped, opened his mouth to say something, then was cut off by another boom. This one closer.

There was a crashing noise at the edge of the camp. And a far-off rumbling that grew louder.

Poko's devil was mumbling. Odessa caught a single muttered word amid the sudden confusion: *Sisters.*

CHAPTER 20

The camp devolved into pandemonium. The devils in the plaza burst into frenetic movement. The devil general shouted for Odessa and the devil, Khara, to be seized, but Odessa was already in motion.

Devils converged on them from all sides. Odessa stood over Khara and the fairy nestled against Khara's chest, her arm burning hot with finality. If she killed enough of the devils, both the devil and Poko may live. The Sisters would save them. Odessa could die happy.

The first devil that rushed them, sword raised, was met with a dagger. Odessa had caught the devil's swinging arm with one hand and plunged the dagger in the devil's throat with the other. She left the dagger buried, its tip grinding against vertebrae, and took the sword before it dropped from the devil's relaxing grip. Her fiery fist charred the leather wrap around the sword's hilt with a smell like burnt hair.

A devil came with a spear, feinting then making to plunge the spear in Odessa's throat. Odessa sidestepped and slashed at the devil's arm, cutting a wide swath of red through its thick muscle.

The rumbling of hooves was loud. From the west, the crash and clamor of battle came sweeping through the camp. More booms rattled the air. Cannonballs ripped through tents and pulverized huts at random. Odessa plunged the sword into the spear-bearing devil's neck, drawing it free from its throat in time to block another incoming spear thrust.

More devils came and she killed them with a brutal efficiency. The sword was in constant motion. Slashing and stabbing. Blood filling the air like a sodden mist. An iron taste clogged her nostrils and filled her mouth. Her entire body began to thrum in a steady rhythm.

When the light of torches and the sounds of war came within a stone's throw of the plaza's western edge, there was a lull in the rush of devils attacking her. Odessa seized the opportunity. Dropping the sword and dousing her flames, she scooped Khara up in her arms and ran. Poko followed close behind. The devil was limp in her arms. A bloody hand pressed against Odessa's armored chest, and Khara quietly groaned.

She sprinted across the plaza, trying to shield the devil as best she could. A spear came snapping toward them and Odessa took it in the ribs, but she continued running until she reached the eastern edge of the plaza. As far away from both the Sisters and the fires as she could manage. Odessa crashed through the door of an adobe hut and dropped Khara on a pile of rushes in the corner of the room.

"Stay down," Odessa said before dragging a table from the other side of the room. She tipped the table on its side and set it to cordon Khara off from the rest of the hut. Perhaps it would block the worst of the cannonballs' spume of shrapnel, or perhaps it would hide Khara from the devil general's soldiers. Odessa could only hope it would do some good, as unlikely as it seemed.

Poko was watching her. "Stay down there with her," Odessa said. "I don't want you to get hit by cannon fire."

"Are you going back out there?"

Odessa said nothing. She didn't have to.

"Please be careful," Poko said quietly.

"I will," Odessa said, although she had no intention of being careful at all. Her side burned where the spear had caught her. Blood ran down her side, wasted. Squandered.

She left the hut as the Sisters began charging into the plaza. Entehlos trampled devils as the Sisters stabbed and slashed from on high. The camp's devils had formed a wall of blades and shields across the length of the plaza and were pushing forward against the tide of riders. Odessa saw the devil's backs as they jostled and stamped their feet before the mass of riders filling the plaza and charging the line.

The first of the Sisters' concentrated assaults upon the line came from the northern side and was quickly repelled by one of the generals' saber winds. The gust knocked several of the riders from the mounts and took the legs out from beneath one entehlo.

When the Sisters came in earnest, the general was at the front of the line, cleaving both rider and mount in two. The wind whipping around him threw large, blinding clouds of dust into the air.

Odessa drew the second of her daggers and went to fall upon the back of the devils' line like a vengeful wraith. As she came closer, the electric buzz of magic in the air became almost palpable. She drew the little strength she had gained since her conflagration and held it, letting it build inside her as she ran. The devils' line was being harried and winnowed, but where the devil general stood it was impervious.

When Odessa came within a few dozen paces of the line and the devil general's back, she let all the built-up pressure loose in a blast of heat that sapped the static of magic from the air. The wind around him died in an instant. Seeing this, the riders were emboldened.

Odessa's feet slowed as the static began to fade into the air. The wind around the general began to twirl again as he cut down another rider. *Shit!* She drew in her strength once more, letting it build and build as lightheadedness began to cloud her mind. Then she let it out in a long exhalation of heat. Holding it as her vision darkened.

The riders broke through the line from the flank and rode through devils like a scythe through wheat. The general spun, shouting in rage as his line began to disintegrate.

The rumbling of hooves rattled Odessa's bones. Entehlos trampled devils not far from where she stood. Her grasp on the exhalation was slackening. Her head spun and her legs were threatening to buckle beneath her.

She was about to tip over when a hand fell upon her shoulder, steadying her.

"I have you," Khara, the devil said. "Do not worry, I have you."

CHAPTER 21

Khara held Odessa as her Sisters rode down the last of the devils. Screams filled the air atop an undercurrent of hoofbeats and crashing iron. Pon-Tor stood among it all, swinging his saber. He took the legs off an entehlo and then cleaved its rider from shoulder to hip. Khara hated standing outside the fray like this. Watching as her Sisters killed and were themselves killed. But it took all her strength to just hold Odessa upright.

Odessa's eyes were half closed and her lips twitched sporadically. But still she kept Pon-Tor's magic at bay. Snuffed it out like a candle.

A spear punched through the armor at Pon-Tor's hip, and he screamed in rage and pain. A scream like thunder. He swung his saber to take the head off the Sister who had stabbed him, but she was gone, already wheeling around for another pass. Sisters circled him now, revolving around him as he spun to face them.

Another spear stuck in his side. He snapped the shaft and threw it at the fleeing rider. Pon-Tor was panting and screaming. Spittle flying from his mouth as he impotently raged. The Sisters continued to harry him, riding in and out of his reach, for nearly an hour. Exhausting him. Toying with him. And the entire time, Odessa remained in her trance. Held in Khara's arms. Sinking into Khara's arms as the night wore on.

Throwing his helmet in an attempt to dismount a fleeing rider who mocked him was Pon-Tor's eventual undoing. A polearm split his skull with a crack and a sickening squelch as it was pulled free. Bits of brain spilled out as he tipped over sideways. He collapsed to his knees, spasming, and the Sisters fell upon him like vultures upon a fresh corpse. They hacked and stabbed and pummeled his still-twitching body. Shouting and cheering as they snapped off his horns and rammed them into his eyes.

"It's done," Khara whispered in Odessa's ear. "You've done it, Odessa."

At first, Odessa made no sign that she heard Khara's words, but soon she was sagging in her arms. All the strength bleeding from her body. Odessa's legs buckled and Khara let her down to the ground, cradling her in her lap. Near Pon-Tor's corpse, a chorus of riotous cheers had begun.

Khara held Odessa for some time, occasionally checking her neck to make sure her heart still pumped. Beneath her skin, her pulse fluttered like the fairy's wings. Quick and delicate.

On one occasion Khara put a finger to her own neck to make sure she was not living some blissful post-death vision. She found her pulse to be steady and strong.

To Khara's disbelief, they were both alive. In spite of the cruel and unjust world in which they lived, and the wickedness of those who inhabited it, both she and Odessa had survived.

She wished they could have remained in that moment a while longer, but as with all good things, it, too, did pass.

CHAPTER 22

Odessa awoke with the taste of blood in her mouth and a tacky feeling on her tongue. A canvas ceiling rose to a peak above where she lay. She was wearing nothing but a thin gown but still she was sweating. She shifted slightly, her body resistant and aching, and the rushes beneath her crackled and snapped.

"You're awake!"

Poko's face filled her vision. They flitted to sit on her chest and lean over her face, staring intently.

"What happened?" Odessa asked. Speaking hurt her throat. The words were like iron barbs tearing up her throat.

"You've been asleep for a week!"

Odessa sat up, her sore muscles crying out in pangs of dull pain. Poko fell backward as she rose and took flight to hover before her. "A week?" Odessa asked, her brow furrowed. "A whole week?"

"A week and two days," Poko said with grave solemnity. "After you did your magic thing, your eyes rolled back into your head and you got all cold and clammy. I told them you needed blood, so they gave you some hearts and stuff like you need, but you didn't wake up. I was starting to think you wouldn't wake up until a few days ago when you started mumbling."

Odessa's mind was turgid and slow. It felt as if her brain had swollen to twice its normal size, so inflamed only one thought could travel through its choked channels at a time. "Who's they?"

"The devils—I mean the Torva." Poko paused then corrected themself again. "The Sisters, I mean."

Odessa rubbed her face with pitted iron fingers. *The Sisters. Just what I need. More devils.* "Where are we?" she asked.

"The Sisters' camp. It's carved into the side of a big mesa. All hidden and fortified. It's pretty nice," Poko said. "But I've got to say, I think I liked our little cave better. As much as I like the fresh air and being able to stretch my wings, I don't like being exposed like this."

Odessa glanced around the small tent, but there was nothing to see but bare rock, rushes, and canvas. It was empty save for her. Outside the tent, there was a voice and the bustle of work and rest. But still she was confused by the situation. "So what are we? Prisoners?"

Poko raised an eyebrow. "What? No, we're guests!" They paused for moment, their brow tightening a bit before it relaxed again. "Well, we're not exactly guests, but we're not prisoners either."

Odessa's mind had begun to warm and pump the lifeblood of thought a bit more fluidly now. "Whether we're guests or prisoners probably depends on whether I take that deal, huh?"

"No, they wouldn't do that! Khara wouldn't let them."

Odessa shook her head. "They're devils. If I don't do what they want, they'd skin me alive without a second thought." Poko opened their mouth to respond, but Odessa continued before they could utter a protest. " Not that it matters. I'll have to take the deal regardless."

Poko's mouth snapped shut and they stared at her, unbelieving. "You will? Why? What changed?"

"What choice do I have? We're here, surrounded by devils. Held captive as their *guests.*" Odessa wasn't sure if that was exactly the right reason. Her head was swimming. Her muscles ached and it hurt to sit even halfway straight. That small exertion was a strain on her overwrought muscles. Her mind vacuous and half delirious, she knew she wasn't wholly correct, but she could not reckon why. So she sat for a moment, trying to ignore Poko's penetrating stare. Drawing scattered thoughts together in a coherent knot. "I want something, Poko. And if I have to kill a god to get it, I'll gladly do it. Because I've had enough of gods. All of them. If I could kill them all, I would."

Poko landed on Odessa's lap and looked up at her. "What do you want? To go home?"

Odessa shook her head, then stopped and thought about it. "I mean, eventually I do. But later. To get what I want, I need an army. I need an army of devils to storm Asha-Kalir and drag Yakun and Tarik out of their little rat's nest so I can beat their fucking heads in." She smiled. She could feel how gruesome a smile it was, but she did not care. "Then I'll go home. And I'll cut Kunza's head off and use it as a chamber pot."

Poko was quiet for a long while. "That's dark, Dessa. Even for you."

Odessa's smile grew less gruesome and more sincere. "Isn't this what you wanted, though?"

"Well, yeah. But I thought your side of the bargain would be a little less . . ."

"Bloody?" Odessa ventured.

"Yeah," Poko said, solemnly. "Bloody."

"I don't really have a choice, Poko," Odessa said, the smile slipping from her face. She looked at her iron hand. Her cursed hand. "Blood is the only thing keeping me going."

CHAPTER 23

Khymanir was a monster. A mass of huge arms, thousands of them at least, constantly in motion. Yakun and Tarik stood in the small, human entrance to the god's palatial workshop. A massive building of white marble stained with blood and grime and soot. Strips of tarnished bronze were inlaid all through the room like rotting veins.

Yakun and Tarik stood watching for a moment longer. Watching as the myriad hands worked clay and carved flesh and tinkered with huge bronze cogs and wheels. Working on a hundred different tasks at once. Watching the god work was an awesome and awful experience. Like watching a sinkhole swallow an entire village.

The only work that the god required of humans was the small things. Things those giant hands could not manipulate. And today there was only one thing required of Yakun and Tarik, Khymanir's newest hands. After the godsdamned girl ran, they had been forced to share their work—what work was not entirely blasphemous conspiracy, that was. And for that, they had been promoted, in a fashion.

Yakun motioned behind him for Tarik, who led four more gaunt slaves into the workshop. Yakun followed them to the ring carved into the center of the massive, vaulted room. A channel ran from the circle to where Khymanir's bulk writhed at the far end of the dingy, dimly lit building.

Tarik lined up the thoroughly sedated slaves inside the circle. His slippered feet made a wet ripping noise every time he lifted a foot from the tacky, bloodstained floor of the circle.

Once they were lined up, the two men backed up to the doorway again as one of Khymanir's hands came and took the slaves in one massive fist. Crushing them all. The sound of bones breaking, tendons snapping, muscles ripping, and skin tearing still made Yakun want to vomit. Even after hearing it happen nearly twenty times a day some days.

Blood poured from between the smooth, pallid fingers and from the bottom of the fist. Splashing upon the floor and filling the channel with blood.

The hand carried the bodies to the other side of the room, where the real work began.

Yakun watched as the fresh blood trickled down the trench in the floor. Making its way beneath the mass of arms and hands to the pool at the far wall. Where the hands worked the blood red clay.

Against the far wall stood a clay giant. Roughly shaped, still sharp-angled and ill-defined, but coming together quickly. It was taller than the tallest building in Asha-Kalir. It had to have been built in a recessed pit dug into the floor, its height was such that even the grand palace could not bear it all without accommodation. It was a conglomeration of clay and blood and bone. And hundreds, if not thousands, of lives.

Merely being in its presence filled Yakun with such terrible dread. Sometimes, usually in the early morning, before he was fully steeled for the day ahead, he would feel as if his heart might stop midbeat, just being in the same room as the bloody goliath.

It was not the sheer size of the abomination. It was its purpose that terrorized him so deeply he could not even escape it in his dreams. Both of them knew what its purpose was without ever being told. They just knew.

It was a vessel. A monumental vessel fit for only one thing.

A god.

PART TWO

CHAPTER 24

In her dream, there was only darkness, pitch black and cold. Odessa stood alone, damp and shivering, in the abyss. Time had little meaning in this place—she stood for an instant and an eternity. She tried to move, but her body was rigid and insensate. Like it was no longer her own. It had been stolen from her. The abyss had bled the life from her. Sapped her of life like the cold drains the body of warmth. Entropy had taken her, and the abyss was as it always had been: still and lifeless.

"Once loosed from its collar, the beast flees to find solace in the home of its enemy," Talara said softly from somewhere far in the darkness. Gooseflesh prickled Odessa's flesh from the base of her spine to the nape of her neck. She had not heard Talara's voice in some time, and it filled her with frigid dread that stilled her heart and made her blood freeze in her veins.

"I allowed you to flee Asha-Kalir in the hopes that you would prosper. That you would consume and become something so much more . . . fearsome. I had hoped your hunger would guide you to further strength. Instead you remained in this dreadful desert, hiding and only taking what little life you could find. Barely surviving when you should have flourished. You have such a boon, and yet you continue to squander it." Talara's voice drew ever closer, dry, cold, and pitiless. The cold turned frigid. The stench of death, cloying and rank, at first subtle and remote. But as Talara drew closer, so too did the dank, putrid stench, until it was so pungent it was a tangible, physical sensation upon Odessa's skin. Cold and wet like a thick, odious fog, its foul residue seeped into her goose-pimpled skin.

"This desert is full of devils. All of them fodder for you to gorge yourself upon. Yet you hid and starved and grew weak. You could have slaughtered whole armies of them, become strong enough to march into Asha-Kalir and rip that old man apart. And I would have allowed it. I would have had Shadows open the gates and escort you to the palace as long as you did not interfere with Khymanir's work. But no." Behind her, Odessa could hear slimy flesh slithering on stone. The stench was so thick, Odessa's eyes watered and bile rose in the back of her throat. Her stony muscles refused her every plea to move and escape. "Instead you taught me a valuable lesson. Freedom is humanity's folly. Given freedom, you will languish and wallow in your misery. You squander all you have and even spurn that which is in your best interest. Humans love to cling to lofty fancies and ideals, yet you remain so intent on mere survival that you can see nothing but what is directly beneath your feet."

Odessa wanted to shout and protest, but no fury could be kindled within her chest. The dank stink of decay had permeated her core, and terror dampened all that sparked her fury and rage. Doused by awesome fear, a small and impotent indignation was all that she could muster within herself.

A large coil of entrails slithered against Odessa's calf. Cold and slimy, the meaty entrail sliding across her flesh left a viscous residue on her skin. "A tame beast can accomplish much, but a wild beast can only survive or die. You need a god to guide you. For you still have a purpose to fulfill, my dear Odessa."

A choked sound rattled in Odessa's throat. An objection strangled before it could take the form of a single syllable. Her throat was constricted. Choked by Talara's very presence. The domineering immensity of her being. The cold had frozen Odessa solid. The stench had seeped into her every pore. And she could sense Talara's bulk behind her. Hear every slimy squelch of her entrail-appendages as she moved. Feel the gusts of warm, fetid breath expelled from Talara's slit nostrils and her slavering, fang-lined mouth.

"Now is not the time for you to speak. You must listen." Talara said. Her words, spoken without force, reverberated through Odessa's body like the rumbling of an approaching stampede. "You have taken up with your enemy. Those who would use you just as the old man did. To them you are little more than a weapon. A weapon to discard when you have been dulled upon their enemies. When you have hacked apart scores of innocent men, women, and children. They will use you until there is nothing left of that humanity to which you so dearly cling."

There was a moment of silence. Talara's warning filled the empty space around Odessa like the oppressive air of an incoming storm. The tightness in Odessa's throat slackened and a garbled whine came out unbidden. Her mouth opened and closed dumbly. Given the gift of speech again, she found she could not find what she wanted to say.

"Sak-Tor," she blurted huskily. "They only want me to kill Sak-Tor. Nothing else."

Talara's breath, hot and sulfurous, unfurled against the back of Odessa's neck. Fat entrails rubbed against the back of her legs. Slick and icy. "Do you truly believe they will allow you to just walk away if you are able to accomplish that suicidal fantasy of theirs?"

"They want to make a deal."

"They want to enslave you." Talara spoke with unyielding authority. "They are devils. Sired by one of the cruelest and most savage gods to ever exist, all they know is bloodthirst. From adolescence, they are reared on scheming and slaughter. Even among their own kind, they show no mercy. Familial bonds—the bond of parent and child even—mean nothing to them. And you expect them to treat you differently?"

Odessa stiffened. "Then I'll run."

Talara's putrid breath tousled Odessa's hair. "Where will you go?"

Before Odessa could respond, the tightness around her neck returned. Only a whimper left her lips. A slithering intestinal tendril wrapped around her shin.

"You have suffered much, Odessa. You have struggled much and received little in return. Save for false promises and betrayal." The immensity of Talara loomed over Odessa. Surrounded her. But in the darkness she could make out nothing. Could not even see the innards sliding along her skin. "I have neglected you. I allowed you to languish in the desert for too long. Starving and alone. I let your talents go fallow. Without ever giving you the instruction you required." Talara's brittle voice held an odd warmth that pried some of the stiffness from Odessa's body. "And now you find yourself in a viper's den." The entrails around her legs slithered higher and then tightened. "Now tangled in their coils, you have few options. But I am here to guide you out of this knot of perils in which you find yourself ensnared. I will guide you to freedom. Guide you to your dear sister and mother. All of this is within your grasp should you do this one thing."

Odessa listened as the goddess told her how to free herself from the devils' grasp. Listened silently even when the tightness of her throat loosened. Engraving Talara's words into her dreaming mind despite the trepidation and outright distrust still gnawing there.

Talara had granted Odessa freedom once. She might do it again. All Odessa knew was that she would be in no one's control ever again.

CHAPTER 25

Unease and disgust lingered like a foul odor after Odessa awoke. Talara's words were lice skittering across her mind and burrowing deep into the soft tissue. The week-old rushes rustled softly beneath her as she roused, sitting up with a soft groan. It was dark in the tent, the only light coming dimly from a brazier of coals in the center. The urge to vomit rose in the back of her parched throat but she forced it back with a dry swallow and grimace. She sat in the silent darkness for a long while. Ruminating on what Talara had told her. What Talara had ordered her to do.

Poko, curled beside her in a basket filled with a soft woolen blanket, was a light sleeper and at the sound of rustling rushes rolled inside their basket to face Odessa. "You're awake?"

Odessa grunted and nodded before dryly clearing her throat. "How long was I out?" she asked hoarsely. She raised her iron hand to rub at a bleary eye before correcting herself and using her other, flesh-and-bone hand.

Poko sat up in the basket and fluttered their wings for a few beats. "Almost two days." They stood up in the blanket, then took to the air, flitting through the dark tent to the copper ewer sitting on Odessa's opposite side, just beyond her reach. The ewer sat burnished in the brazier's glow. "Actually it might have been two whole days. You were only half awake for a few hours before you really were out, but I think it still counts." A ladle sat in the ewer, its handle curving out above the wide mouth. Hovering, Poko took the ladle's handle and rose. Water splashed onto the dusty rock as they brought Odessa the swinging ladleful of water.

Odessa quickly took the ladle, cupping its bowl in her hands, and drank. The water was cool and soothing, dousing the arid dryness that made her mouth feel tacky and made her throat itch. She drank the ladle dry, both quenching her considerable thirst and hoping to compensate for Poko's wastefulness.

"I thought I told you to wake me in the morning," Odessa said, scratching her scalp through a nest of bed-matted hair. She had only been awake a few hours when drowsiness had taken her again two days before. Since she had first awoken beneath the tent's canvas roof, she had existed only in brief respites of wakefulness between long bouts of deep, insensible sleep.

"I tried," Poko said, landing beside her on her rushes. "I screamed and shouted and jumped on your chest. I even slapped you around a little." They frowned. "Nothing."

The thought of Poko's tiny hands striking her kindled a small ember of irritation in her chest, but it was snuffed out as quickly as it had come. She was too tired and weak for such strong emotion. Her fingers absently combed through her frizzy, tangled hair. "How many days have we been here?"

"Almost a week."

Odessa frowned. "I can't stand it. I can't stand being an invalid like this. I'm not even a person at this point. I'm a wraith that appears for a few hours here and there." Her fingers worked at her knotted braids to no avail. In the back of her mind were vestiges of her dream, like the stains of soot after a fire. "One of these days I'm going to wake up with my throat cut. These devils will see I'm of no use and be done with me. And I won't be able to do a thing about it. I won't even be aware of it happening. I'll be sleeping and then I'll just . . ." Her fingers snagged in a tight knot. "Stay there. In that horribly empty dark."

"They won't do that," Poko said sternly. "Khara said they'll help us. She wasn't lying either."

"Have you seen Khara since we got here?"

Poko was quiet for a moment. Then they said, with some reluctance, "No."

"We don't even know if she survived."

"Of course she survived!" Poko said indignantly before going quiet. Their words came out a heartbeat later, softer now and almost entreating. "She was all right when we started for this place. I mean, all right considering what happened to her. She couldn't have died."

"She was missing fingers and bleeding all over. Any one of those wounds could have gone sour and poisoned her blood." For a moment, Odessa thought she could feel Talara's cold touch creeping up her spine. *If she is dead then the deal might be off. And if that's the case then it's all off. Either fight or run. And I'm in no shape to do either.* The chill spread from her spine across her back, and she shivered. *I'll have to convince them myself then. Somehow take control of this situation.*

Without becoming their slave. In the dimness, the tent walls seemed to be closing in. Drawing near to ensnare her, swallow her up, and smother her.

"If something like that happened, we would have heard something by now."

No we wouldn't, Odessa thought. *We're prisoners. Prisoners aren't privy to such things.* Her hand, having given up on untangling her hair, fell in her lap and clasped its iron counterpoint. She was already beginning to feel faint and tired. "Maybe you would have heard something, not me. Have you been out lately?"

"No, I've been by your side the whole time," Poko said, but there was a note of something left unsaid. A touch of unease in their tone. The devils made Poko nervous as well. Nervous enough to not want to be caught alone with them, she thought.

The heaviness of exhaustion pulled on her aching body, and Odessa said no more on the matter. There was no more to be said. All that could be done was to wait and see. And prepare for whichever eventuality took shape.

"I'm tired," Odessa said. "I'm going to just lie down for a short while. Wait until breakfast." Her stomach was a tight ball in her abdomen and pangs of hunger occasionally clawed at her ribs, but it was not breakfast her body truly hungered for.

Poko watched as Odessa lay down on her rushes, concern plainly visible on their face in the scant light. "I'll try to wake you up if you fall asleep."

Odessa grunted in gratitude and, curling in a ball with her arms wrapped about her, she closed her eyes.

It was the scent of porridge that woke her from fitful sleep. She had not seen a devil since the night she had broken Khara loose from her imprisonment, so when her eyes fluttered open to see a maroon face with two horns as black as night leaning down before her, she jerked upright with an iron fist cocked back.

The devil lurched back, dropping the bowl of porridge she had held. It didn't drop far and landed upright with a curt, delicate clatter. In its fall, a bit of tawny colored porridge had spilled over the bowl's edge and splashed onto the ground.

A spear was suddenly at Odessa's throat. Another devil, in full scale and helm, stood at Odessa's feet. The devil who had dropped the bowl, a young-looking girl in a beige tunic, ran to shelter herself behind the warrior.

"Put that fist down," the spear-wielding devil hissed. "Now."

The urge to rip the spear from the devil's hands and beat her over the helm with the haft made Odessa's arm freeze for a moment in that raised position. Her armored arm was heavy, making her shoulder quickly ache. Her arm trembled slightly, but she kept her fist cocked back. A heat kindled in her tight chest, and Odessa's eyes flicked over the spear to the hands holding it then to the eyes that bore into her. Narrow eyes, as red as arterial blood, filled with distrust, distaste, and disgust.

"Get that spear out of my face," Odessa said through a teeth-grinding snarl. Her fist lowered, but her arm remained tensed and poised to lash out in an instant. She gathered what scant strength she had and prepared her weak, atrophied legs. She had not stood for more than a few moments or a few stumbling steps since arriving at the devils' camp. But if she had to, she could. She could feel it in the marrow of her aching bones.

Before either one of them could say or do a thing, Poko was fluttering between them, waving their arms. "Stop!" they said, hovering to face the devil. "She didn't mean anyone any harm! She won't do anything—she was surprised is all! So please, put your spear down, I'm begging you."

"Tell her to put that hand down," the devil said, staring at Odessa. "And to stop looking at me like that."

Poko turned to Odessa and hissed, "Put that fist down, Dessa. Are you trying to get us killed?"

Odessa took a deep breath, her nostrils flaring with mounting fury. She wanted to kill the devil. To rip her to shreds. And the little devil cowering behind her. To tear through the entire devil encampment. Burning and slaughtering. The smell of smoke and blood filling the air. But in Poko's pleading eyes, she grounded herself and acquiesced, lowering her arm to her side.

The spear withdrew from her neck.

Odessa's fury still raged in her chest, but she did her best to quell its infernal uproar. She took a slow breath and licked her lips. Her gaze drifted from Poko to the warrior and then to the girl. "You . . ." she started. "You startled me." She swallowed and, after sucking in a breath through her teeth, said with a sigh, "I apologize."

The warrior, still eyeing Odessa, looked unconvinced, but she said nothing further. She only gave Poko and Odessa a sullen look before turning to usher the terrified girl out of the tent.

Poko watched them leave, then turned to Odessa. "What was that about?"

Odessa turned from them and lifted the bowl of porridge. The bottom of the bowl was somewhat warm. The porridge was thin and watery, the color of rust. Her stomach began to twist and churn with nausea. "She startled me." She lifted the bowl to her lips and sipped. The porridge was warm but bland with a faint metallic taste. The devils knew she needed blood, and the porridge was their means of administration. By its taste, she knew it was entehlo blood. The fact that she could differentiate blood by taste disgusted her profoundly.

"I'm not talking about that. I'm talking about after she startled you. You were trying to pick a fight!"

Odessa took another sip from the bowl. A gag tickled the back of her throat, but she restrained it. Her body refused food, wanted only blood, and compromises had to be made. "They stuck a spear in my face as soon as I woke up. I was a bit upset."

Poko eyed her, dubious. "All that talk about devils killing us in our sleep and it's you who's trying to get us killed."

"I said I was sorry. What more do you want?"

Poko sighed. "Nothing." They settled down on their bed in the basket. "Make sure you finish that porridge. You're looking skeletal."

Odessa ate her porridge in silence. The little blood in her porridge was barely enough to keep her godsblood from cannibalizing her body. It wasn't lifeblood.

Her arm, beneath its iron carapace, was beginning to pulse with sharp stabs of bright, searing pain. She would need to kill soon. Her hunger needed to be fed before it consumed her instead.

CHAPTER 26

Odessa was sitting on her rushes, running a finger along the runes of her iron hand when Khara entered the tent, pushing the flaps open with hands encased in thick bandages. She wore a loose, dark blue tunic, which made her violet skin appear deeper and darker, and a wide belt cinched at her waist. Her entire left hand was encased in a bulky wood splint bound with leather and bandages, while her right hand was a lump of bandage with only her splinted thumb rising from the wrapped fabric.

"You're awake," Khara said with a weak smile, the tent flaps closing behind her. Hollows had begun to form around her eyes and cheeks. The short stumps of horn on her forehead were sealed at the ends with a dry, brown paste. She limped across the tent, stooped over slightly as she walked. Her hands held near her chest, she looked like a scolded child. A child accustomed to beatings.

"You're alive," Odessa said, a muddled flood of emotions washing over her. Relief and pity; vague resentment and weak exultation. Much had been lost to save Khara from her captors, and Odessa still did not fully believe she had done the right thing in saving her. But seeing the wan smile on Khara's haggard face was somewhat convincing in its own right.

Poko circled the air around Khara's head, cheering and pirouetting about. "You're alive! I was so worried! We thought maybe your wounds got infected or something and you had died! We hadn't heard anything since we got here, they just bring us food and leave. Day after day, so we didn't know," Poko babbled.

"I apologize for taking so long to see you. My, um . . ." Khara raised her bandaged hands up for emphasis and continued with a pained, despondent expression. "My hands took longer to mend that we had hoped."

"Oh no, there's no need for you to apologize at all!" Poko said. "We understand. We were just worried."

"How are they?" Odessa asked. "Will your hands heal?"

Khara smiled sadly and raised her lump of bandage. Her splinted thumb waggled. "Well, this one, I'm afraid, is a bit too far gone." The stump lowered. "But my left hand should regain most of its dexterity if it heals according to plan."

"Which hand is your dominant hand?" Odessa ventured, already sure of the answer but asking anyway.

Khara raised her stump. "It would appear my sword- swinging days are over," she said, a false smile curling the corners of her mouth. Her eyes belied the smile's falsehood. They were deep pools of dark sorrow. The color of a dying sun as it's smothered by a pall of thick clouds.

"I'll give you mine," Odessa said, with a forced smile of her own. "You can take the whole damn arm if you want." Khara's pitiful state had drawn an unfamiliar compassion from her. Kindness straining from disuse over the harsh months spent in the desert. Like a vestigial muscle cramping upon its first use.

"Were it only possible," Khara said. She gestured to the ground in front of Odessa. "May I sit? I'm still not very steady on my feet yet."

Odessa nodded. "Of course."

Khara sat cross-legged across from her with a wince and a huff of breath. She settling into the least uncomfortable position she could find, then set her gaze on Odessa. Eyes sober and earnest. "I want to thank you for what you did. Sincerely. If it weren't for you, I would be dead. But not before I'd been tortured and exposed to a multitude of agonies. I owe everything I have and everything I am today to you." She clasped her bandaged hands before her and bowed at the waist until her broken horns were pressed against the dirt. "From the deepest parts of my being, I thank you. I am in your debt forever."

Odessa's face grew warm and flushed. "Get up," she said, waving a hand at Khara. "You're welcome, just get up already." As Khara rose, Odessa saw Poko fluttering behind her, smirking. "And don't worry about debts or whatever. I have enough of those already. As long as your deal still stands, we're even."

Khara was quiet a moment, her face gone stony. "About that," she started slowly. "I laid the groundwork when I left to find you, but the deal isn't as set in stone as you might think."

"What do you mean?" Odessa asked sharply.

"What I mean is, if I hadn't been caught and . . ." she raised her hands again for emphasis. "Mutilated like I have, our deal would be an almost sure thing.

But in my present state, I've lost some standing with Remaka and the rest of the Elder Sisters. It will take some convincing. It's still possible, mind you. I want to assure you of that. But it will take more finesse than I had previously thought."

Poko cut in, fluttering beside Khara's knee. "Why did you lose standing? It's not like you asked to get caught."

"I staked my reputation on finding you, Odessa, and bringing you here to kill Sak-Tor. And I failed. Instead I allowed myself to get captured." Khara's eyes fell to the ground. "Sisters died to get me back. Odessa, the reason I left in the first place, nearly killed herself to get me back. I allowed myself to get caught and interrogated. I should have chewed off my tongue and died before I let them begin prying answers out of me. I failed in every conceivable way."

"You still got me here," Odessa said. "Things may have gotten a bit complicated in the middle, but I'm here now."

"That's not of my doing. You came to free me of your own volition and got yourself swept up in this mess by your own choice."

"Oh, that's shit. Do you really think I would have done any of this if it weren't for you?" Odessa asked.

Khara didn't say anything. She only continued studying the dusty ground.

"And who's to say the rescue didn't help our cause a bit? We must have proved that I'm at least somewhat useful to them. There's one less of Sak-Tor's bastard sons walking around—that's proof enough for your Sisters, no?"

"I suppose so, but you also nearly got killed in the process."

"Come on, I didn't nearly get killed. I just exhausted myself. I have to get my strength back is all," Odessa said dismissively.

"How can I help you get your strength back?"

Odessa's eyes were almost magnetically drawn to Khara's hands, but she resisted the tug and instead met Khara's gaze. "You know what I am. What I need." Odessa's iron fingers tapped her knee, suddenly full of nervous energy. "I need blood. I need a sacrifice."

CHAPTER 27

Poko's pale face was drained further of color at Odessa's words. Or, rather, just one word: *sacrifice*. But Odessa could not think of another word for what she needed.

Khara, on the other hand, did not so much as flinch. "What sort of sacrifice? We don't have many beasts to spare. Half of our riders have lost their entehlos."

"Not animals. Animals don't have enough in them. Not enough life. Not enough power. I need something big. Something drastic. As half-dead as I feel now, I need something like catching a bolt of lightning." Odessa found the words were coming quickly to her lips, urgency and sudden zeal bringing them cascading from her mouth. Forcing her to consciously slow them and parse through them lest she appear too eager for blood. Khara was watching her, rapt and attentive, but Poko's eyes held suspicion and a mix of pity and disdain. Poko knew she needed blood but perhaps they had never realized just how much she needed it. How much she itched and ached for it. Did not know the empty feeling that cracked ever wider inside her. That emptiness that gaped wide and abyssal even after feeding. Odessa wiped a bit of spittle from the corner of her mouth, giving herself enough time to compose herself and temper the roaring hunger inside her to a low whine. "I need a person. Whatever I take from the dead, it's purer in people. More potent."

Khara nodded thoughtfully. "We took few prisoners after I was freed. Anyone who did not swear fealty to the Sisters was summarily executed, but we did take some." She frowned. "I doubt Remaka and the others would approve of you feeding, so to speak, on one of our prisoners. The few prisoners we took either have information we want or are suitable hostages. We are effectively exiled guerrillas in this barren land. We do not have much of anything in excess, I'm afraid."

"I would only need one," Odessa said. "If you could convince them to spare me one prisoner." Shame began to flood her cheeks with warmth at the ghastly proposition she was so excitedly presenting. But it was necessary. Without it, her body would soon begin to fail her. The poison in her veins would burn her from the inside out. The throbbing in her arm grew sharper and dug deeper the more she thought about her need. The pulsing stabs were concentrated in her shoulder now and sent knives of white hot pain down through the bones of her arm to her fingertips, as well as up into her neck and across the right side of her chest. "If I could have one prisoner, I could convince your Sisters. I'm sure of it. All it would take is one. If I can have one, I could get my head straight. And this damnable weakness and constant pain would go away."

"Would blood suffice? I believe I could take a cupful from them without much undue contention."

"It might allow me to subsist a while longer. But it won't edify me like lifeblood."

Poko stood up from their place beside Khara, pale and sickened. "I'm sorry, I can't listen to this anymore." They took flight and hovered, a hand to their thin, frowning lips. "It's one thing when it's self-defense or when I don't have to hear, but this is—This is ghoulish." They shook their head. "I need some air." Poko darted across the tent and out through the flaps before Odessa or Khara could respond.

The tent was quiet for a time. An awkward, bloated silence. For Odessa, the silence was heavy with shame and disgust.

"Poor thing," Khara said, still turned toward the flaps no longer fluttering after Poko's exit. "They have a kind heart. Unfortunately this is no place for kind hearts nor innocent souls such as theirs."

"They're not so innocent," Odessa said with false levity. "You know how we met? They tried to eat me."

"I don't know if I believe that. Have you thought that maybe you're just bad at first impressions? Because as I recall, you were close to killing me when we first met." Khara smirked.

A trace of a smile spread across Odessa's lips. "No one's perfect."

Khara smiled, her sharp teeth poking out from beneath her lips. "I suppose that's true." Her smile faded a bit as her gaze fell away. Drifting to her broken hands then back to Odessa. Meeting Odessa's gaze with sober solemnity. "Why did you change your mind? After our first meeting, that is. What possessed you to sneak into a heavily guarded encampment to save someone you had wanted to kill but a few days ago? I don't understand it."

Odessa shrugged. "I don't know. Poko convinced me, I suppose."

Khara raised an eyebrow. "I myself don't find that very convincing."

Odessa eyed Khara for a moment, surveying the earnestness in her hard features. "Do you really want to know?"

"Yes." Khara nodded. "I do. Truly."

"I didn't think I would really get to you at all. I thought they would cut me down before I even reached the entehlos." Khara was watching Odessa intently, absorbing her every word. Odessa withered under Khara's gaze. Odessa's eyes fell away to her own hand, bound in runed iron and filled with poison. She sighed. "I thought I would die. And I was fine with that. I was more than fine with it. I think that was what I wanted the most. To die doing something decent, I suppose. I don't know, I wasn't really thinking clearly." Her iron fingers closed into a fist then opened, grating with every movement. "I haven't been for a while, I think."

There was another awkward silence. To Odessa, this silence seemed somehow deeper. It was a quiet that packed the ears and weighed upon her shoulders. Khara was still looking at her, she knew. She could feel her gaze. A pitying gaze, Odessa was sure. Or one of disdain for such weakness. Or betrayal. Her rescue had not been born of noble intentions. It had been little more than a serendipitous byproduct of a convoluted suicide attempt.

When Khara spoke, she spoke softly. "Do you still want that?" Her words were soft and gentle. Words that caressed and coddled. "Do you still want to die?"

"I don't know."

"I think you do know," Khara said. "Why would you want that blood if not because you want to continue living?"

Because I have a monster in me. A monster that craves nothing but blood and it's driving me mad. Odessa shrugged, wanting to put her thoughts to words. But she was ultimately unable to do it. To admit how powerless she was to the hunger. She could not bear it. She could not admit to herself that the tainted hunger had hold of her. That all her efforts had not been enough. "I suppose you're right," she said quietly.

"Say it."

Odessa looked at Khara, quizzically. "Say what?"

Khara uncrossed her legs and shifted to sit on her knees. A sudden intensity in her eyes, soft and bright like a sunrise. "Say that you want to live."

"I—" For a moment, Odessa was too taken aback to utter more than that. "I want to live."

Khara smiled a wan, joyless smile. "Good. That's very good." Her bandaged hands rose to the right side of her belt. Pinched between her flat palms, she drew a small antler-handled skinning knife from its sheath and held it out.

"What are you doing?"

"You said you need a person." Khara extended her hands and the knife pressed awkwardly between them. "Take me."

"Stop it," Odessa said, eyes fixed on the knife. Horror began creeping like a night's frost into her heart. Horror at herself. Because a part of her was so very willing to take the knife and plunge it into Khara's chest. Odessa's throat began to tighten and go dry. "Put that away."

"I wouldn't be here if it wasn't for you, Odessa. You saved me." Khara's expression was steadfast and supremely earnest. "Allow me to return the favor now."

Odessa's iron fingers twitched then tightened into a tight fist. Her hand vibrated with a building pressure. The pulsing of her arm quickened with the racing of her heart. "Stop it, Khara," her choked voice said, sounding distant to her own ears. In her mind she saw vividly her own hand taking the knife. Ramming it to the hilt in Khara's chest. Stabbing again and again. Blood spraying in the air. Spattering across her face in crimson dots of fire. Then she would be satisfied. Contented in the splendor of the kill. The purest bliss.

"I am offering you a deal right now. Take of me what you need and kill Sak-Tor. I know you can do it." She extended her hands farther in a jerking thrust and the knife tumbled from her precarious grip. It clattered on the stony ground before coming to a rest at Odessa's feet. Khara looked at it, then back to Odessa. "Take it." Her voice was quiet. Almost pleading. Her face was blank save the placid insistence in her eyes. "Take the knife."

Odessa watched as her iron hand slowly extended. There was the hushed scrape of metal against stone. Her fingers gingerly wrapped around the antler handle and she lifted it from the ground. The blade was short. No longer than her index finger. But long enough. One upward thrust beneath the bottom of the sternum was all it would take. Pull the blade out and Khara's life would come pouring out in a torrent of splendid scarlet. The blade quivered in her trembling hand. She looked from it to Khara, who nodded in return.

"Do it." Khara laid her hands gently in her lap and closed her eyes. She was serene. The deep, quavering rise and fall of her chest the only sign of her fear.

Odessa rose onto her knees, knife clasped in two hands. Pain and fatigue forgotten. Her blood ran hot. Her mind buzzed and sparked with sunburst dynamism. Just the prospect of blood enlivened her tattered body.

Her eyes were trained on the point at which she would drive the blade. The hollow beneath the sternum. In her mind, the blue tunic was already darkening with her spilled blood. She could see Khara's bandaged hands clutching at the hole in her chest. The bandages becoming red and wet before falling away, limp and lifeless.

The muscles in her arms tensed. Her fingers tightened around the knife's handle until they hurt. Her breath came in quick bursts through her nostrils. Blood rushed like the sound of the ocean in her ears. A roaring cacophony drowning out everything but the need. The craving. The hunger.

She bit her lip until she broke the skin and continued even then. The taste of her own blood was bitter. The pain held her anchored. Kept her from being swept away in the ecstatic maelstrom of bloodlust. Her eyes misted with frustration. Her fingers tightened further on the knife. Shuddering and shaking with strain.

Then, with great will, the pressure building within her broke and came hissing out of her in a long, deflating sigh. Finger by finger, her grip loosened until the knife fell to the ground again. The hands remained there in the air for a moment, trembling. *I almost killed her.* Shock and horror chilled her blood. *I was a second from killing her. I wanted to kill her. I wanted to kill her so much.* Revulsion turned her innards to a churning mass of acid and bile.

"What's wrong?" Khara asked, her serene resignation replaced with concern.

"I can't do it." Odessa shook her head. "I won't do it."

A sad smile graced Khara's lips. A relieved yet disappointed smile. A smile of contradiction. "How long can you last without a sacrifice?"

"I don't know. I probably have a few days before I start really burning up. After that it won't be long, I don't think."

"Take just a little blood from me then," Khara said. "Enough to keep you going at least."

Haven't you bled enough? Odessa thought numbly as Khara rolled up her loose sleeve, exposing a muscular forearm replete with the faint memories of faded scars. Without thought, Odessa's hand found the knife. She drew close to Khara. "Are you sure?" she asked in a dry whisper.

Khara nodded, holding out her arm to expose the veins of her wrist.

Odessa put her left hand on Khara's arm near her wrist and held it still. Khara's skin was warm. The flesh underneath was firm. Against her palm she could feel Khara's pulse, quick and strong. Slowly, she brought the knife up to Khara's arm. The point hovering above the bulge of an artery in her wrist.

For an instant, in a flash of horrible presentiment, she imagined nothing but opening up Khara's entire arm from crook of elbow to wrist and lapping up the blood as Khara's life flooded out. Odessa's teeth found the ragged spot of lip she had already bitten and bore down upon it. The pain was sudden and exquisite.

Carefully, Odessa brought the knife's point down and pricked the skin above the vein. Before she could do anything more with it, she dropped the knife. A dot of blood welled up in the pinprick, then spilled over the ridge of the artery in a small, slithering drop.

Without thinking, Odessa pressed her mouth to Khara's wrist and licked up the drop before it could slide any farther. The blood was hot and coppery.

Her lips pushed against Khara's warm skin and she drank greedily. Her tongue lapping up the blood as it came. A rush of warmth flooded her body. Energy tingling through her body. A faint strength seeping into her muscles like a warm rain into dry, sunbaked earth.

When her stomach felt close to bursting, Odessa drew away, wiping her mouth with the back of her hand. Khara was pale, her skin gone a pallid mauve, and her eyes were distant and unfocused. But when she noticed Odessa's gaze, her eyes focused and she smiled. "How do you feel? Better?"

Odessa put a hand on Khara's wrist to stop the pinprick's bleeding before Khara lost any more blood. "I do," she said. "Thank you. You don't know how much I needed that."

Khara's smile widened. "I'll try to get you a prisoner but for now you can take from me whenever you need."

Odessa shook her head. "I shouldn't have even taken what I did now. You need your blood to heal."

Khara snorted derisively. "The way I am right now, my blood would be more useful to you than to me."

"Shut up," Odessa said with a thin wry smile. "Just be quiet and rest for a while. You've got no blood in your head. It's making you stupid."

Khara obliged her, leaning against Odessa when the strain of sitting upright became too much. Odessa sat with Khara for a while, squeezing her wrist and holding it long after the bleeding had stopped. It was comforting, Khara's weight leaned against her. But in the back of her mind, at the base of her skull where her baser faculties went about concealed beneath thought and the pretensions of humanity, there lay unease. Unease scraping at her nerves as it paced compulsively in those hidden recesses of her mind. Discomfort and anxiety brushed against the back of her neck like cold spectral fingers.

After a while her thoughts drifted along a familiar path once again. A well-trodden path that brought her first to memories of Tarik. Of furtive kisses in the shadow of Khymanir's palace. Of his hands tracing the lines of her body in the dark. His silhouette in the doorway as he sat strapped in a chair with a metal arm fused to her flesh and innocent blood pumped in her veins.

The path brought her naturally—unavoidably—to Yakun. Yakun and his lies. Yakun and his gnarled hands on her skin. Roving. Molesting.

When Poko returned to the tent, Khara lay on Odessa's rushes, still sleeping. Odessa, meanwhile, barely registered Poko's return. She sat a short distance away from the sleeping devil, skinning knife in hand. Running her fingers along the blade's flat face. Letting the touch of hard iron anchor her fast in her ruminations. As she thought again and again of Yakun and Tarik. And how hot their blood would be as it spilled from their open chests.

CHAPTER 28

Wreathed in cool, dank energy, Ayana's fist sank deeper into the oozing putrefaction of the spore column. The column shuddered as she focused on the decay roiling like a mirage around the bare skin of her arm. Numbness nipped at her curled fingertips and at her knuckles. Her arm, from elbow to fist, throbbed. A hole, black and oozing, gaped around her arm. Quickly widening as her rot gnawed and melted the column's dead and gnarled flesh. Bits of green and black flesh dropped onto her skin and slid to the pale, fleshy ground.

Teeth bared, she slid her fist farther into the slimy pit she had hollowed out. Sinking nearly to her shoulder in the massive tower's hard-packed, stringy innards. Her fist unfurled and her fingers dug through the sludge of decaying meat until they found the sinewy cord running up the length of the tower. The column, almost twice as large as the first column she destroyed, had a core as wide around as her middle. Her fingers ripped into the hard, striated strands and they began to soften and fray, pulling away from each other as she dug her nails in deeper.

Sinewy strands turned to sludge around her fingers. Taking a handful of hard-packed, fleshy cord, Ayana forced more of herself into the rot pulsing through her arm. Focusing and condensing it in her tightened fist. The energy pouring from her skin like blankets of thick steam.

Decay ran up and down the column's core with malignant rapidity. The column groaned and shifted slightly. The hollow around her arm was now nearly large enough for her to crawl inside it. Ayana continued pouring her focus into her fist. Her arm was covered with black slime and gobs of rotten flesh. The stench of rot was so powerful it made her eyes water despite her predilection to the musky, fetid stink. The wall of inert flesh, so cold and lifeless, gave off a strange odor as it rotted. An unnaturally harsh smell somewhat reminiscent of burnt hair and feces.

A section of the column above her sheared off from the face of the wall with a wet ripping sound. Ayana ripped her arm from the wall and leaped back. The slab of rotting meat hit the ground in front of her. Its impact made a heavy, muted thud as it splattered in a heap of sick, purple-tinged flesh upon the column's mounded roots.

More flesh sloughed off the column and fell to the ground. Ropes secured to the top half of the column, anchored in place with spikes the length of her forearm, were pulled as the tower began to shudder and cant to the side.

Ayana ripped her fist free from the wall of blackened flesh. There was a wet sucking noise as the gaping wall of meat attempted to hold her. The pungent, heady stench of rotting spore column pervaded the air now, coating Ayana's mouth and throat and clogging her nostrils.

There were shouts of alarm and calls for the men at the perimeter to run. Two pairs of men guiding the column fell away from Ayana and the line of warriors arrayed behind her. Groaning through masks, their backs twisted as the column's base crumbled into meaty chunks and the upper half began to lean drunkenly away from Ayana.

The column's hollowed-out bulk shook the earth as it fell with a distinctly wet and meaty thud. Its interior collapsed, and the column disintegrated upon impact, pieces of putrid meat flung into the air or sloughing off the huge heap of flesh that now stood nearly twice as tall as the men who had hauled it to the ground. A cloud of spores filled the air above the fallen column and drifted lazily downward.

"Get back!" Ayana called to the men still holding the ropes. In the fog, her voice was muddled at a distance greater than an arm's length. The men remained in two clusters a short distance from the outer edges of the fleshy mound, pulling their rope's anchor free from the pile of gore, reeling it in from that meager distance. Pale motes as fine as sand fell on their heads and shoulders. Collecting in the curls of their hair and in their eyelashes. Yet they continued their work, one man reeling the rope in while the other man coiled.

Idiots! The cool aura around Ayana's hands and arms dissipated in an instant, giving way to the frigid, bone-deep cold of the spore-thick air. She made her way for the column's base, waving the men away. *I told Kunza this should be a Shadow's work only. I told him!*

"The spores are still alive!" she called, although they were not exactly living. The men looked up as she crested the column's base. Looking at her with blank, baffled eyes. She ripped the mask from her face and shouted, "Get away from the column! Now!"

The men's eyes remained bewildered for a heartbeat longer and then widened with realization. Both pairs of men backed away in a hurry, shaking spores from their hair and wiping their faces with the spore-covered hands.

Ayana glanced at the column's stump as the men stumbled away to take up their arms again. In the pit at the center of the stump was a deep, black hole where the core had spread into the earth. Its roots sinking deep into the dirt. But her rot had taken the roots whole. She was sure of it. This spore column was entirely destroyed. In her weeks of destroying spore columns, she had learned one immutable fact: their roots were resilient and ran deep.

Screams drew her attention. The screams of men and the chest-rattling bass of a garbled bellow tearing itself from a marred and melded throat. Hurried, heavy footfalls softened by the fleshy ground.

Through the mist she could make out a Blighted giant's form looming before a few of her warriors. The warriors surrounded the stooping giant, dodging its swiping limbs and prodding with careful spear thrusts. But the bellow had not come from a giant's throat. It had been far too deep and too loud. Too animalistic.

Emerging from the murk came a shape taller than the giant and as wide as a man is tall. Its head sat atop a thick neck and it bore a high arched snout terminating in a mouth of slobber and foam and flat, gnashing teeth. Loose folds of pale brown skin hanging from its head, neck, and flanks disguised what it was in its prior life. The beast plowed into a warrior, lowing in hysterical fury as its hooves pounded the warrior into the flesh-strewn dirt.

"Retreat!" Ayana cried as the Blighted beast whirled on the Shadows that came darting from the mists to strike it down. Its swinging head knocked one Shadow aside as two more rounded its flanks, hacking and slashing.

Ayana's beastfolk were at her side, all three of them pressed against her and bristling with agitation. They ushered her around the rampaging Blighted beast. A knot of warriors and Shadows soon formed around her, moving like a school of fish through the mists.

"Retreat!" Ayana repeated, straining her voice to pierce the muting fog. "To me! Retreat!" Her heart was pounding. The rush of blood was loud in her ears, drowning out her words and her thoughts. They had never been faced by a Blighted creature so large. It very presence forced her to confront a worrying truth: there was no telling what monsters lurked in the mist. They had already seen all manner of corrupted people and animals. But there existed worse things in this world. Much worse, Ayana knew.

The beast was on its gangly knees. Her Shadows made to behead the blood-ied thing as it lunged and snapped and bucked on the ground. Even grounded, the thing was taller than the Shadows.

Amid the jostling of her army in retreat, Ayana attempted to take a count to see if the bulk of her men and women had regrouped, but in the fog and bedlam, it was no use. She was particularly worried about the warriors on the perimeter, but there was little she could do now but shout as they skirted past the beast and made for the world yet untouched by the Gray. That, and pray that all her war-riors followed.

The toll of her exertion and the fog's constant sapping of her strength had begun to make her lightheaded, but she pushed on, a hand on the jackal-headed woman's back for support as they trotted.

Killing Blighted as they fled, they did not slow until the fog had thinned enough to see across the plains to their camp. It was then that her men and women tore off their masks and could finally breathe freely, sucking in deep breaths of joyously pure air.

The spore columns' detritus had completely dried on Ayana's arm by the time they reached the perimeter guard at their post a stone's throw from the receded wall of fog. Not far from the perimeter guard were Ur-Mak's masons and a contingent of slaves as they began to put up the wooden framework for the rammed-earth wall that would divide the Gray world from Talara's paradise. The wall would stretch from the Slateseer Sea in the east all the way to the Coatlahara Mountains in the west. The bones of Azka, his dead sons, and his Chosen, engraved with sigils of Talara's make, would be arrayed along the length of the wall as a bulwark against the Gray.

The wall's construction would take years. Long, arduous years of constantly destroying spore column after encroaching spore column. Years of breathing in spores and feeling the stagnant air sapping her of warmth and life.

The Gray's advance came with the creation of a forest of spore columns. Hundreds of them spread out across the plains north of Noyo. Saplings and gargantuan towers of flesh weaving a tapestry of fog across the land. Their roots forming a mess of lifelessly probing fingers beneath the earth. And it was her responsibility alone to stunt that forest's growth. She and she alone could do it.

At the camp's entrance she dismissed the warriors to bathe and purify them-selves in ash and blood. Each human detachment she took into the Gray had to be replaced after no more than four hours. After four hours, a human would begin to cough up bloody sputum and their nose would begin to drain con-stantly. Their eyes would turn red and swollen and their vision would start to blur. Shadows had no such impediments, but Kunza had limited the number of

Shadows Ayana could take with her as she cleansed the deeper, more developed reaches of the Gray. He had said Talara required them for a different purpose, but to Ayana's mind there was no greater purpose for them than the destruction of the spore columns.

She and her beastfolk made their way through the increasingly cramped camp. With the introduction of Ur-Mak, along with his masons and their slaves, the camp had grown into a sprawl of tents and goat pens.

Ayana entered Kunza's tent and found it empty. Pausing a moment in the flapping doorway, she wandered inside to wait for him. The map in the center of the room, the focal point of the sparsely decorated tent, was littered with hundreds of dots and crosses. The Shadows scouting out the Gray lands had been meticulous in their search for spore columns. And there was no shortage of spore columns to find. At most, Ayana had destroyed seven in one day and that was when she did not have to worry about the constitution of human warriors. A drop in a Gray ocean.

Leaning over the map, she found the spore column she had just destroyed. It sat just above a smattering of crosses. The small indentation she had personally carved into the Gray. The tiny hold she had scratched and clawed into its unyielding approach. More than sixty crosses were clustered in a wide arc over the camp's position. Taking the crow feather quill from its holder, she dipped it in the pot of soot ink and carefully crossed out the spore column's dot.

After Ayana lounged about the tent for nearly an hour, taking the time to clean the decayed flesh and blood from her body and occasionally perusing the map and trying to divine what Kunza's next plan would be, Kunza returned.

"I did not expect you back so soon," Kunza said. Ayana thought she detected a note of reproach in his voice. "I hope you have not waited long."

"No, I just got here," she said. "Now what's the plan? You said it was changing."

"Not changing. Not really."

Ayana, sitting cross-legged on the floor, sat up straighter and eyed him. "What's happening?"

Kunza crossed the tent and sat across from her. "The plan has not changed. The wall will rise on schedule, and you will clear the columns according to the grid."

"What has changed then?"

Kunza licked his lips and took a short breath as he searched for the words. "I'm afraid I must leave for some time. So Ajatunde will be taking over the ritual and day-to-day leadership of the camp in my stead."

"You're leaving?" Ayana asked. "Where? And why? Why now?"

"I'm needed in Asha-Kalir. Sak-Tor masses along the river for a siege and at the Khymanir's current rate, the vessel won't be ready by the time the devils are at the gates."

"And how is that your problem?" Ayana asked sourly. "Isn't our work more important?"

"Without Asha-Kalir, our supply of flesh dwindles and our work suffers," Kunza said curtly. "But most importantly, Talara wills it." He looked like he wanted to say more, but they both knew there was no reason to waste another word. The Goddess's will was absolute.

"The Goddess knows best," Ayana said, resigned and irritated. To have Talara's will thrown in her face was like a slap across her cheek. She understood the importance of Talara's will better than anyone. Ayana's faith was steadfast and to have it besmirched so casually infuriated her. She rose. Her muscles, having relished their respite, ached in protest. She had rested enough. There were more spore columns to destroy. More men and women to lose to the Blighted. More grief like an iron band tightening around her chest. And she would have to bear it alone.

She supposed that was also Talara's will.

But if a queen should suffer so her people would prosper, Ayana thought that could she bear it.

CHAPTER 29

Kunza had thought he knew fear. He had stood before Talara on the mount. Faced a wrathful god and survived. He knew true, existential fear. He knew dread. He knew the fear of the soul. But on his way to Asha-Kalir he was assaulted by a different sort of fear. An inborn fear he had never encountered before until he was hurtling through the sky, clinging desperately to a hammock strung around Ketabi's neck. He was curled in the hammock against the soft, luxurious fur of Ketabi's throat. The thin air struck him through the thick strands of rope that formed his woven womb, blustering and brutal. He shivered and pressed his face into Ketabi's fur. Beneath him there was nothing but air and a very long fall.

He had thought he would be riding on Ketabi's back or something similarly dignified. But Ketabi would not allow a mere man to straddle him, so concessions had to be made. Now Kunza cursed himself and his concessions. *Damn this war, I should have just walked. I'd sooner walk a thousand deserts than fly like this. I'd crawl a thousand deserts. Devils or no, my dignity be damned, I don't care. I'd crawl.* His fingers tightened around the ropes that held him secure. *As if I have any dignity left. This flight is the most undignified thing I've ever had to do in my entire life. In a way, I hope I fall before we arrive in Asha-Kalir. It would spare me the embarrassment.* As soon as he thought of falling, his stomach began to churn, and he regretted his foolishness.

Damn you, Ketabi. I should have had your brother take the throne, you bastard. Better yet, I should have blown up all of you arrogant little godlings with your father. Let Talara's true dedicants lead. Not some upstart puppet. He gritted his teeth against the cold and his own reckless thoughts.

Crammed beside him in the hammock, his two Shadows were silent. Behind their bronze masks, their blank eyes stared down at the distant desert rolling beneath them. Impervious to fear. But Kunza was a man. And to be a man was to know fear. To know it as surely as one knows himself. So in keeping with his humanity, he held onto his fear like a lover. Focusing his entire being on the fear. Of falling. Falling for long agonizing minutes. Watching the ground sweep up to meet him. He clung to his fear until he grew sick of it. Until its very existence repulsed him.

Fervently embracing his fear like an old lover he had grown to loathe, he bore down upon it. Thinking of nothing but falling and striking the ground in a cloud of sand and arterial red mist. Thinking of nothing but his own death. Because beyond death, Talara awaited. His Goddess would take him in open arms.

In his embrace, he squeezed the life from that old lover, fear, until there was nothing left but acceptance. Physically, an innate primal fear still tickled him at the nape of his neck and sent shivers of cold down his spine, but mentally it had no longer held its domineering sway over him.

He cursed his moment of weakness but only partially. For overcoming such weakness was the true test of man. It was what made humanity human. That struggle to overtake such base, inborn flaws and become a purer, more godly being. Through strength of will and faith alone.

The descent into the city was sudden. Kunza's stomach rose up into his throat as Ketabi began to drop. His fingers tightened around the hammock's rope until his joints ached. He cast a glance behind him to see the cityscape—rooftops and streets like cobblestone rivers—rising fast. Ketabi was plummeting straight down to the palace. Kunza buried his face in Ketabi's fur and grimaced. The sudden flood of fear mixed with fury. *Damn you, Ketabi. You're doing this just to make me feel weak and helpless. To make me look like a scared old man.* He smothered his fear again, letting resolve take its place like a cold rain washing away the dust and grime of a long journey. *It won't work. I won't allow you to make a fool of Talara's chosen emissary. I will make you regret this little display. One day.*

With a great flap of his bronze wings, Ketabi suddenly slowed their descent and landed lightly in the plaza of Khymanir's palace. As soon as Ketabi's paws touched cobblestone, Kunza's Shadows were slicing the hammock's ropes. As the ropes gave way and the hammock's outward facing side unfurled, Kunza began to climb down the hammock like a rope ladder. The Shadows attempted to assist him, but he dismissed them with a hiss.

"Welcome, Ketabi, Sovereign of Noyo," Bukoris's voice came from behind him as he climbed down the hammock. "Asha-Kalir thanks you for personally delivering the Priest of Ashes in our time of dire need. My Eminence knows the importance of his work in Noyo and offers to you His most gracious thanks for your generosity in lending us his aid."

"It is my pleasure. I humbly accept your Eminence's thanks." Ketabi bowed his head and Kunza dropped with it, his foot suddenly touching the ground. He let go of the ropes and steadied himself. Brushing the dust and hair from his dark robes, he turned and faced Bukoris. Behind Bukoris, before the massive skull of a long-dead god, stood two men, one old and one young. Kunza bowed.

"Thank you for coming, Kunza," Bukoris said, stepping forward. His plumage looked duller than it had been the last time Kunza had seen him. And his avian eyes looked weary. "I hope you do not take offense, but I must forgo the rest of the formalities and leave you in the care of our soulweaver, Yakun."

"No offense taken," Kunza said. "I am anxious to get to work."

Bukoris bowed, then hurried past him to Ketabi. His thin dry voice chattered, engaging the god in a discussion of the war effort as they made their way across the plaza to some exquisite lounge for honored guests. Where Bukoris and the rest of Asha-Kalir's most distinguished would grovel and beg for wartime aid from the new Sovereign of Noyo.

The old man quietly stepped forward, his loose-hanging robes the color of cornsilk swishing across the cobblestones. His skin was white like curdled milk. Blue eyes blazed from red-rimmed hollows in his haggard face. Tangles of white hair had been swept back from his face and tied in a knot. A long, unruly beard flared from the bottom half of his face like a white corona. He extended a hand, the joints swollen and knobby. Kunza took it. The old man's grip was firm. Unflinching against Kunza's hand and the cold might that lay within it. Unfazed in the presence of Talara's blessing.

The old man's stare pierced Kunza. Not so much as a moment's hesitation before staring into Kunza's smoldering eyes. "I am Yakun," he said, releasing Kunza's hand with a nod. "I am glad to have you. We have heard you have some great experience with the binding of soul and flesh."

"By Talara's grace, I have been fortunate in my craft."

"I'm glad to hear it," Yakun said, his voice totally devoid of anything approaching gladness. "We need more experienced hands if we are to finish before the devils start crawling over the city walls."

The young man stepped beside Yakun and bowed. His skin a coppery brown, his hair straight and black, and his eyes deep and dark, the young man was a native of Asha-Kalir. His eyes were tired, dark bags beneath them. And they would not meet Kunza's gaze. "I am Tarik," he said, his head cast down in deference. "A pleasure to meet you, sir."

Kunza nodded, then said to Yakun, "I am happy to lend my aid in your Eminence's work, but I'm afraid your bird's letter was a bit unclear as to the finer details of what exactly is needed of me."

"I apologize for the vagueness. Times of war call for a great deal of discretion." Yakun paused and glanced back at the palace. "It was also a quite hastily written letter. Our Eminence ordered me to send for you immediately without, at the time, deigning to let me know why. Since then, the problem for which we require your expertise has become more apparent." Yakun gestured for Kunza to follow him as he started for the palace. "Come, I will show you."

Walking past the giant skull and into the palace, Kunza's curiosity simmered to a boil. A vessel fit for a god. What a massive undertaking. Unthinkable in its scale. The grandness of such thought. What earthly materials could hold the entire essence of the divine? The Kusa sisters had only small portions of the divine within them. Ayana had to be submerged in the pool at least once a week to keep her body from succumbing to the rigors of her god-touched blood. What could hold a god's entire being?

He followed the two soulweavers down long, high-ceilinged halls, turning left and right through a maze of enormous corridors until they came to a pair of bronze doors dominating the entire wall at the end of the hall. As they approached, the rattling and clicking of chains and pulleys sounded from somewhere. The doors began to draw slowly open, cracking wide enough for them to enter.

The room was massive. But as he entered alongside the two soulweavers, Kunza's attention was drawn to but one thing: the god at his work. He had never seen a being such as Khymanir. A heap of arms and hands, some massive and some tiny like those of a child. The god was as tall as some of the larger buildings in Noyo. At its center was a mound of flesh, myriad bones shifting back and forth beneath its loose skin.

Khymanir's red-stained hands worked with a grotesquely fluid grace, reaching with handfuls of wet, blood-red clay or sculpting with painstaking but somehow effortless finesse. The hands, all of them, beneath their red stains, bore the bright streaks of divinity spiderwebbing up their fingers like veins of sunlight. Staring at their fingertips and reaching up their wrists.

With Khymanir's massive bulk in front of them, only the top portion of the vessel was visible against the far wall. Above its shoulders remained unobscured by the tangle of writhing limbs. It was a vaguely human shape but broader and more muscled than any living man he had ever seen. Its face was a rough, half-formed approximation of a face, but in the hollows of its eyes glowed two brilliant orbs of lapis lazuli veined with gold. Stone eyes devoid of life but holding within their luster the potential for something more. A vacancy waiting to be filled.

Tarik came close to Kunza's side and whispered, "If he speaks to you, it may feel strange or could even hurt, but try to not recoil from it. It only makes it worse."

Kunza gave the young man a curious look, scarred brow furrowing as much as it could.

"Look," Yakun said, drawing Kunza's attention. He pointed to the god. One of Khymanir's many arms, one of the longest, beckoned them impatiently forward. "He wastes no time. That much can be said for old Khymanir." Yakun's mumbled words were a blatant insult in the presence of a god. Kunza expected one of the hands to come sweeping from across the room and snatch the old man up by his head, but his words went ignored.

Kunza moved across the long room, the soulweavers following a few steps behind him. Passing long work tables filled with knives and tongs and bloody pieces of flesh and organ. The walls were lined with shelves holding great copper cisterns and tall glass jars filled with blood and offal. The entirety of the vast, vaulted room, with its fine marble and well-worked bronze, was covered in a pervasive layer of filth. The stink of decay had seeped into the room's every niche and pore. It brought to mind Kunza's hut in Kalaro. Before he had moved his workspace into the subterranean temple when he had done all of his bloody work on the dirt floor of his hut. That thought, that his work was at all similar to that of a god's, almost made him chuckle aloud.

Halfway across the room, set into the floor, was a bronze-inlaid circle covered in dried blood. Kunza skirted around it while studying the exquisitely refined runes and sigils inlaid at various points along the circle's outer edge. Along the circle's inner edge was a deep channel carved into the floor. A channel that ran from the circle across the room to the giant vessel in construction.

Edging around the circle, Kunza and the soulweavers were within the reach of Khymanir's longest arms had he been so inclined to reach out and snatch them up. The god towering over him as he approached, Kunza could not help but watch with awe the myriad hands at work. Most of them angled up and away from the approaching men, busy with clay and small bronze implements. The arms moving independent of one another like a nest of snakes tangled at the tail. Some of the arms were as wide at the wrist as he was around the waist.

He stopped halfway between the circle and the bulk of the god's body. The fleshy core amid the mass of arms. He could see now how the god supported himself. Beneath his body were a few stout arms holding his weight off the ground. Knot-knuckled hands splayed against the marble, the bones twisted and deformed by centuries of constant pressure.

A hand half as tall as a man squirmed from out of the press of arms. A long, emaciated arm stretched and extended the hand in a loose fist towards them. A hand unstained by red clay, its glowing gold veins were in full display as it approached.

Yakun and Tarik stepped aside as the hand came within a few paces of Kunza. Leaving him alone with the hand.

Fingers unfurling, the hand rose and presented its palm to Kunza. In the center of its gold palm was an eye. Red-rimmed and twitching. The hand's golden veins radiated from the bloodshot eye, the light a stark contrast to the dark, lusterless eye set in the center of the palm.

The eye, after a moment's whirling and twitching, settled fixedly on Kunza. Its iris was a shade lighter than black and served to draw his gaze into the pure black pupil. The eye's gaze bored into him as he stared back into the deep well of dark that lay within it.

Pressure swelled at the back of his head. Like something burrowing beneath his skull. Something probing at his brain. Like cold, filthy fingers working their way into his head. Forcing between the folds of his brain. The pressure grew, extending to the front of his skull as well. Until it felt like his head might burst. His temples began to throb.

"Kunza. Talara's pet," an internal voice said. A voice totally devoid of warmth and emotion. Its words were slow and unmodulated. The syllables stretched awkwardly in a monotonous drone that grated against his mind.

Transfixed by the eye's hypnotic gaze, Kunza spoke aloud without realizing. "What do you require of me?"

"The circle. Beneath the vessel's feet. Its completion requires the full attention of a scrupulous man." Khymanir's voice was loud in Kunza's head. The pressure dug deeper in his brain. Psychic fingers stabbing into the center of his mind. "The old soulweaver, Yakun. He does not comprehend the vast amounts of power the circle must hold if the weaving is to be successful. His experience is limited. Based on capturing a portion of divinity. Not its entirety." Kunza's knees began to buckle as the throbbing at his temple swelled. The pounding made his scarred eye sockets ache. He ground his teeth together and in himself found the dark, quiet place where Talara's love resided. Her sanctuary made manifest within his soul. By her strength, he steadied himself.

"Yakun does not truly wish for the circle's success. He thinks only of his own survival. He cannot be trusted with such a pivotal task. But you, Kunza. You must finish the circle. So that I may finish the vessel in time. Can you do it?"

The pressure abated just enough to allow Kunza a moment's respite to think. Such a circle would be similar in design to the circle within the temple's sanctum. But infinitely more precise. Every detail would need to be perfect for uninhibited divinity to flow into the vessel. If anything was askew, even by a hairsbreadth, there was no telling what would happen. The entire city could be blown to rubble for all Kunza knew. "How much time do I have?" Kunza asked.

The psychic fingers knuckled his mind roughly and he winced. "The devil's entire host has massed along the Darrood. Surrounding the city. Razing villages and fields. The preliminaries of the siege are already underway. And when it comes, our walls will not withstand Sak-Tor." Then the psychic fingers were gone. Kunza's thoughts rebounded, free from the pressure and now pouring forth in a cascade of doubt and anxiety.

He glanced back at the circle in the middle of the room. The circle in which the catalyst would be primed before it flowed into the binding circle. The binding circle within which a god would be bound. A circle that would need to withstand the full force of god's unrestrained might.

Kunza looked into the unblinking eye. Sure that the eye's all-encompassing gaze could see the doubt within him. Binding a bit of a god's divinity to someone already blessed by Talara had been an easy enough task, but this endeavor so thoroughly strained the bounds of rational thinking he could not even fathom a circle ever holding together long enough to bind a god. Stone and metal had limits. Definite limits that could not be bent or stretched. There was only so much magic and power these physical things could hold, and that fact was simply incontrovertible.

The eye watched him blankly. *As if I have a choice one way or another.* Kunza's shoulders slumped wearily. *My Goddess's will be done.* He resigned himself to the insurmountable work ahead of him. "I'll begin at once."

CHAPTER 30

Odessa's legs trembled and she braced herself against Khara's shoulder. The few steps from her bed to the tent's flaps had been an arduous journey for her atrophied legs. She had drunk from Khara once more and had gathered some of her former strength, but her muscles had gone soft in her infirmity. Khara pushed a flap aside with her diminished hand and led Odessa outside the tent for the first time since arriving at the camp.

The tent had been pitched at the end of a long cave beside a paddock of entehlos. Past the entehlo pen and a cluster of tents, the mouth of the cave gaped wide. Across from the cave's open mouth was a sandstone cliff pocked with similar, but smaller, caves.

The cave's mouth stretched wide, allowing faint daylight to filter inside. The far end of the cave was obscured by tents, ruined buildings carved from stone, and the lively bustle of devils.

"What do you think?" Khara asked as she and Odessa took a few careful steps along the stone wall of the paddock.

Poko fluttered behind them, casting glances here and there. Having already left the confines of the tent multiple times now, Poko was unimpressed by the view.

Odessa stopped and leaned against Khara once more, breathing heavily. Fatigue hung over her like a pall of thick chainmail. Just standing took a considerable effort, but Khara and Poko had been insistent that Odessa at least step outside the tent. And Odessa had been too tired to argue. "What is this place?"

"Some ancient people fled here after Ogé's death. His most devout and most loyal, I assume. They tried to build a refuge here but were wiped out before they really started."

They began walking again, slowly making their way toward the nearest of the ancient buildings, a squat square building extending from the cave wall. "How did you all find this place?"

"Since Sak-Tor's campaign in Asha-Kalir, the Sisters had been roving about and hiding wherever Sak-Tor's forces were not. A few months before I finally deserted, some scouts out foraging in a village caught wind of a group of refugees hiding in some caves northeast of the Severed Pass. Within a week, the Sisters had consolidated most of their roving bands here." Khara gestured, beaming with gentle, amiable pride.

Odessa eyed a rust-colored stain on the ancient wall as they passed. "What happened to the refugees?"

Khara's beaming dimmed. A frown flickered over her face for the barest instant, then disappeared. "They're gone."

Devils watched them pass, lifting their eyes from their work or poking their horned heads out of tent flaps. Sharp features drawn. Eyes narrowed. Suspicion darkening all of their faces. Anxiety brushed up Odessa's spine. She could feel the contempt and the hate in their gazes. All of it concentrated on her. The brunt of their focused disdain cowing her in her weakened state like a pelting rain crushing a withered plant. If their ardor were fomented in any capacity, she would be torn apart. The entire camp would be upon her like hyenas on a lone calf.

"Here, this way," Khara said, leading her between a row of tents. Nearer the cave mouth, the tents receded, and soon the contemptuous stares were behind them. Khara led Odessa to a row of flat stones arranged a fair few paces from the cave's mouth. Odessa collapsed on a stone, her already aching muscles immediately loosening in relief as soon as she sat down.

Khara sat down beside her as a soft, sidelong breeze coming through the canyon grazed their faces and tousled their hair. "The fresh air will do you some good."

"It's nice to smell anything other than my own stink," Odessa said.

Poko landed and sat on her shoulder. "Hopefully this breeze blows some of it away. Because I don't know if I can take another night of it. Our tent's like a rotten egg filled with dung that's been sitting out in the sun for a few days."

"Oh shut up!" Odessa brushed Poko from her shoulder. They hovered in the air, snickering. The sound of their laughter had a strikingly musical quality.

Khara smiled softly, her distracted gaze drifting from Poko and Odessa to the canyon walls opposite them. In the dim niches there could be spied the shapes of devils. "I'm afraid I did not bring you out here for the air," Khara said, turning her attention to Odessa. "Remaka wishes to speak to you tomorrow."

"Tomorrow?" Odessa balked. "I can barely take two steps without grabbing onto you for support. How can I convince her that I can help kill Sak-Tor when I can't even stand up by myself?"

"She insisted. There was nothing I could do. I've delayed it as much as I could, but it did little good. What sway I had is gone. My reputation is as ruined as my hands." Her bandaged hands shifted, folding over one another in her lap. "I'm sorry I cannot do more, Odessa."

"What about the sacrifice? If I could just have that, I would have enough strength in me to show Remaka and the others my merit."

"I tried. They would not even consider ceding a prisoner to you."

"Shit," Odessa hissed, striking the rock beneath her with an iron clout. Chips of rock burst from the stone and clattered to the ground. The exertion of bringing her heavy arm to strike the rock brought her heart to a painful, lurching gallop for a moment. Her iron arm sagged and she slumped on the rock. Mind clawing at scattered bits of thought, desperate to find some alternative she had overlooked. In the state she was in, there was nothing she could do to convince the Sisters she was anything more than deadweight and another mouth to feed. Even if she was not debilitated, there was still no guarantee Remaka would listen. Khara had greatly overestimated the Sisters' willingness to enlist the aid of a tainted human. No amount of blood-steeped strength would change their minds if they had a mind to just kill Odessa and be rid of her. Or if their rebellion was in a dire position, perhaps they would offer her to Sak-Tor as a means to broker a truce. Instead of killing her, the Sisters might keep her with the other prisoners until they had need of her. That was where her true usefulness lay. As a political prisoner. A scapegoat. Odessa had killed scores of Sak-Tor's devils. Hundreds maybe. Her head would be a most persuasive bargaining chip.

Odessa's thoughts assailed her, one after another, battering her into a frothing paranoia. She needed to leave this place. Take off with Poko immediately. Find her own bloody sustenance and her own way out of this barren, godsforsaken desert. Talara's words had been no more than empty promises. There was no way of extricating herself from this den of vipers short of a hasty and headlong retreat.

"There must be some way of convincing them, right?" Poko asked. "Weakened or not, the things you've done already speak for themselves, Odessa. They would be stupid not to listen to you."

Khara shook her head. "I'm afraid the things she has done thus far are a hindrance as well as an advantage. Odessa is a divisive figure in the Sisterhood. Opinion is split whether she is an ally in Sak-Tor's opposition or a threat to all Torva."

A defeated sigh escaped Odessa's mouth. "I've killed a lot of your people. Of course they wouldn't want me around." Her hands clenched into tight balls. Her head sagged from her slumped shoulders. "It was a stupid idea." Internally, her mind screamed its own disjointed mantra. *Escape is the only option. I have to leave and leave now. Escape now. Go.*

"It was not stupid." Khara's voice was firm. "If I had not gotten captured, I could have brought you here with fanfare and laid a solid foundation of support for you. But I have fouled it all and now even those who were amenable to you are wary of your involvement. All because of me. My inadequacy has left a stain on your standing in the Sisterhood."

For a moment, Khara's self-pity sparked in Odessa embers of wanton anger, but they were quickly smothered in the dense shroud that was despondency's claustrophobic, ever-constricting embrace. Such despondency was a heavy, suffocating sensation closing around her and it brought to her mind the knife she had held before her chest. Remembered the overwhelming urge to plunge the dagger into her own chest. Wanting nothing but escape. All that had come from a despair so absolute Odessa had thought she had no other choice but to die by her own hand. But this feeling was different. It was a deflating constriction, but it was not the total weight of a cruel world pressing upon her. Its grasp was weaker.

There has to be something we can do before tomorrow. Maybe a bazak or a goat would be enough. Enough to get on steady feet at least. She played with the idea but ultimately knew that a single animal's life would not be enough. The hunger consuming her from the inside out had reached a critical juncture. The cracks in her physical body were forming. Spiderwebbing cracks widening to gaping fissures. The weakness and pain were only the preliminary symptoms. When the fever and delirium came it would be too late. She would be lost in that vast emptiness again. Sinking forever. And this time there would be no rising from the abyss. Even now it called to her. Called to her in an infernal buzzing drone that reverberated through her bones. The vast, formless presence that called the abyss its home awaited her return. Tendrils churning the darkness, ready to take her and never let her slip away again.

"What about an animal?" Poko asked as if they had picked it from the swirling bedlam of Odessa's thoughts. "That might be enough to hold you over right?" they asked Odessa.

"Maybe." Odessa looked to Khara. "Are there any entehlos or bazaks or anything like that going to slaughter? Even a chicken would do at this point."

A small smile twisted Khara's lips but her demeanor as a whole was still dejected and uncertain. "I asked our de facto steward the other day and was told no, but perhaps we shall have better luck today."

Poko fluttered into the air, cheerful. "Let me do the talking then. I can be very persuasive."

Khara rose to her feet, her smile warming with a faint ghost of genuine mirth. "By all means. I am sure you could do no worse than I already have. When I asked, she looked at me like I'd asked to cook her first born for dinner."

Khara came to Odessa's side and offered her an arm. Odessa took it and unsteadily rose. Her legs trembled, having grown stiff from the few minutes of inactivity. "A camp like this must have a few old beasts puttering around, waiting to be culled."

"Beasts such as that were put to the stew pot many months ago. There's no pasture for the beasts, so we only keep what we can feed. Most meat we have is foraged from nearby villages and the few caravans that still come through the pass."

Odessa stopped, holding onto Khara's arm. "How close is the nearest village?"

"There is a village only a few hours' ride to the south, and a group of nomads and herders were camped out a half day's ride east." Khara eyed her suspiciously. "Why do you ask?"

"If I need a beast, I should go to the source, no?"

"And how do you expect to accomplish this? Are you going to walk there?"

Odessa steadied herself a bit and looked fixedly at Khara with a subtle smile. "You're going to take me."

Khara snorted. "Do you think Remaka and the other Sisters are going to let me, a disgraced cripple, take you, a guest in detention, to raid a village? We would have better luck with the steward's first born."

Odessa cast a quick, furtive glance around the cave. No one was near them. No piqued ears listening from tent flaps. "We wouldn't tell them. We take an entehlo after sundown and come back before anyone's noticed we left."

"You make it sound so easy." Khara shook her head dismissively. "We wouldn't be able to get an entehlo out of the paddock without being seen, let alone leave the cave. There are guards stationed everywhere. We'd be spotted before we reached the bottom of the canyon."

"There must be a way. A secret cave exit or maybe you have friends who might look the other way?"

"There's no way. There's not an exit unguarded and no one would be willing to risk their own hides so I could sneak you out of camp. It is not possible."

The cracks were widening as Odessa's hunger opened wider, screaming for satiety. *I don't care if we're seen, I just need out.* "Fine," Odessa said, a bit curtly. "We'll figure something out." She let go of Khara's arm and started back toward the tent. "I'm tired. Go ask the quartermaster about the beasts. I need to lie down."

Walking away, indignant rage guttered and took flame in the emptiness of her hunger-wracked body. *I'm leaving tonight. I'm getting what I need no matter what. I don't care who I take it from. I need it and I need it now.*

The soft, susurrus flapping of Poko's paper wings followed her to the tent, but the fairy did not say a word. The noise trailing her added kindling to the flames of her fury, and the urge to whirl and smack Poko from the air came like a sudden rush of bile up her throat. To crush the fairy in her fist and wring the blood from their mangled body into her mouth. She dismissed the notion with cold dispassion and an alarming amount of difficulty. Her iron hand remained tensed for a quick, brutal strike no matter how she refused the urge.

I need blood soon. Or I'm going to lose myself to this damnable hunger. I won't die. It won't allow me to die. It will make me into a true and total monster before that happens.

CHAPTER 31

Night poured into the cave like ink into an inkwell. Total darkness enveloped the camp. Inside their tent, Odessa lay grimacing and groaning on her rushes. Stabbing pain jolted up her arm into her shoulder in alternating swells of pulsing agony. Poko ministered at her side, but there was little they could do but whisper hushed consolations and wipe the sweat from her brow with a damp cloth.

"Godsdamn it," Odessa hissed, spittle flying from between her grinding teeth. "I can't take this anymore."

The pain had come not long after her discussion with Khara. As if in retaliation for not sating its bloodlust, her body betrayed her. Screaming its displeasure in bursts of bright torment. She could barely think for all the constant pain. The pain receded only occasionally. Ebbing enough for her to catch her breath before it came again, twice as furious.

"Just hold on," Poko said, dabbing her sweat-dappled temple with the rag. "They'll be coming with another bowl of porridge any second now. That'll help."

"I don't need fucking porridge! I need blood!" Another wave of electric pain arced through her arm, and she stiffened with a choked moan. The cords in her neck bulged. Her lips pulled back from her grinding teeth in a terrible grimace. Her quick breaths whistled through her clenched jaws like the last desperate breaths of a wounded animal. *I'm going to die. This pain is going to kill me.*

The swelling pain filled her head like a dense, scalding-hot gas. Blotted out all thought for a moment. Beneath her tightly shut eyelids, a deeper, more complete darkness took hold of her. For a fraction of a second, she was gone. Sinking again.

A hand shaking her shoulder ripped her from the darkness. Khara knelt beside her, the stump of her hand roughly shoving her shoulder back and forth. "Odessa?" she said. "Odessa, are you there?"

Odessa's unfocused eyes whirled. Shapes moved behind Khara in the dimness. Vague figures she could not be sure were actually there. Or had they come from the abyss? Perhaps some of the shifting shadows that churned in that infinite darkness had followed her in the waking world. Psychopomps to drag her back to the void.

Khara turned to the figures, holding out a bandaged hand and saying something too quickly to Odessa to comprehend. One of the figures came and took Khara's hand. A devil with a knife pricked Khara's wrist. "Here you go," Khara said, pressing her wrist to Odessa's lips. "Drink it. Hurry and drink it." Odessa's lips mashed against her teeth as Khara pressed her wrist harder against her mouth. Then the tang of copper found its way onto Odessa's tongue and her hunger took over. She drank feverishly. Her mind clearing more as she lapped up the hot blood beading from the pinprick wound. Her head filling with a buzzing electricity. Odessa leaned forward into Khara's arm and drank deeply.

In her ravenous gluttony, Odessa's teeth found Khara's skin and bore down.

Khara's arm jerked a bit, but she did not pull free from Odessa's teeth. But the momentary recoiling of Khara's arm gave Odessa enough of a start to pull free from the intensely ravenous desire filling her head and body with a thrumming vitality. She pulled her mouth from Khara's arm. "I'm sorry. I didn't mean to . . ."

"It's fine," Khara said, placing her bandaged stump on the spit-smeared pinprick on her wrist. "More importantly, are you all right? Do you feel better?"

Warmth seeped through Odessa, buoying her beleaguered body with energy. "Better," Odessa said. Her eyes moved from Khara to the devils arrayed throughout the tent. Eight devils in full armor. "What's going on?"

Khara smiled. "You will have your blood. Sansehra, a Sister of mine by our father's blood, was going to lead a raid on the nomads tomorrow but I convinced her to move the raid to tonight. Isn't that great?"

Odessa's heart, enlivened by the warmth of Khara's blood, quickened. "I get to come on this raid?"

"As long as no one says anything, yes." Khara gave the devils around her a facetiously stern look.

"Are you coming too?"

Khara looked at Odessa with a quizzical expression. "In my current state, what use would I be on a raid?"

Odessa could feel the eyes of the other devils on her. Devils she did not know and did not trust. "I need you," Odessa said after a moment. "Even with your blood, I can barely walk more than a few steps by myself."

A genuine smile warmed Khara's face. She shook her head. "There are ten Sisters going with you, each of them with two working hands. They can help you."

"No," Odessa said, staring unblinking into Khara's eyes. She needed someone there with whom she could place at least a modicum of trust. Riding into the desert with a band of devils she did not know was a foolishly reckless idea, even for her. "I need *you*."

Khara was quiet a moment. A thoughtful expression on her face. "Fine. I am not so feeble now that I cannot still ride."

Poko came fluttering near the two of them, wringing their hands. "Are you sure about this?"

Odessa nodded. "Absolutely," she said. "I've never been more sure of anything in my entire life."

Odessa's armor was returned to her, its missing scales replaced. Her helmet had been adorned with two horns, ostensibly sawn from some unfortunate devil's forehead, so she could blend in with the devils as they left the camp. Wearing the armor again came with a welcome familiarity and comfort. A certain strength came with donning the armor. In its weight upon her shoulders she found an unmistakable confidence.

The party saddled their entehlos. Odessa saddled a soot-colored female that kept nudging her with its snout every time she bent to cinch the saddle's girth or adjust the stirrups. Once the saddle was secured, she helped Khara astride the entehlo, then climbed behind the devil, taking hold of her waist as she situated herself awkwardly in the saddle made for one. She sat pressed against Khara's back, her body angled uncomfortably against the saddle's flared back.

Khara had the reins pinched between her splinted thumb and bandaged stump. When the party was prepared, she spurred the beast forward and they rode single file out of the paddock and toward the cave's mouth. Guards stationed at low stone fortifications set along the ledge watched the party as they passed. Dark eyes following them. Odessa could feel their eyes upon her. Most certainly wondering why a warrior would be riding double. The line of riders moved past one such fortification toward the mouth of a narrow path leading along the edge of the cave down along the cliff's face. Odessa's breath remained imprisoned in her chest as they rode by. Her body was tense. Expecting hands to grab her by the leg and drag her from the saddle. It was not until their entehlo was past the fortifications and starting down the path that cut into the end of the cave's mouth did she release her breath and sag in the saddle, relieved. They picked their way slowly down the path, navigating its slope and sharp switchbacks by torchlight.

Their torches cast long, stretched shadows upon the cliff walls. Ghoulish shadows flickering upon the stone like ghosts dogging their slow descent.

Once they reached the bottom of the canyon, they formed two columns and started eastward at a hard gallop. Odessa's arms tightened around Khara as she jounced in the saddle. Trying to squeeze the saddle between her legs, her feet bounced against the entehlo's flanks with its every galloping step.

After a short while, Odessa leaned forward and said as quietly as she could over the pounding of hooves, "What is this raid for?"

"The nomads did not provide us with the livestock we require. A quarter of their herd was all we asked. But they fled. So they will lose the herd and their lives."

Odessa sat back in the saddle, frowning as an uneasy excitement rose within her. A guilty, primal exhilaration. She tried to think of the nomads not as people but as a faceless enemy on the run. They were prey. They were sustenance.

They rode hard and in silence. The pounding of hooves a multifaceted drumbeat in the desert stillness. The steady drumming of war's approach. Of death come by hoof and blade.

In the murky dark, an uncertain amount of time passed, Odessa's strength ebbing away with every passing minute. Soreness simmered in her backside and the inside of her straining thighs. She clung tighter to Khara's waist, as if she could siphon some of the devil's strength through touch.

When, peering past Khara's side, she saw campfires in the distance, a gruesome giddiness stirred in her belly. The hunger roused now raked at her insides. Scratching furrows in her ribs as it widened in anticipation.

The devils must have shared her excited anticipation, for as they neared the campfires, they began to trill and whoop. Crying out and proving their presence over the shortening expanse of desert between them and their prey. The two columns split and fanned out to encircle the fires. Shouts came from the camp, but they were drowned out by the sudden roaring of devils shouting their fury into the night.

In a sweeping line of hooves and iron, one column fell upon the camp. Tearing through tents and trampling those within. Odessa leaped from the saddle and landed roughly, her knees buckling. She tottered and righted herself, then drew one of the devilish knives, wielding it with her iron hand.

"Odessa!" Khara shouted, still astride the entehlo. But Odessa did not hear her. The smell of fear and blood was already in the air. A harbinger of what was to come like the sharp scent of an approaching storm.

Fires rose throughout the circle of tents as torches tossed upon them set the goat's hair sheets aflame. A shriek split the raucous air. Odessa tottered on numb, aching legs. Searching for prey in the deep shadows cast in the night by burgeoning fires.

Figures in the reddish glow were scrambling for spears and staves and knives or running into the dark to be cut down by the circling riders. Bazaks bellowed somewhere in the pitch-black night.

Odessa moved on loose, buckling legs. Stumbling through the bedlam. Nearly being run down by a charging rider. A nomad was running between two tents. Stopping at a collapsed tent and tearing at the sheets as hot embers rained down upon them.

Her hand clamped onto the nomad's shoulder, and she rammed the dagger into their back. A sharp, raspy gasp. Odessa twisted the blade, and the body stiffened and jerked. Hot blood poured over her iron hand. Flooding into the runed channels. Burning power flowed through her arm. Converging in her center. Filling the cracks that had formed inside her. Mending them with molten strength. Her arm began to pleasantly throb. In the center of her chest, a tight ball of heat grew. Stoked by the heat of blood.

She ripped the dagger from the nomad's back and let the body fall to the ground. The smell of smoke and death filled the air around her with an electric buzz. Evaporating life all around her. Steeped in death, she could feel the energy beginning to seep through her pores. Breathe it in and drink of its potency.

Her head was filled with a rushing flood of need and hunger. She ran with the agility of a great cat and killed with a razor's keenness. Blood sprayed into the air all about her. Raining down in showers upon drought-stricken soil.

Raptured in her own bloodlust, the slaughter ended all too soon. The nomads had numbered few and they had died quickly, without much resistance. Her blood pounded for a while after the last nomad was killed. Stalking about the burning wreckage, searching for living prey. All the while, absorbing what life drifted among the whirls of smoke.

Only when the spilled blood had lost the last of its potency and the energy abuzz in the air had dissipated did Odessa see the corpses for what they truly were. As triumphant devils tossed their corpses into the fires, she saw their faces. The faces of men, women, and children. She saw her mother and father and sisters in those dead faces.

After the thrum of bloodlust had receded, then came the shame. Guilt pouring in a flood that chilled her to the marrow. Drowned her in the horror that her own hands had wrought. The terror that she had knowingly taken part in. The atrocity she had relished so madly. But as her bloodlust receded, so too did her guilt. No more than a fleeting pang in a numbed extremity.

CHAPTER 32

Odessa remained in a sickened trance for some time. Wandering through the death. All the while drinking in the carnage.

A hand drew her gently from her stupor. Khara's hand taking her own bloody iron hand and pulling her from her stunned daze. "Odessa," she said. "You should sit. Rest. You've done too much."

Allowing herself to be pulled along, Odessa complied from a liminal state of being. Her mind not yet regaining its full faculties, she followed Khara through the ring of fires and the pervading stench of burning hair. The entehlo they had ridden lay just outside the fires' glow, half on its side, half upright. Its sooty coat taking a reddish cast like a dying ember. Khara sat Odessa down beside the beast, her back reclined against the entehlo's. It sighed and shifted a bit as Odessa's weight settled against its back.

By the time Odessa had taken a seat, her vacuous thoughts had solidified. Congealed like cold grease. Her iron fingers flexed, still tingling with renewed vigor. That was when she noticed Khara's hand still holding her own. A bandaged hand like a mitten pinching her insensate fingers.

Khara sat down beside her. Firelight warmed her dark skin and caught in her eyes, turning the copper in them to a molten bronze. "How do you feel?"

Odessa opened her mouth. It had gone dry. "I feel good. Strong." The words were listless and devoid of sentiment. The lifeless husks of true statements. Physically she was fine. Better than fine now. But on a human level, in the realm of emotion and vague principle, she felt as she had after every raided caravan. The emptiness.

Not hunger, but a spiritual emptiness. A hollowness. She thought she became, in a way, incorporeal during those hollow times. A disembodied spirit shirking the terrible weight of their sins. Allowing her to feel indistinctly the guilt and shame of what she had done, but at a distance. Muted and hushed like faraway screams.

In the nomad's camp, devils were tearing apart the last few unburned tents. Torches moved in the darkness outside the camp. Distant hoots and hollers as the devils rounded up the bazaks to be herded back to the devils' cave.

Khara turned Odessa's hand in her own. Inspecting it in the dim firelight. Still tacky with blood, its runed channels held within them a soft, lambent glow. A crimson shimmer fading from the congealing blood. Barely perceptible but there nonetheless. The blood was still acting as a catalyst to drain dissipating life from the air. Khara's eyes traced the swirling runes. "This is truly a work of art," Khara said softly. Reverently. "Is it of Asha-Kaliran make?"

"Yes," Odessa said coarsely, drawn further from her disembodied fugue. "I was deceived by someone I thought I could trust and this is the result." She pulled her iron hand from Khara's grasp a bit too sharply. Holding it aloft, she turned it back and forth. Fingers curling and uncurling. Making a fist then relaxing. "They put rivets through my flesh and anchored spikes into my bones. The metal is fused with my skin, so even if I was able to rip this thing off me, I couldn't without skinning myself."

Khara's eyes never left the iron hand. "Why would someone do that to you?"

"They wanted me to become a godkiller." Odessa's voice took a grave, sharp tone. Her fingers closed into a tight fist. The iron plates grated together.

"I did not know that," Khara said quietly, her eyes falling from the hand to Odessa. "I suppose I've done the same, haven't I? I've pushed you into the same dreadful position you were in previously."

But I won't be anyone's godkiller. Not Yakun's or yours or Talara's. Odessa's hand dropped heavily into her lap. "As long as you can keep your end of the bargain, it's not the same. Not at all." *No one's going to put a collar on me ever again. Not a man or a devil or a god.*

The entehlo behind them rolled onto its side a bit more, grunting. Breaking the skim of tension solidifying around them.

"If we can convince Remaka tomorrow, whatever is in my power to give you is yours," Khara said.

"And if we can't?"

Khara looked at Odessa, her gaze intense and unyielding and genuine. "Then we flee."

The entire ride back to the devils' camp, Odessa thought about Khara's words. Her mind was ill at ease. Khara was an odd variable in her reckoning of the situation she found herself in. All too amiable, the devil was after something. Odessa knew that. But still, Odessa could not help liking the devil. The insidious bitch's company was pleasant and warm in a time when all she had grown accustomed to was harsh and cold. But the devil's motives were what Odessa could not precisely pinpoint. Were it just to have Odessa kill Sak-Tor, she could understand that. But there was more. An underlying motive she couldn't entirely distinguish, nor trust. And Khara's plan to flee together if Remaka's meeting did not go as planned only solidified that distrust. It made no sense. What purpose that would serve, Odessa could not figure.

She probably said that to further gain my trust. It's all an act, Odessa thought. *I'm sure this Remaka is behind all of this anyway. The result of tomorrow's meeting is preordained. It's all theater. But for what purpose? Is all this really for Sak-Tor? Or is there more? Is there something I'm missing?*

The entehlo galloped steadily beneath her. Her grip around Khara's middle was looser than on the journey out to the nomads' camp. Revitalized, her legs and her core tightened and relaxed with the rocking of the entehlo's strides. In a compact mass ahead of them trotted the herd of bazaks.

Ruminating on her suspicions, Odessa tried to beat back at them. Half-heartedly swiping at the doubt hanging about her like a dense cloud of mosquitos buzzing around her head. Trying to tell herself that perhaps Khara's kindness was genuine, but such thoughts were easily lost in the buzz of suspicion and distrust.

She's just being kind, she told herself sternly, but there was a distinct lack of conviction in the thought. Instead, there was an almost pleading quality to it. She wished it were true. Desperately wished Khara's kindness were genuine. But such fancies were dangerous intoxicants. They dulled the senses and provided nothing but a false sense of security. *Tarik was kind. Yakun too. They're all kind until they're sticking the knife in your back.*

They arrived back at the devils' camp just as dawn's rosy fury was bleeding over the horizon. The bazaks were herded up a second path up the back of the mesa while Khara, Odessa, and the few devils not herding bazaks made their way up to the cave. The devils had been in high spirits the entire ride, but with dawn's approach, the good humor had faded and was replaced with a weary quiet.

The entehlos huffed and labored up the path, as tired as their riders. The guards at their stations watched the riders noncommittally as they filed past on their way to the paddock.

In the paddock, Odessa slid from the entehlo's back amid jostling beasts and dismounting riders. She hesitated a moment, wanting to head for her tent. To find solace in the tent's isolation and allow herself some time to think alone and without the constant press of devils all about. But she lingered and, after a moment, held out her hand to help Khara down.

Khara pressed her bandaged stump to Odessa's outstretched hand and hopped down from the saddle.

"Thank you for this," Odessa said begrudgingly. After just that small thanks, she could feel her ill will faltering. Softening and weakening like hard-packed snow beneath a midday sun. Despite her best efforts, sincere gratitude came welling up from the cracks. "Without this, I would have died. Slowly and painfully, and soon."

"I owe you my life. It was the least I could do." Khara's face was bright and genial even in the dimness of the cave. Exhaustion had begun to sink into the hollows of her face, but her eyes were unaffected. They glittered in the dark cave like twin bits of topaz. "You have saved my life twice. Did you know that?"

Odessa furrowed her brow then shook her head.

"I had planned on deserting Sak-Tor's army for a long time. Many months. Years. But I never did. I had resigned myself to my wretched fate. But then I saw you. On the battlefield. Bringing Pash-Tor to his knees. Ramming a spear into his skull. Things I never thought I would see. And done by a mortal. A human woman." The topaz gaze glimmered. "You inspired me. I doubt I would have ever taken the leap had it not been for you. So do not thank me. Your presence here, now, is thanks enough."

Odessa's suspicion crumbled further. Around them, entehlos were unsaddled and brushed but Odessa and Khara remained apart from it all. "How did I do all that? How could I have had such an effect on you? I don't understand."

"It is good that you don't," Khara said softly. "Being a Torva woman is slavery. And I say that as a warrior. One of the lucky ones. I was born and raised a slave and for the longest time I took it as a fact of life. Sak-Tor and his sons owned me. The only thing I could do was become strong and fight ferociously so that I could avoid the worst of their abuses and delay the inevitable." Khara stepped close to Odessa. Intense emotion burning in her eyes. Her scent, the smell of iron and leather and sweat, was mellow and rich. "That is how you saved me. You showed me that women like us can actually fight and win against them. Divinity and higher magics be damned, they can be killed."

Odessa was stunned silent for a moment. "All I did was kill a devil."

"A single human woman killed him. Do you not understand how extraordinary that is?"

"I'm not human anymore. Not totally."

Khara snorted. "That does not matter. The ratios of blood, human and otherwise, in your veins is a trivial thing. You are you. You are the woman who killed Pash-Tor. You are the woman who rescued me from my fate as breeding stock.

Wholly human or not, what does that matter? I carry mixed blood in my veins as well, but I could not have brought Pash-Tor down by myself." Khara reached and clumsily took Odessa's hand in hers. She held it, the hand of only flesh and bone, and squeezed it between her mangled, bandage-wrapped hands. "You are unique. I knew that as soon as I saw your face beneath that ill-fitting helm. I knew you were my salvation."

Odessa pulled her hand away. "You're mad," she said, uncomfortable and flattered all at once.

The intensity of Khara's gaze dimmed and flickered. She drew back a step, hands clasped before her chest. "I'm sorry. That is a lot to lay at one's feet all at once, isn't it?"

"I'm not your salvation. I'm nothing close to that. For anyone. I've been many's damnation and I suppose I'll be that to many more if your Sisters don't kill me first." The distrust had begun to solidify into something colder and more rigid. A wall of cold detachment. A monument to alienation and aversion erected in her mind. She turned from Khara and bent to uncinch the girth at the entehlo's belly. "I'm not whatever you imagine me to be, so stop forcing your ideals and fancies upon me. I'll kill your god but not because I'm some once-in-a-millennia savior of devilkind. There is nothing more to it. I'm a killer and a stealer of life. That is all I am."

Girth uncinched, she lifted the saddle from the entehlo's back and turned to push past the stunned devil.

"I did not mean to push anything onto you," Khara said as Odessa passed.

Odessa paused a step from Khara. "I know you didn't." She glanced at Khara, whose bright eyes were now dark and withdrawn. "I just don't want you to have the wrong idea about me. I am not anything to you but a killer of your people. I may be of some use, but I am nothing more. Do not forget that."

Odessa turned and shoved her way through the press of entehlos and devils. From within the walls of her detachment from these devils, the frustration and resentment she felt for Khara and her mad idolatry dwindled quickly. By the time she had left the paddock, dropped the saddle with the other, and made her way for the tent, it was nothing but cool embers of vague discontent. She regretted the harshness of her words, but they needed to be said, she assured herself.

The devil had some sort of sway on her to have her feel this way, Odessa reasoned. To have her feel such extremes. Familiarity and compassion. Resentment and suspicion. She wondered how she had allowed a devil to affect her so, then dismissed the notion. None of that mattered now.

The sun's rising had cast a soft pallid light in the sky above the canyon, which still languished in shadow. Reaching out to open the tent's flaps, Odessa wondered if she would be alive to see the setting of that sun.

CHAPTER 33

Khara was quiet when she came to escort Odessa and Poko to meet Remaka, the Sisters' Matron. Tension like a thunderhead loomed heavy over them as they made their way through the network of tents. Poko fluttered between them, quiet and confused by the shift in mood since the raiding party left.

Odessa, having bathed for the first time since she had arrived in the camp, and having, with Poko's help, untangled and washed her knotted hair, felt none of the self-assured confidence she had expected to come with her renewed strength, a bit of grooming, and a clean tunic. She walked as she had up the Stairs of Ascension that fateful day when her first life—her better life—ended. Walking with a churning unease in her stomach and heavy dread dragging at her ankles. If the devils did not take the offer, then Talara's schemes would not bear fruit. And Odessa's life as a free woman, free from the scrutiny of both men and gods, would die. Unborn and unrealized.

At the back of the cave was a long stone building. Its walls, blank and adorned save by the crumbling erosion of time, adjoined the cave's ceiling, making it a tall, looming structure in the cave's relatively low and cramped space. A sheet of dark orange felt hung in the wide doorway. Two guards in full armor and helm and armed with halberds stood on either side of the door. They glared at Odessa and Khara as they approached.

Khara stopped outside the doorway. "Are they ready to see us?"

One of the guards nodded while the other guard scrutinized each of them. Eyes scouring them for weapons or perhaps a bomb. Even Poko, dressed in a silvery tunic with not so much as a single pocket, was not spared the guard's narrow-eyed scrutiny.

They stepped through the doorway, Khara first and then Odessa, into a dark, smoky room. Wide braziers were placed intermittently throughout the hall, but they did little to alleviate the gloomy atmosphere that pervaded the soot-stained room.

The hall's ends held stores of food and weapons. But the center of the hall was empty and dominated by a dais lit by two massive braziers. On the dais sat five devils in chairs formed from bone. Femurs and humeruses formed the legs and seat, while the backs were comprised of vertebrae and ribs spread wide so they curled around and almost embraced those seated within them. Khara and Odessa walked slowly to the dais, with Poko flitting nervously behind them. Their iron-soled boots clicking loudly.

They stopped before the dais and the unyielding stares of the devils before them, then kneeled with their heads bowed. Poko kneeled on the ground between Odessa and Khara, their small hands trembling ever so slightly. Odessa wondered why they were so nervous. It was not as if the devils wanted their tiny head.

"Khara and the fairy. You may rise," a terse, commanding voice said from the dais. It was the voice of a big cat rumbling its dissatisfaction. A predator's voice.

Khara and Poko did as they were bidden, looking unsure.

"Step away from the human, if you would," the voice said, not exactly a command but not at all a suggestion either.

"May I ask why, Matron Remaka?" Khara asked.

Odessa glanced up to see the devil seated in the center of the dais level a chilling glare in Khara's direction. "Because the Elder Sisters and I have no questions for you or the fairy. Your presence is immaterial now. We all know your position on the matter—there is no more to be said by you."

Khara nodded. "Yes, Matron. Of course." She glanced at Odessa, worry and regret in her expression, and then at Poko. They both stepped back a few steps. Poko landed in Khara's cradling hands and sat nervously picking at their lips.

"Now," Remaka said, her voice echoing in the hall. "Odessa. Raise your head."

Odessa did as she was told and looked at the Matron of the Sisterhood of the Daughters of Ana Yuma. Remaka was a massive figure cut from the reddest sandstone. Standing, she must have been at least two heads taller than Khara. Her shoulders were broad and muscular. Beneath the thin, almost gossamer silk of her clothing, something between a tunic and a kaftan, her muscles were ripplingly apparent. Her hair was the color of a rich wine and cascaded down the dark blue of her silks in multiple braided plaits. But it was her face Odessa's eyes were drawn to. Deep lines creased the dark, ruddy skin around her mouth and at the corners of her eyes. Her eyes were dark, almost black, and pierced Odessa's wary gaze with unwavering intensity.

"Have you recuperated sufficiently?" Remaka asked, her words sharp and pointed. "Khara has been quite adamant that your condition would not allow our questioning. But to my eyes, you appear quite hale and hearty."

"I am feeling much better," Odessa said, wondering if Remaka knew about her involvement in the night's raid and hoping such thoughts were not made apparent on her face.

"Ah, I'm glad to hear that." Remaka leaned back against the cushioned ribcage of her chair and crossed her legs. The hem of her garb lifted to expose boots of exquisitely tooled leather and fur studded with small rounds of turquoise. Her large, wiry hands gripped the knobbed joint of the chair's armrest and she looked down at Odessa with clear distaste. "Now let me ask you, Odessa, now that you are well enough to answer. How many Torva have you killed?"

The question struck Odessa like a punch to the stomach. Worry gripped her heart and dread made her stomach sink and twist like a dying water snake. She opened her mouth and found it unable to make sound. All the breath had evaporated from her lungs. She swallowed and tried again. "I-I do not know."

"Can you guess?" Remaka asked. "A dozen perhaps." Her hand waved noncommittally. "Two dozen? Perhaps even a hundred? Venture a guess for us, please. How many of our people have you killed to drink their lifeblood?"

Odessa's heart thudded traitorously in her chest. This meeting was not going nearly as well as she had hoped. "Anything I have done to your people, I did not have a choice. The Asha-Kalirans used me. They put a collar around my neck and—" Odessa started.

"How many?" Remaka's voice cut her off with two sharp words like cracking snaps of a whip.

Odessa's mind whirled, unsure of what answer the devil wanted to hear. Or if her answer even mattered. "Less than a hundred," she said, uncertainly. If the number of devils she had killed truly numbered less than a hundred as she had guessed, it would have been fairly close to it.

Remaka's eyes continued boring holes into her skull. As if she were probing Odessa's mind for the truth of her words. "How many of these hundred did you kill after you left the auspices of Asha-Kalir?"

A tightness congregated around Odessa's throat. Nervous fear wrapping its hands about her neck and slowly squeezing. "Less than half," she said hoarsely.

"How many less than half. A quarter of them? An eighth?"

"Maybe a quarter."

"And these were killed without a collar around your neck?"

Odessa stiffened. "I was hunted. I had no choice."

"Could you not have left this awful desert? Fled and been free instead of ambushing and slaughtering our Sisters still deluded and in Sak-Tor's thrall?"

"Where could I have gone? The Severed Pass is under Khymanir's control, the north is plagued by the Gray, and I have no idea how far the desert stretches southward. What choice did I have but survive in this godsforsaken desert any way I could?"

Remaka regarded her for a moment, cold and silent. "I want to tell you a story," she said, shifting forward in her seat. "When I was a child, there was a place my tribe would always camp during the warm months. Fertile pasture for as far as the eye could see. Some copses of hardwood along the stream. Picturesque. But one season, there came a pack of wild dogs. Hungry, savage dogs. My tribe lost four children to them. I was not allowed to go anywhere without my mother or an aunt with me. The tribe spent weeks hunting these dogs, but they were elusive. I believe we had even moved to greener pastures before the last of them were exterminated. So now I ask you: if you had been there and one of those dogs came to you with its head bowed, submissive and sheepish, would you trust it? Would you invite it into your home? Would you let it lie beside your family's bed?"

"Of course not."

"Yes, of course not." Remaka smiled, a smile that was both sour and pitiless. "Now I am going to be candid with you, Odessa. I do not trust you. I do not like you. I do not care how useful you may prove to be. I believe if you were given the chance, you would betray us in a heartbeat to save your own hide."

"I risked my own hide to save Khara. Does that mean no thing?"

Remaka glanced at one of the devils sitting beside her. An older woman, thin and severe with skin the color of slate. There was an exchange of glances, quick and cursory, then Remaka's gaze returned to Odessa. "It may prove to have some meaning. So let us speak of it. What brought you to Khara's aid? Why did you risk life and limb after her capture?"

"Khara promised me protection." Odessa paused, feeling Khara's presence only a step or two behind her. The kind, pleasant presence she had leaned upon in her infirmity. The presence she had so quickly begun to doubt and resent as soon as her strength had returned to her. "And she was kind to me."

"Why were you not captured alongside her then?"

"I initially rebuffed her proposal. But I changed my mind."

Remaka nodded. "And her proposal. She promised you protection. Was that all she promised you?"

"Just protection. An alliance," Odessa said. "And friendship."

Remaka's lips formed a tight, bloodless line. "Friendship? That's quite . . . interesting."

"Yes, that was my initial reaction as well," Odessa said.

The tension in Remaka's face relaxed just the tiniest bit at that. "What made you reconsider this offer? Rushing into a Torva camp alone is quite bold for just an offer of friendship."

"Poko, the fairy, convinced me. They can be very persuasive."

Remaka's gaze shifted behind Odessa to Poko, lingered, and then returned. "Khara seems to think you can be of some great use to the Sisters. Is she correct in that regard?"

Odessa nodded. "I believe I have already proved that I could be quite useful. The general in the camp, the one who held Khara—I was able to deaden his magic while your Sisters brought him down. I believe we all can see the value in that, no?"

Remaka's expression was stony and impassive. "And that deadening of his magic, that is what left you bedridden for weeks, yes?"

"Yes but I was already depleted before doing so. And I did not have any time after the skirmish to replenish myself."

"Replenish yourself with Torvan blood, correct?"

Odessa grimaced and was unable to bring herself to reply.

"Do you truly think you could nullify Sak-Tor's magic they way you deadened Pon-Tor's? The magic of a full-blooded god is almost unlimited. Sak-Tor, even in his sleep, wields magic of a magnitude many times greater than any of his sons could ever hope to muster."

The tightness around Odessa's throat had spread and now bands of fear constricted her chest as well. "Given I have enough lifeblood in my system, I believe I can. At least for long enough to allow your Sisters to deal him a grievous wound."

Silence filled the hall like a cold draft. Remaka stared down at Odessa, probing again with that sharp, dark-eyed gaze. "And what exactly do you ask in return?"

The tightness dug deep into her flesh. Squeezing the air from her lungs for a moment. "I would ask for a contingent of your finest warriors to aid me in a raid."

"What sort of raid?" Remaka asked coldly.

"My village's ka-man corrupted my people, killed my father and my uncle, and has held my mother and sister hostage ever since. I want them back. And I want his head on a spike."

"You want our aid to kill an old medicine man?" Remaka asked.

She wanted to mention Yakun and Tarik. Their names welled up in her throat. But within the walls of Asha-Kalir, she knew they were out of her reach. Remaka would not sanction an assault on Asha-Kalir so Odessa could kill two men. She consoled herself with the thought of punching through Kunza-ka's thin chest and ripping out his still-beating heart. It heartened her. "Yes. That is what I want."

Remaka was quiet again. "In exchange for a god's head, that is quite generous of you."

Odessa could feel Khara and Poko behind her. Their hope warm and buoyant. "There is one more thing I would need."

Remaka's eyebrow raised. "Is that so?"

"Yes," Odessa said. "I would need Khara's mutilated hand to be made whole. There must be some sort of apparatus or prosthetic that can be built for her. I know little of your people, but I do know your kind are industrious."

"I suppose that could be arranged," Remaka said, a suspicious glimmer in her eyes. "So those are your terms?"

Odessa nodded. "Yes, they are."

Remaka stood from her seat. The other Torvan women followed suit. "Then I believe a deal has been struck. You will have your family and the ka-man's head along with an apparatus for Khara's hand in exchange for your aid in Sak-Tor's subjugation and death." She stepped down from the dais and stood before Odessa, a hand extended. "Are these terms acceptable?"

Odessa rose. Remaka stood nearly double Odessa's size. "They're acceptable." Odessa took her massive hand. It was like shaking hands with a stone statue.

"The deal has been struck then," Remaka said. "Down with Sak-Tor, may he rot for all eternity."

CHAPTER 34

After being dismissed and watching with rote reverence as the Elder Sisters descended from the dais, Odessa turned to Khara and Poko.

"You didn't have to do that," Khara said softly. "You didn't have to get me a hand."

Odessa shrugged. "I had a little leverage. Why not use it?"

Khara smiled. "Well, thank you."

"It's nothing," Odessa said, still not totally believing the deal had been struck. Not believing she would soon be fighting alongside a horde of devils to kill a god. For now, she coasted on a thin, fragile euphoria. Emboldened and feeling strong.

"I still can't believe you made it out of there with your head intact," Poko said, darting in front of Odessa and Khara. "It didn't start off so great for you, you know?"

Odessa's face was cracked by a sliver of a smile. The relief of avoiding failure's bite was intoxicating. "Yeah, I know. I was the one she was sizing up for a noose."

The three of them were in good spirits as they neared Odessa and Poko's tent. Khara's quiet reservation remained but a small, almost timid smile stretched her lips.

A few steps from the tent, Odessa stopped. Her hand shot out and stopped Khara. The tent's flaps waved slightly as if blown by a breeze. Her body tensed and she began to drop into a quasi-crouch when a horned head poked out from the flaps. A face the color of lavender in full bloom. Two horns curled over her head like twin tusks of ebony.

"It went well, I take it?" the Torva woman asked Khara. Odessa thought she recognized her from the raid but beneath the helms all the warriors had looked more or less the same.

Khara eased Odessa's iron arm down from where it had barred her and said, "The deal is struck."

The Torva warrior's face warmed and a grin spread across her lips. She pushed through the tent flaps to reveal a large clay jar cradled in her arms. "I thought this could be a decent consolation if your meeting went sour, but it will taste much sweeter in celebration."

"What is that?" Khara asked, stepping forward. Poko followed curiously but Odessa remained behind, her elation withdrawing in the face of encroaching apprehension.

"A fine red wine that the nomads were hoarding." The Torva woman held the jar out for Khara to inspect. Khara took the jar reverently in wrapped hands. The Torva woman gestured to Odessa. "Come! Drink! We have much to celebrate!"

Odessa, a jittery sensation crawling up her spine, followed Khara, Poko, and the woman into the tent.

"Who's your friend? I like her," Poko said, buzzing around Khara as she carried the jar to a rug laid out next to the stoked brazier.

Khara carefully set the jar on the ground beside the rug and straightened. "Oh, yes, I forgot. This is Sansehra, one of my sisters by blood. She is the one who guided me to the Sisters. If it was not for her, I would still be one of Sak-Tor's dogs."

Sansehra scoffed. "I just pointed you in the right direction." She looked to Odessa and Poko, as amiably as an old friend. "I had been trying to get her to leave for months. Years. She would not go. She said she had an obligation to the women in her shield wall." She took a knife from her belt, knelt beside the pot, and stuck the knife's blade in the resin-sealed space between the jar's mouth and the stamped clay stopper. "Then suddenly she tells me she must go. Immediately. So I asked her, 'What changed your mind?' Naively thinking my words may have finally gotten through the cracks of her thick head." She pried the stopper free and flicked it aside with the flat of the blade. "Alas, that was not the case. Instead she told me she'd had a premonition on the battlefield. In a stroke of miraculous revelation, she was glimpsing our people's champion. Mind you, while this was happening, I was knee-deep in entehlo guts, trying to keep my head on my shoulders." Having let the jar breathe a moment as she spoke, Sansehra poured a splash of wine into three earthen cups. Khara and Odessa sat down on opposite sides of the rug and Poko landed cross-legged in the center.

"Come now, we do not have to speak about all that," Khara said, glancing at Odessa as she spoke with a flicker of hot shame.

Sansehra handed Khara a cup and gave one to Odessa. "Why not? You had a religious experience at the sight of her. I believe that is quite a fine topic to discuss over a few cups."

"It was not a religious experience," Khara said curtly, not able to look in Odessa's direction. "It was not anything as grand as that. It was just hope. And hope was something I had not felt in a very long time."

Odessa raised the cup to her nose. A sour, vaguely fruity aroma struck her. She took a tentative sip and the taste of spoiled fruit and vinegar assaulted her. She recoiled. "Do you actually drink this?" she interrupted.

Both Khara and Sansehra looked at her, surprised. It was then Odessa could see the familial resemblance despite the differing shades of their skin. The sharp eyebrows and high cheekbones. The same narrow amber eyes and prominent noses. "Do your people not drink wine?"

"We have palm wine, but it's not like this," Odessa said. "Palm wine has a stronger smell, sure, and I don't think it tastes that good but at least it doesn't taste like pure vinegar."

"It is an acquired taste," Sansehra said before taking a long swig. When the cup was drained, she smiled with a mouthful of red teeth. "Delicious."

Khara took a drink. "This isn't bad at all. Why did those nomads have it? They were bazak herders. This is a fine wine."

Sansehra shrugged. "They were saving it for us maybe."

Odessa took another, longer drink, swallowing the wine with a grimace. This time she could make out some muted tones of fruit beneath the acerbic harshness.

"Hey, I want some!" Poko said, fluttering to Odessa's shoulder.

"I do not know if that's such a good idea," Khara said. "It's quite strong. As small as you are, a sip might drop you right there."

"I'll be fine!" Poko said, gesturing for Odessa to bring the cup toward them. Odessa did as the fairy bade and tipped the cup slightly so Poko could lap up a drop as it came creeping toward the rim. When the liquid touched their lips they jerked back, spitting. "That's foul! It's gone bad!"

Odessa tipped the rest of the cup into her mouth and swallowed, feeling a warm flush spread across her cheeks. By the time night came, they had drunk nearly half the jar and were shouting and laughing. Khara and Sansehra spun and kicked in a lively dance that, in their drunkenness, looked more like a shared hysteria than choreography. Odessa lay sprawled on the rug, laughing at their sporadic, stumbling twirls as the tent itself spun in slow revolutions. Poko, after a few more sips, had fallen asleep and been placed in a sock which had then been pinned to a tent pole.

Khara's hair fell loose across her face as she stumbled across the tent to Odessa. "Come!" she said, extending her broken hands to Odessa. "Dance! It's fun!"

Odessa waved away Khara's hands. "You call that dancing? I thought you two might have got ants in your trousers."

Khara frowned as best she could through a wide, drunken grin. "Come now! Don't be such a curmudgeon!" She reached down to take Odessa's hands. Odessa took her wrists to avoid Khara's broken fingers and allowed herself to be pulled to her feet. Both of them swayed for a moment.

They laughed and they danced and for a moment, all that existed was the inside of the tent. Their shadows flickered against the canvas as they danced and sang and forgot the world outside those thin, flapping walls.

CHAPTER 35

Kunza was crouched beneath the looming vessel, scraping at a deep groove in the floor with a thin rasp. He glanced over at the opposite end at the hunched old man, Yakun, stopping to watch him for a moment. He had suspicions that the old man was not as careless and inept as his failure to finish the circle had suggested. Kunza suspected him of a subtle sabotage. An accumulation of small mistakes compounding to ruin the intricate workings of this unprecedented magic. Now it seemed most of Kunza's day was spent watching over Yakun's shoulder.

Blood dripped down from one of Khymanir's hands and fell beside Kunza in a fat splatter. Tarik, the young soulweaver, was still bringing Khymanir his bodies for the final bits of sculpting. All that was left was the rune work upon the vessel. A task only Khymanir's dexterous hands could manage.

At the far end of the god's workshop, Khymanir's bronzeworkers were hauling in sacks of charcoal and crates of bronze ingots and benches with a crank connected to a set of tongs and an array of holes drilled in an upright draw plate at the opposite end through which hot wire would be drawn and thinned. He turned back to his rasp and began scraping at the burred stone at a bend in the channel. There was little time left for the stonework. When the bronzeworkers had their wire ready, he would have no choice but to step back and let them do their work. Once the wire was set in the channels, there was little more that he could do to the stone. The circle would be finished, functional or not.

Fingers aching, he set about his work. His bag of tools rattling and clattering at his belt. His robes girded around his thin legs. Going as fast as he could. Following the channel's path and meticulously surveying every line and angle. Gauging depth and slope and the smoothness of the stone. Hurrying perfection. Time was running out.

Outside the city walls, devils massed. Massive war machines lumbered to hammer at the gates. Scores of devils sharpened their blades to better hack through the innocent citizenry of Asha-Kalir. Gnashing their teeth in anticipation of the slaughter.

CHAPTER 36

Sak-Tor has begun moving with earnest to lay siege to Asha-Kalir. He means to have the city before the Darrood floods in approximately two months' time, " Remaka said. The hall was filled with Sisters whispering to one another. Remaka and the Elder Sisters stood upon the dais, waiting for the murmurs to recede. Odessa, Poko, and Khara stood in the back of the hall, listening quietly. Sansehra and her raiders were clustered in the crowd in front of them, whispering amongst themselves.

"The Darrood River is already his. Fore and rear fortifications are under construction around the entirety of the city. If it were not for the city's cannons and its clay men, its walls would have already fallen." Remaka paused, looking out at her Sisters before her. A resolute mettle in her hard, knitted brow. "If Sak-Tor is allowed to take Asha-Kalir, which he, if given time, will, there will be no stopping him. The subjugation of our sisters still in his thrall will not end. Behind the walls of Asha-Kalir, with an army of clay soldiers at his disposal, he will be untouchable." Remaka paused, weighing her words. "If we are going to put an end to his tyranny, it must be now."

Hearing this shocked Odessa, but no one else in the hall seemed surprised at all. It was a forgone conclusion that Sak-Tor would take Asha-Kalir. Her confidence that she would be able to stop Sak-Tor's magic dwindled. Guttering like a new flame in a strong gust of wind.

A few weeks had passed since her meeting with Remaka, and Odessa had only been able to consume life twice since then and both times had provided her only one or two kills by her own hand. She could still but only function. If she tried to draw flames from herself, they would be but tiny, sputtering tongues of sickly yellow.

"Our only chance of taking Sak-Tor is by isolation and surprise. But even by striking from the rear, reaching Sak-Tor through ambush will have us routed before we even catch sight of the bastard."

A chorus of low murmurs rose throughout the crowd.

"For now, we must weaken his supply lines, soften his rear guard, and gain intelligence. We need to know where he will be at all times. This is the time for subterfuge and deception. Sak-Tor will tear down those walls if he is allowed within an arm's length of them. It is only a matter of time— all able bodies must make haste for Asha-Kalir immediately."

Odessa and Khara glanced at one another, exchanging a look of apprehension. Throughout all of the Sisters' camps, their forces numbered little more than a few thousand warriors. The whole host of Sak-Tor's army totaled almost one hundred thousand even after the Gray's whittling of their numbers. It would take a miracle for the Sisters to get within a day's ride of Sak-Tor, let alone kill him.

After Remaka's announcement, Odessa and Khara made straight for the blacksmith before she began tearing down her forge.

"Is it done?" Khara asked as they came upon the open area where the forge had been established. A massive anvil stood opposite a round, low-chimneyed stone bloomery. A grindstone and a trough of silty water were placed within arm's reach of the anvil. A rack of spears and swords stood along the cave wall. A heavy wooden workbench wrapped around the workspace, cordoning the forge off from the rest of the cave. Iron implements covered the surface of the bench along with bits of armor and weapons.

The blacksmith, Harsuth, was nearly as large as Remaka, with sharply curved horns and a permanent scowl. She had been collecting her scattered tools when they arrived. She dropped a pair of tongs upon her workbench with a clang and sighed angrily. "I have barely had a moment to breathe after the meeting and you're here bothering me."

"If we're to leave before sundown, I will need it."

"Your hand's just barely mended."

"Not this hand." Khara raised her fingerless hand, each individual stump now wrapped in a patch of thick canvas, and wiggled her thumb. Its range of motion was still poor but better than it had been. "Look, it has completely mended."

"Those stumps are going to bleed like a hog's slit throat the moment you put on the apparatus."

"No they will not. They are nearly totally healed."

Harsuth sighed again. "I do not have time for this." She bent and dug through a crate beneath the workbench. Flipping aside layers of oil-stained cloth, she reached inside and drew from the crate an iron contraption like a gauntlet with a blade, sheathed in a sleeve of iron, lying flat against the top of the forearm so its point sat above one's knuckles.

Khara's eyes were wide. "Is that it?"

Harsuth nodded. "Put your hand out. Have to see if it fits."

Khara extended her hand, pulling the sleeve of her tunic back to expose her arm from the bicep to her waggling stumps. Harsuth slid the gauntlet contraption over her arm and tightened a few leather straps. Harsuth moved to Khara's hand and adjusted the iron glove fitting over the back of Khara's hand. An iron bar laid in her palm so it rested in the crook of her thumb and palm while another bar, this one raised a hairsbreadth from her skin, was situated above the calluses at the top of her palm.

"You see this lever?" Harsuth asked, pointing a soot-stained finger at the raised bar. "If you take your stumps there and squeeze that lever to that palm bar, that releases your blade here." She turned Khara's arm over. The blade ran along Khara's entire forearm, from elbow to knuckles, and was sheathed beneath a sturdy plate of iron. "So when you depress that lever, make sure your arm is pointed down so the blade falls into place. And make sure you hear a sort of *ker-chunk*, all right? That is how you know it's secured and it won't go sliding back in when you're swinging."

Khara turned the gauntlet over and back again, admiring its craftsmanship with an almost loving adoration. "This is wonderful. I-I cannot thank you enough." She looked at Harsuth, eyes bright and alive. "It's a work of art."

"It's a rushed job," Harsuth said, waving away Khara's compliments like she was swatting away a fly. "Hopefully I can get my hands on it again before we get too involved in god-killing. It's too heavy. You're not going to be able to move it around the way you would want to. It will take some getting used to until I can fine tune its weight and balance."

"It's perfect," Khara said, smiling. "Can I try it?"

Harsuth put her hands up and backed away a few paces. Odessa did the same. "Just step away from my bench," Harsuth said, gesturing away from the forge toward the cave's wall. "Go over there and let it go. Just in case it comes flying out like an arrow."

Khara stepped away from them and stood next to the rack of spears. Holding the gauntlet out from her body and angling it downward like she was lifting a heavy pail, she squeezed the lever. The blade whispered out of its sheath like a lunging viper. A gleam of polished iron flashed. The blade froze with a heavy click, extending so its tip nearly scraped the cave floor.

"Wow," Odessa said. "That's amazing."

Harsuth was standing with her arms crossed over her apron-laden chest. "It's not bad for a first attempt. But it will get better. I can already see it."

Khara was slowly moving the blade back and forth. Testing its balance. A slow slash and then a thrust. An upward cut. Each movement coming faster and faster. "It feels pretty good."

"Now try and sheath it," Harsuth said. "Depress the lever and hold your arm up. Let it slide back until it clicks."

Khara did as she was told, and the blade slid back into its sheath as quickly and easily as it had come out. It took a little jiggle of her arm for the click to secure the blade, but Khara was not concerned in the slightest. She walked to Harsuth, arms opened wide. "Harsuth, you beautiful bitch, I love you."

Harsuth took her hammer, a tool with an almost impossibly large head atop its handle, and raised it as Khara approached. "If you take another step, I'll take the top of your head off."

Khara stopped and lowered her arms, smiling. Harsuth's hammer-wielding arm slowly fell and she, too, began to smile, strained and tight-lipped.

"Thank you," Khara said.

"You're welcome. Now get out of here. I've work to do."

Khara grinned wider, then returned to Odessa's side. Her eyes kept falling to the gauntlet on her arm. Odessa and Khara left Harsuth and her forge just as the bustling of the camp reached its apex. There was much work to be done.

Khara and Odessa were packing up the tent and loading entehlos and bazaks with supplies and provisions. By midday, the entire camp was dismantled and prepared to migrate, splitting off into a series of groups. All of them making their way, directly or indirectly, toward Asha-Kalir.

Khara and Odessa were assigned to a party of roughly one hundred warriors, led by Sansehra and her raiders, heading northeast. After nearly two weeks' hard travel, they arrived at the banks of the Darrood. Far north of Asha-Kalir, where the wide Darrood wormed its way through the uneven foothills. Khara and Odessa lay at the crest of a steep embankment sweeping down to the riverbank. To their left, where the ridge fell away more gently, was a stream feeding into the Darrood.

The sky was a dark, stony gray. The water's surface, like hammered tin, rolled and undulated in its gentle perambulation. The Gray was thicker to the north. Another week's travel northward would take them to the outskirts of Blighted land. The land from which Sak-Tor and his people had fled.

The river narrowed here between the foothills, but from bank to bank it was still so wide even if the oldest and tallest tree in the Arabako Forest had been felled across the river's span, its thinnest, most intrepid branches would only just brush the opposite bank. Odessa and Khara watched the water flow ever onward below them. Splashing and tearing around the skuttled rattan fishing boat the Sisters had placed on the far side of the river. Over the course of a day, they had sunk a log three quarters of the way across the river and buried one end of it deep into the rocky riverbed. Slanting upward against the current, the other end of the log protruded just slightly over the water's surface like a crocodile lying in wait. Around this log they had piled driftwood and branches hewn from the log to create the illusion of a fledgling logjam. And upon this log, angled toward the center of the river, they had skuttled the boat. Ramming its hull onto the log like a fish on a spit.

The bodies of the fishing boat's owners, denizens of a nearby half-deserted village that was now looted and razed, had been tossed from the opposite bank and allowed to float and beach themselves a short distance downstream to add to the authenticity of the ruse.

Odessa's gaze kept returning to the body of a man caught in a clump of reeds. His legs bobbing up and down as the river bade him onward downstream. She had killed that man. As he begged for his people to be spared. Offering her and her devil compatriots anything they wanted if they would only let him live. His children, all four of them, had succumbed to disease over the past year. His wife was all he had left in the world. She had been standing a half-step behind him as he pleaded with her inside their small, domed hut. Holding onto his hand, trying to pull him away from the armored monster in the doorway. Now she was somewhere farther downstream, swept away from her husband forever.

Khara nudged her with the side of her gauntlet. "They're coming," she whispered. Both Khara and Odessa eased back from the ridge's crest, melting into the coarse grasses. The dozen or so Sisters on the ridge alongside them did the same. A huge boat, something between a barge and warship came around the bend of the river upstream. Dozens of oars bristled from its hull, dipping into the water in a slow, steady rhythm. A thudding staccato drumbeat echoed through the foothills and down the watery corridor. Like the faraway heartbeat of a giant.

The ship slid across the water, slowly gaining speed as the river narrowed. Approaching the point where the stream intersected the river. Hidden in the reeds, two small hide-stretched canoes lay in wait in the stream. A call came out from the ship's bow, ordering the helmsman starboard around the obstruction. As the ship approached, Odessa could easily make out the glinting bronze of cannons along its low gunwale. Five cannons on each side.

When the ship's bow passed, only a stone's throw before them, the Sisters sprang into action. Odessa rose to her knees, nocked an arrow, and let it fly in the span of a few seconds. Sisters rushed onto the ridge, throwing grappling hooks into the ship's rigging. Teams of three and four hauled on the ropes as the ship's oars began ripping into the water.

The two canoes slid from the stream's mouth and the river's current pulled them toward the struggling ship. A canoe sidled along either side of the ship and at each oar hole in the hull of the ship, they threw small, loosely tied bags of lime dust into the oarsmen's deck. Filling the deck's stagnant air with a fine mist of particulates. Halfway across the ship's length, the oars began to fall limp or jerk inward as the oarsmen coughed and hacked and tried to flee to the main deck.

The volleys upon volleys of arrows kept most of the cannon crew unable to man their weapons, and the ones that did reach them were too late. When the ship was in reach, Sisters came with long planks spiked on either end and let them fall with heavy thuds upon the ship's deck.

Odessa and Khara were among the first on the planks. Charging down the steeply angled plank as the ship bobbed and swayed against the ropes holding it grounded.

The warriors on the ship's deck were forming lines of spears when the oarsmen, human slaves with manacles around their ankles, came stumbling blindly from the lower decks, hacking and wheezing with red, swollen eyes.

Odessa shoved past a coughing woman and ran her spear into the neck of a warrior still bent over one of the starboard cannons. She turned to see Khara leaping from the plank, her blade unsheathed and gleaming. She parried an incoming spear, darted forward, and punched her blade into a warrior's neck.

"Do not kill the slaves!" Sansehra called from the plank.

More Sisters poured onto the deck. The wood was soon soaked with spreading pools of blood. Boots stepped and slid through the pools as blade and armor clashed. As blade ripped flesh and spilled more blood onto the deck.

Odessa was able to kill two more warriors before the skirmish was over. The last warrior was clouted over the head with a club and then stabbed through the armpit before falling against the gunwale. Her blood poured from her nose and mouth and splashed into the dark water below.

While the wheezing, snot-dripping slaves were being lined up at the bow to have their eyes washed out, Odessa and Khara made their way to the companionway hatch leading below deck. A fine mist still drifted up the stairs. Khara wiped her blade clean and let it slide back into its sheath as they looked down the stairs into the swirling white mist below.

"Might have poured those little bags a bit heavy, no?" Odessa asked. "How long will it take to air out?"

"I don't know," Khara said. "But I do know we need to move this ship before another boat comes."

Sansehra came beside them, wiping blood from the blade of her sword with a rag. "We will have to let the sails down. See if we can catch a breeze."

Khara paused, considering the still air against her skin. "I'm afraid we might be out of luck when it comes to that."

Sansehra sighed. "There is no such thing as a perfect victory. We will give it a while longer to air out, then the slaves go back down and we turn this behemoth upstream." She glanced around the deck, scanning faces. "Now I have to find our little spy, Poshta. She said she would make herself scarce once the fighting started."

"You don't think she would be below deck, do you?" Khara asked.

"Not on the oarsmen's deck. Probably in the cargo hold if she is not hiding somewhere on the main deck. If that is the case, she will just have to sit and wait for the air to clear like the rest of us."

"The dust won't filter down to the cargo hold?"

"Godsdamn it, I don't know," Sansehra snapped. "Maybe. She'll have to hold her breath and close her eyes then." She shook her head and sighed. "I'm going to look for her. You two start stripping bodies and scrubbing the deck." Sansehra left them and made her way aft to the raised afterdeck where the ballista sat, head dropping forward like a weary animal's.

Khara exchanged a wide-eyed look with Odessa. "I didn't mean to rile her up like that."

Odessa shrugged. "Battle is a stressful time. And she's got a boat full of poison. I'm sure she's just a bit touchy right now."

Khara nodded and they went to begin stripping, looting, and dumping bodies into barrels to be stored below deck. The work of the wicked was never done.

CHAPTER 37

Half of the slaves were at least partially blinded, but they could all still hold an oar. Once the dust had mostly settled, they were ushered down the stairs with rags covering their noses and mouths. Dry rags were used to wipe the oars and oar benches clean.

The ship slowly and arduously worked its way upstream where the river widened so it could turn and head straight up the river, while the nude bodies of the slain floated downstream toward Asha-Kalir.

Poshta was found in the cargo hold with three other defectors. Poshta had told the Sisters of the ship and its cargo weeks ago. She emerged from the packed cargo hold, flustered and coughing with watery eyes. To Odessa she looked remarkably young for a Torva warrior. Ayana's age perhaps. "What was that?" she asked loudly.

"Lime powder," Sansehra said. "I had to get the oarsmen to drop their oars."

"And you couldn't have sent me word of something like that?"

"Who told you to hide below deck?"

"Well, did you want me to hide above deck where the killing was?" Poshta said, her defectors clustering behind her.

Sansehra shook her head resignedly. "No. No I didn't." She looked at Poshta, a weary, pleased expression coming over her face. "I'm just glad you are in one piece."

"So am I," Poshta said. "But what do you think? Will the ship do the job?"

"I should think so. But I'm more concerned about the cargo," Sansehra said, looking over Poshta's shoulder into the farthest depth of cargo hold. Sacks and clay pots of all sizes and whole salted sides of meat were stacked in compartments throughout the hold.

Poshta led Sansehra and the rest of her small retinue into the far reaches of the hold. In a walled-off section of the hold was a floor-to-ceiling stack of huge clay pots as tall as a child and as wide as a tree trunk. Sansehra pried the lid from one and sniffed. Even Odessa, from the back of the retinue, caught a whiff of the acrid, oily odor. Sansehra sniffed and scrunched her nose before pounding the lid back into the jar. "This will do. This will do very nicely." She grinned at Poshta. "You've done a great service to the Sisters, my dear. A great service, indeed."

The ship headed north up the Darrood until it reached the mouth of the Khire River, which it followed westward until the sun was nearly hidden behind the mountains so very far to the west. The ship anchored near a sandbar between two low hills dotted with trees and dark, withering vegetation. For dinner, they ate a hearty meal of lentil soup and salted meat with a hard brown bread. Odessa ate little, for the richness of the meal made her want to gag. But the little she did eat was savory and pleasantly hot.

After dinner, Odessa and Khara sat on the afterdeck with a horn of pilfered wine, their backs against the frame of the ballista. Dark shadows gathered beneath the sparsely wooded hill before them and between clusters of brush and grass. It had been a while since either of them had seen such greenery. Even in the dark, it was a comfort just to see the silhouettes of trees against the dingy gray-black sky of night. Odessa thought Poko would have loved seeing the green of trees and grass instead of the drab desert of the Sisters' new main camp.

The smell of grass and water was fresh and invigorating after months of inhaling desert dust and entehlo shit. The lingering smell of blood and death were the only anchors to their reality. To the war that they were waging. The ship rocked softly against the river's gentle current. Tiny lapping splashes against its hull like whispers in the night.

Khara took a sip from the horn and passed it to Odessa. "So, you have been with us for a while now," Khara said, her voice fluid and on the verge of slurring. "What do you think of us devils?"

Odessa took a sip of tart wine. "You're fine, I suppose."

"We're fine? That's it? Just fine? You have nothing else to say? Good or bad?"

"You've been much better to me than my last . . ." Odessa trailed off, unsure how to continue. "My masters? My owners?" She passed the horn to Khara. "You devils have been fine to me."

"I've been meaning to ask . . ." Khara took the horn and held it without taking a drink. "Your last people, they were the ones who put that iron on your arm, yes? They were the ones who deceived you and prepared you to become a godkiller?"

Odessa nodded. "Yes. They were the only people I thought I could truly trust after my father died and left me with this poison in my veins. Yakun, he was a friend of my father's. A fellow conspirator. He told me I could be cured in Asha-Kalir. Instead, I was collared and made to kill so I could grow stronger and more bloodthirsty." Odessa glanced at the horn. "Are you going to take a drink?"

Khara shook her head and gave Odessa the horn again. Odessa took a long sip and returned the horn to Khara. "I wasn't just collared physically," Odessa continued, looking out into the shadowy grasses as they swayed and bounced in the breeze. "There was a young man working with Yakun and Azdava. Working on their supposed cure. His name was Tarik. And I . . . I was fond of him. Very fond of him. But he was just another leash around my neck. To keep me in line. The carrot as opposed to the stick. Another tool to keep me killing for them."

Odessa's hand went to her iron arm, fingers tracing the rune work. "Then after I had killed more than my fair share, they drugged me and put this blasted thing on my already ruined arm. And they pumped me full of blood. The blood of innocents I thought I had saved. Force-feeding me like a duck before slaughter." Her fingers traced the runes up to her elbow. Warmth had spread across her cheeks and down her neck as pleasant drunkenness seeped into the weary parts of her soul and relaxed her tense, overwrought spirit. "Can I tell you something? Something Poko doesn't even know, I don't think."

"Of course."

"Yakun, the old man I thought I could trust. The old friend of my father's. The one who taught me how to control my fire." Odessa stopped there, a blockage rising in her throat. She steadied her breathing and tried to quiet the sudden patter of her heart. "He touched me. Not at first. Not for a while. But after I was with him for a few months, he started. Just a little at first. A hand on the shoulder that lingered a moment too long. The back of his hand accidentally grazing my breast when reaching for something. But it didn't take long before it got worse. He started saying that he needed to inspect my body to see if the godsblood in my arm was spread elsewhere. So he could poke and prod at my chest." Odessa swallowed hard. Her eyes lost focus and her hand fell away from the rune work into her lap. "But it didn't stop there."

"Of course it didn't," Khara said softly. Barely audible. Her hand reached out slowly and tentatively and she rested her fingertips on Odessa's left arm. "It never does."

"The thing is, I could have broken his neck at any time. I could have torn his head from his shoulders and crushed it between my hands. But I didn't. I let him do it to me. I allowed this to happen to me. So what does that say about me? Am I just weak? Or what, did I want it to happen?"

"No. You're not weak. And you did not want it. In no way, shape, or form did you want that. He was someone you trusted, and he took advantage of that. He used it like a weapon so you couldn't do anything. You cannot blame yourself for not stopping him. You're strong but he had power over you. And he used it insidiously. It is no one's fault but his. And I hope he pays for it."

"I hope so too," Odessa said morosely.

"I'm glad you got away from all of that," Khara said.

Odessa shrugged. "I just didn't want to be used anymore."

"And that took bravery," Khara said, squeezing Odessa's arm. "It is not easy leaving something like that. That is why I waited so long to leave Sak-Tor's army."

Odessa raised her head and turned to look at Khara, whose gaze was firm and unwavering but filled with a somber understanding. "Did something happen to you?"

"Almost," Khara said. "It almost did. I was injured in a battle around two or three years ago. A club struck me in the back, and no one was quite sure if I would be able to walk again. Our healer thought my spine was broken but there was too much swelling and bruising to be sure, and I was in too much pain to do much more than moan and groan and sleep. But during one of those times when I found myself in the valley between waves of pain, I overheard one of Sak-Tor's sons, I don't remember who, and our healer. They were outside my tent talking about me. Talking about my recuperation. The son asked our healer how long it would take for me to get back on my feet if I was able to walk again. The healer told him a few months at least. So he tells her he would like to impregnate me while I was infirmed so I could carry the child and give birth while recovering, since I was already going to be out of commission for a while. And he said it as if it were just a matter of efficiency and not rape. And the healer said nothing in my defense. Only said she would have to see how bad the damage was before any decisions could be made. Can you believe that?"

"That's horrible," Odessa said. "I'm so sorry, Khara. I can't believe they would even talk about that."

"That's the world Sak-Tor had built for himself. We women are just breeding stock to him and his sons. We warriors have our duty deferred for a time, but if you are a remarkable warrior like my mother was, then you become a prize to them and they never let you go. You cannot just bear their children and be done with it. They keep you like a trophy and use you until you're just a husk of a woman." Khara took a drink, then wiped her mouth with the back of her hand. "Do you know what they do to women who try to run or shirk their duty in some other way? They cut their legs off at the knees. And it has to be at the knees and not the hips—otherwise the pelvic muscles get loose and it's not as pleasurable for those sick, sadistic bastards. That was the world I was born into, Odessa. So when I say, I know it's hard to escape a situation like that, I mean it, truly. Our relationships and our obligations are like manacles sometimes. Collars that you have to slip free from eventually."

Odessa's eyes misted. "I'm sorry that I didn't trust you at first. It's hard for me to trust anybody now. Even Poko sometimes. Even myself. Or especially myself." She shook her head. "I'm sorry."

"Don't apologize," Khara said. "I came on too strong too quickly. I projected my own feelings onto you and did not see you as a real person. You were just this idol to me. An idea I could follow without thought or worry. If I had you to guide me, I was at least not totally lost. In a way, I was using you. And I'm sorry for that."

"You don't have to apologize. I understand."

Khara shifted, leaning toward Odessa. Her shortened hand slid down Odessa's arm to her wrist. Her head came down to rest upon Odessa's shoulder. "I know you do. And I understand you," she whispered, her breath hot with alcohol.

They stayed sitting there for a long while, leaning against one another. Khara fell asleep first, snoring softly, her shortened finger stumps entwined with Odessa's fingers. Odessa tried to stay awake, listening to Khara's gentle, whistling breaths. Waiting with dread for the sun to begin its ascent. But she fell asleep long before dawn, her chin resting on Khara's head.

The Sisters on watch duty walked around them throughout the long night, mercifully leaving them to their restful slumber without disruption. For they all knew the toll of war. And one had to take comforts as they came. They were few and so very fleeting.

CHAPTER 38

Odessa awoke with Talara's words echoing in her mind: "Steel yourself and you may find yourself in paradise yet. All transgressions can be forgiven, all sins are within my domain. The day is upon us. Cleanse yourself in the blood of devils and be reborn. Your sister and mother await your return."

Three days had passed since they took the ship. Three days of anchorage in a sandy tributary flowing south into the river. Hidden from the river by a sharp, meandering bend in the stream, they awaited word from Remaka. Their messenger had left on an entehlo the morning after the ship's hijacking and was due back any day now.

Odessa slid from her hammock as the morning bell chimed a second time. More than sixty Sisters were packed into the cramped sleeping quarters at the forward end of the oars deck. Three layers of hammocks were strung up on either side of a narrow aisle through the room. Hanging between the wall and posts set in short intervals across the room.

Odessa pushed past Sisters climbing down from the uppermost hammocks, rubbing bleary eyes, or stretching sore and aching muscles to join the current of Sisters moving down the aisle to the main oars deck.

Through the doorway of the sleeping hold, Odessa passed the slaves still chained for the night to loops of iron bolted into the floor beneath their oar benches. They slept sprawled on their benches or on the ground beside them, their manacled legs always twisted toward the rings in the floor. Most of the powder had been swept away, but the slaves bore burns from its remnants. Their skin reddened and leaking. Their eyes weeping constantly.

One slave watched her as she made her way for the hatch to the main deck. Hate burning in his eyes. To him, she was a human who had betrayed her own kind. And perhaps that was exactly what she was. But she had been betrayed first. Forsaken by all. What other choice had she but this?

On the main deck, the warriors mustered. Those on the second half of the night's watch filed down the hatch to the hammocks, Khara among them. As Khara passed the gathering troops, she gave Odessa a tired, wry smirk.

All throughout muster and her small breakfast of last night's soup and bread, Odessa wondered when the Sisters' hospitality would run dry and they would betray her. She could not help parsing through the memory of her meeting with Remaka. The ease with which Remaka had accepted Odessa's terms. Once Sak-Tor was dead, they would have little use for her. Even still, Talara's whispered orders were clear in her mind. To bring the Sisters to Asha-Kalir and to Sak-Tor. To have them swarm the Conqueror God as an ill-fated diversion. Because both Talara and Odessa knew Odessa's magic-snuffing ability would be as a breeze is to a wildfire when pitted against the conflagration that was Sak-Tor. But she would make a show of it and convince the Sisters that his magic was weakened. Then, the Sisters would die after being torn to pieces by Sak-Tor's magic, allowing Asha-Kalir's counterattack to take Sak-Tor's head in the short, bloody instant the brunt of his magic was averted from the city. While his magic ripped through Khara's people, Asha-Kalir would unload upon him and his forces. Only then would Odessa truly unleash what little magical suppression she could muster—after the Sisters' blood was spilled.

Odessa wondered if she would really be able to betray the Sisters. For Talara's sake, no less. The idea of doing anything for Talara made her skin crawl, but what choice did she have?

As long as she could keep Khara from harm, she thought she could do it. She could betray the rest of them. Have them dashed upon the walls of Asha-Kalir. Crushed between red clay and devil flesh. But no harm could come to Khara. Of that, there was no debate in her mind. No matter what happened, Khara could not be hurt.

She dipped a crust of bread into the shallow pool of soup still in her bowl. *Wouldn't the deaths of everyone she's cared for hurt her? Wouldn't Sansehra and Remaka and all the rest dying in vain hurt her?* The hard, half-stale bread sopped up the soup and grew soggy in her hand. She let it sink into the pool of broth and set the bowl aside. *She would move on eventually. And Sak-Tor will still die, just by Khymanir's hands. So they wouldn't be dying in vain. It would be a noble sacrifice.* Just thinking those thoughts made the soup in her stomach turn sour.

It's not as if I have a choice. There is no way we can kill Sak-Tor. His entire army is massed around Asha-Kalir. We have no chance of even getting within a stone's throw of him. The Sisters are going to die anyway. All I can really do is keep Khara safe and save ourselves. She looked across the deck at the Sisters busy at work scrubbing the deck and cleaning the cannons. Soon they would all be dead. And there was nothing she could do about it but use those deaths to save herself and Khara.

The messenger returned later that day, riding along the riverbank on a heaving entehlo. When the rider reached the ship's ladder, she leapt from the back of her foam-mouthed beast and scaled the ladder in moments.

"Where is Sister Sansehra?" the messenger asked. She was short, only a bit taller than Odessa, and thin as a reed.

Sansehra pushed through the crowd gathering on the deck. "I'm here. What say Remaka?"

The messenger drew a piece of parchment, folded and sealed with dark red wax, from a satchel hanging at her side. She handed it to Sansehra, then collapsed against the gunwale, sweating profusely beneath her lamellar jerkin.

"Someone take her below deck and get her some water and something to eat," Sansehra said as she broke the parchment's seal with a flick of her sharp nail. The messenger was escorted below deck as Sansehra read, her eyes dancing over the page.

Silent for a moment, she folded the parchment and held it between her hands. The crowd around her waited with bated breath.

"Remaka and her retinue will be here by day's end. Tomorrow we are bound for Asha-Kalir."

For a while, that was all Sansehra said. Then as if she had awoken from some semi-conscious state, she straightened and looked around at her warriors. "This ship must be spotless when the Matron arrives. I want all hands on deck. The ballista must be in perfect working order. I want the bowstring replaced, I want the winches and springs and stand joint cleaned and oiled. All cannons must be cleaned and the cannonballs stocked on deck. And I want the ballista fully stocked as well. Every shot we have, I want to be stowed on this deck. This ship will be battle-ready for the Matron's arrival, understood?"

The crowd cried out in the affirmative and saluted before scattering groups to fulfill their tasks. Odessa scrubbed the deck, rubbing a brush over the bloodstains sunk deep into the wood.

Remaka came with a retinue of most of the Elder Sisters and thirty warriors. They rode their entehlos up the gangway to be lowered into the hold with a crane and sling. Already the ship had nearly one hundred entehlos packed in the forward half of the cargo hold where the livestock were quartered, three to a stall. Odessa wondered if the new arrivals would even fit. They would have to wander the rest of the cargo hold, stumbling about as the ship lurched and pitched.

All of the Sisters on the ship stood assembled in rows of twelve as Remaka inspected cannons and ballista in the fading light of day. They remained there as she and the Elder Sisters, led by Sansehra, went below deck. Odessa stood in the back row, her guts sinking more and more as the sun lowered beneath the mountain peaks. She wished they could have stayed anchored in this tributary for a week longer. More than that. She wanted to stay there until Asha-Kalir fell. Until Sak-Tor took his armies elsewhere. Until the Gray came south to choke the life from the lot of them.

A few moments later, Remaka and Sansehra and the Elder Sisters returned to the main deck. Remaka's dour face was sharp and somewhat pleased. As she made her way to the front of the assembled warriors, Odessa caught what looked like a glint of fanatical excitement in her eyes.

Remaka stopped before her warriors, looking up and down the rows with an expression of pride. "My Sisters," she said, voice seeming to rumble across the deck like the thunder. "Tomorrow, we embark to do the impossible. Tomorrow, we avenge the mother of our people and all of our sisters throughout history who have suffered at the hands of Sak-Tor and his foul brood. We stand to put an end to it all. We stand to correct all that has been perverted by his wickedness.

"I will not lie to you. It will not be easy. But steel yourselves and have faith. Sak-Tor bleeds like any other, and we will make him bleed. Whether we succeed or fail, he will bleed. And that is a victory in and of itself, my Sisters. We will make him bleed and he will remember who we are as we scream our rage into the smoke-filled air. For as long as he lives, he will remember the Daughters of Ana Yuma."

Remaka paused, a grim smile etched into her stony face. "But I believe he will not have to remember for long." She moved, beginning to pace back and forth across the deck, a few steps in either direction. No, I have faith, my Sisters. I believe in us. I know Sak-Tor will die tomorrow. I feel it in the marrow of my bones." Her voice began to rise, to crescendo. "As surely as I know the sun will rise in the morning, I know it will rise upon Sak-Tor's final day. Sak-Tor and his sons will die by our hands so no more of our mothers and sisters and daughters will have to suffer. No more will our women suffer their torments. Tomorrow we unleash upon them generations of torment. Tomorrow, we let our fury be known! Tomorrow, my Sisters, we rage!"

Remaka's speech was met with assenting shouts and howls of brash conviction.

Beside Odessa, Khara howled. It was a throaty, animal sound. Like a dog howling at the sky. Her eyes were wet and glassy.

Not for the first time, Odessa felt the outsider.

The shouts and bravado, to Odessa, sounded like a cocksure yet bittersweet funeral dirge.

CHAPTER 39

The ship cut through the water like an arrow. The oars cut through the water with the shouts of their helmswoman. A drum's quick tapping setting the brisk, frenetic pace. The slaves bending forward and snapping back in time with the drums.

They left before dawn and now, past midday, they were passing the fields and villages Odessa had passed when she had first come to Asha-Kalir. The fields were barren. The villages ruined cinders. She stood at the gunwale, watching the ravaged riverland as it swam past.

The city walls loomed in the distance. Plumes of smoke rose above the city. The boom of cannons came one after another like the rumbling of a stampede.

A blockade was fast approaching, a line of ships with their cannons and ballistae aimed upriver. Their ship slowed a far distance from the blockade, coasting on the current alone. Poshta was at the bow with a long horn into which she blew three plaintive bleats punctuated by a few quick blasts. Then she waited for the reply, Sansehra beside her. Remaka remained below deck, hidden from any prying eyes upon the blockade. On the deck, a heavy tension had built in the atmosphere. A static growing between each body busy at work. If the blockade divined their deception, the ship would be blown to splinters before they could do so much as load a cannon.

The reply came as a sequence of loud horn blasts. "What does that mean?" Sansehra asked, not looking away from the blockade.

"They're letting us through," Poshta said, relief deflating her tensed frame.

Another series of blasts followed and Poshta cocked her head. "They're telling us to hurry."

The ships making up the blockade were moving, parting so they might pass through the center. The ship's oars cut through the water again, and the ship resumed its course downstream.

"That is one barrier overcome," Sansehra said quietly.

The ship passed through the blockade and Asha-Kalir loomed nearer. Odessa could see clearly now the absence of the giant warriors that had stood watch at the entrance of the city's waterway. Massive boulders of sheared and obliterated rock blocked the massive bronze gate. A pile of red and lichenous green rising from the dark waters. Against the white of the walls, the mountain of rubble rising from the water was a stark and brutal contrast.

Spread throughout the stretch of river before them was a fleet of ships. Dozens of them. All of them firing cannons and ballistae toward the city. Cannon smoke hung over the water's surface in gray, wispy blankets.

Over the riverbank, across the pitted and torn fields and ruined huts, a vast plain of black armor and bristling spears stretched toward the horizon. And it was moving. Despite the volleys of arrows and booming cannon fire, the army was moving ever closer to the walls. Charging in a mad dash. And amid it all, one body towered taller than the rest. In the middle of the battlefield, Odessa glimpsed for the first time the figure of the Conqueror King. He charged forward at the head of a large column flanked by his sons astride entehlos. His massive strides outpacing the entehlos around him. A cannonball rocketed and disintegrated in a burst of dust and bits of stone.

The ship pulled up close to the western bank, and Sansehra looked to Odessa expectantly. Many eyes turned to her. Exerting upon her a dreadfully overt pressure. Remaka came from below deck in full armor and leveled Odessa with a sharp, piercing gaze.

"Do it now," Remaka said. "If we don't stop him here, the walls will come down and it will be too late."

Odessa nodded and looked out over the battlefield. But her eyes were drawn to the riverbank instead. In the burnt ruins of warehouses along the river's edge, she spied three of Talara's Shadows. Waiting for her betrayal to aid in her escape.

Odessa drew her eyes from the Shadows and trained them on the massive god in the middle distance. His horns flared from his head. The horns of some infernal ibex. She drew in a breath and tried to feel in the air the static of his considerable magic. But there was nothing. He was much too far away. But it was for this very moment she had told them she could nullify his magic at a distance. She would tell them his magic was dampened when it wasn't. They would unload on him. Cannonballs and ballista shot full of incendiary sludge rocketing toward him. And they would do nothing but distract and divert the devil horde long enough for Asha-Kalir's sortie to repel the assault. Then Odessa and her Shadow escort would join the sortie and nullify Sak-Tor's magic in earnest so he could be captured.

Her fingers tightened on the gunwale's railing. Beside her, Khara watched her, hope and concern in her expression. Those eyes boring a hole in Odessa's traitorous head. *All I have to do is say it's working. Or nod. Just nod. Then everything falls into motion and I just have to run.*

Odessa's head sagged. "It's not working. He's too far."

"Shit! Godsdamn it!" Remaka hissed. She turned to Sansehra and ordered, "We're going to have to mount up. I want the entehlos saddled and the hull breached right this instant."

I doubt I could even stop his magic if I was right next to him. I don't have enough strength in me. I barely have more than I did when I was starving in a cave. No, I have even less than that.

Khara's hand touched her back. "It's all right. It was a long shot anyway. We'll just get closer."

"I don't think I can do it."

Khara pressed close to her, her hand on her back moving to her shoulder as she held her. "Yes, you can. I know you can."

"I don't have enough in me. I didn't get enough." Khara looked at her, cool and composed with a compassionate warmth kindled in her eyes. Odessa looked over the battlefield to Sak-Tor, now halfway to the city walls. His four arms pumping, each of them wielding a different weapon the size of a human. His magic deflecting and splintering oncoming arrows as if they were leaves caught in a gale. Cannonballs bursting apart like clods of dry mud. He was a monster. How could she hope to stop magic like that?

After a few more strides, Sak-Tor stopped and screamed words that were lost in the bedlam. His massive foot stomped the earth, and even from such a distance, Odessa felt a wave of magic ripple through the air. Intense and potent. Like an aftershock of a faraway earthquake.

The ground beneath Sak-Tor's foot churned. A wedge shape of twisting earth spread toward the wall. Large chunks of clay and sod rising and falling as the earth canted and twisted at the bloodthirsty god's beckoning.

When the wedge of churning earth reached the wall, the white stone began to crack and groan. Dust fell from the wall and soon pieces were falling to the twisting earth beneath it. The center of the wall began to buckle. Then it fell. An entire section of wall crumbled to the dirt.

There's no stopping him now. He'll be in the palace within the hour. He's out of our reach.

She thought of Yakun and Tarik meeting the Conqueror God in some palace hall. Sak-Tor tearing them apart and destroying all their foul work. Destroying the bleeders and the other tortured souls in the dungeons of Asha-Kalir. A brutal and bloody mercy. And she wondered if perhaps the fall of Asha-Kalir wouldn't be such a bad thing.

Then a thought struck her. Her iron fingers drummed on the gunwale railing as her reeling mind twisted strands of errant thought into something cohesive. Something feasible.

"I've got it. I know what to do."

By the time the hull of the cargo hold was breached and gangways were placed, Sak-Tor and his army had already poured into the city. The sounds of wanton slaughter and destruction came from beyond the walls, a terrible cacophony of screaming and crashing.

Nearly the entirety of the army of Sisters rode down the gangways. Odessa and Khara rode alongside Remaka at the head of the charge. All of them stone-faced and focused. The lives of every Sister were balanced upon the razor's edge of Odessa's hastily constructed plan. Splashing through the shallow water and up the battle-churned riverbank to race across the battlefield, they chased Sak-Tor into the city. To the palace.

CHAPTER 40

Every Red Clay Warrior in the palace was congregated in Khymanir's work-shop, arrayed around the walls, halberds and pikes readied. Kunza stood beside the vessel's circle, a few of his Shadows around him.

Khymanir was in the center of the room, sitting on the catalyst circle. Completely motionless. The myriad arms folded in a tangle of knob-elbowed limbs.

At hearing that the city walls had fallen, Yakun and the boy had fled to the lower levels. As if they'd be safer secreted away with the bleeders. There would be no hiding from the horde of devils pouring through the city streets. Their only chance of survival lay in the carved hands of the vessel.

Kunza scanned the circle beneath the vessel's feet. Scouring the deep chan-nels in the marble for any imperfection he might correct before the time came for the circle to be put to use. The bronze wire set along either side of each channel gleamed in the dimness.

Set in a pool within the intricate whirls of bronze, the vessel's feet stood inert. Each foot larger than Kunza. From its feet to its head, the massive clay figure was covered in an infinitely complex labyrinth of runes and sigils. A maze of fine, flowing script. Myriad hands had inlaid each rune and sigil with bronze wire. The god's fingers had handled the lengths of still red-hot wire with a deli-cate grace nearing reverence. Bending them into shape and setting them in the barely wet clay. So now, finished mere hours before the hordes broke through the walls, the hulking figure shone in the dim light. More than a ton of bronze adorned the vessel. And precious gems were set into the center of rune carved in its arms, legs, and hands. Finished, the vessel looked like a man of impossibly broad proportions. Its arms and legs were thick and round. Its hands were large and bore six fingers. Each of them studded with a different gem. Its chest was too wide and deep, more like the trunk of some primeval tree than of a man. A wide neck rose from round shoulders, giving the vessel the look of a man permanently mid-shrug. The head atop it all was mostly a blank canvas for tightly spun runes radiating from around its piercing blue eyes and a pair of perpetually frowning lips. The hint of a flat nose in the center of its face gave it the vaguest notion of humanity. Looking upon the vessel filled Kunza with a dreadful awe.

A crash came echoing down the palace halls. A booming thud and another crash followed soon after. A roar of voices and footsteps upon polished marble. The clash of bronze against iron. Iron and clay and flesh. Bodies hitting the floor. Khymanir's guards winnowing away as much of the devil horde as they could. All of this far away in the sprawl of palatial halls. Kunza glanced at the massive doors at the other end of the workroom. Barred with thick planks of hardwood that would be turned to splinters in an instant before Sak-Tor's brutal strength and magic.

Kunza eased away from the circle. His Shadows drew closer around him as he stepped to the right side of the room, near a large bronze cistern. There was further crashing and clashing and screaming in the palace. *Have faith, you feckless old man,* he told himself. *Talara would not have sent me here to die at the hands of devils. The circle will work. The devils will die here.*

A crash came far closer than any that had preceded it. The sound of a blast. Splinters and shrapnel filling the air. Heavy footsteps pounding the stone outside the heavy doors. Kunza reached within himself and found Talara's strength. Took hold of it. The cold ebbing through him soothing his doubts and his fears. He slid the obsidian knife from its sheath. The aching of his finger joints quieted as Talara's cold resolve seeped to his fingertips. Her power coalescing around his hands. Hands made for sacrifices and the creation of new life. Not for doling out death to blood-lusted devils.

The doors at the end of the room burst open in pieces of twisted bronze and splinters. Ripped from their hinges, the doors, in multiple warped pieces, flew into the center of the room. A few of Khymanir's largest hands swatted them away, knocking them against the walls and into his own Red Clay Warriors, crushing one and shearing an arm from another.

Devils in black armor poured through the door, a cloud of dust swirling around them as they came. Khymanir remained sitting in his circle, his arms once again motionless. His Red Clay Warriors stood at attention still as the devils fanned out and formed a wedge in front of the doorway.

From behind the cistern, Kunza watched the hulking body fill the doorway. Nearly as tall as Khymanir, Sak-Tor had to stoop for his long, recurved horns to clear the top of the door frame. He was as tall as three men stacked atop one another. Powerfully muscled, his four arms were like huge, gnarled tree trunks. He wore no armor but a lamellar skirt of iron and dark leather. His skin was a purple as dark as a night sky. Gold and silver bands were twisted around his four biceps and a gorget made of gold wrapped around his neck and lay across the front of his chest as if his throat had been cut and from the wound had poured gold. But all along his body were veins of a purer gold. Divinity shone in bright streaks like lightning across his forearm and chest and down his legs. Around his dark eyes was a tangle of glowing capillaries, sun-bright and furious. But along the marks of the divine, small swollen lumps were beginning to bulge out from beneath his skin. One side of his face seemed to sag slightly.

In his four hands he wielded two clubs and two curved swords, each of them longer than a man was tall. Sak-Tor pointed one of the swords at Khymanir and shouted, "Khymanir!" His long drooping mustache and forked beard twitched and trembled as he shouted, his yellowed fangs bared. "You have hidden behind your walls and your clay toys for far too long!"

Khymanir remained still save for one hand. One small hand moving, an eye in its palm staring blankly at Sak-Tor. In an instant, the Red Clay Warriors along the walls leaped into action. Shadows hidden in the ribs of the vaulted ceiling slid down the walls and darted to engage the devils.

"Coward!" Sak-Tor boomed. A sweep of his arm and three Red Clay Warriors were rubble. The air around him began to howl, a burgeoning cyclone at his feet whipping up dust and bits of red clay. "While the rest of us are choked by the Gray, you sit here and play with your paltry statues. You do not deserve godhood!"

The dingy white marble beneath his feet cracked and shifted. Then the floor in front of him exploded in a cloud of dust and pearly white shrapnel. Khymanir's arms wrapped around himself as shards of rock tore through his skin.

Any Red Clay Warriors or Shadows in front of Sak-Tor were battered to bits and thrown back in pieces. The ground in front of Sak-Tor was a ragged crater, but he cleared the gap in seconds, leaping over it all to land in front of Khymanir's bleeding form.

Hands snapped forward to grab Sak-Tor. To throttle him. Sak-Tor hacked them off in two swings. "You are weak," he hissed, breaking an arm with a club. The crack was wet and satisfying. "You are nothing."

He plunged a sword through the tangle of Khymanir's arms into his fleshy core. Khymanir stiffened, his arms twitching. Then a swarm of hands took Sak-Tor's arm. Drawing him closer. Pushing the blade deeper into Khymanir's body.

"Get off me!" Sak-Tor growled, ripping his arm free and the blade from Khymanir.

Khymanir collapsed in a heap. His arms twisted beneath him or jerking spasmodically. His fingers twitching in quick bursts. Blood poured from Khymanir's core, splashing onto the marble in a crimson cascade. Filling the shallow grooves of the circle beneath him. A red river running through the channels.

The air in the room chilled and became heavy. Kunza recoiled behind the cistern, hoping more than anything that the circles would hold. The air whipped and screamed, enveloping the circle in rushing energy. Sak-Tor stepped back, his weapons raised. "What is this?" he shouted. "Khymanir, you cretin, what have you done?"

The howling wind swirling around the circle's perimeter strengthened. The room grew colder. Kunza could feel energy ripping past him. Drawn to the center of the room and the maelstrom. He leaned against the cistern, the bronze icy against his skin. The air had thinned. It was hard to draw breath.

Khymanir's blood flowed along the floor, dripping into the pool and filling the binding circle. A slow trickle ran along the bottom of the channel.

Sak-Tor charged toward the circle at the center of the room, but the spinning energies rebuffed him like a wall. He screamed in rage and slashed at the churning air. The cyclone had become so dense with energy, the blade bounced off.

When the first trickle of blood had reached the second pool and touched the vessel's toe, a lambent glow like an early morning sunray began to crawl up the vessel's foot. From flowing rune to flowing rune, the light crept upward. And then the other followed suit as the pool continued to fill with blood.

Sak-Tor raged on at the cyclone of pure divine energy. The floor around the circle splitting and bursting. But the maelstrom only grew in intensity. Pressure building within it. Building and building until it could take no more.

Kunza prayed.

CHAPTER 41

Odessa leaped from her entehlo in the middle of a narrow hallway. She and the devils had followed Sak-Tor and his host all the way to the palace, riding through the wake of his destruction. Having split off from the main host in its pillaging and slaughter, she had led them down halls she would rather have forgotten.

The staircase winding down below the palace was cramped. Odessa took the steps two and three at a time, bounding down them, yet she still felt Khara and Remaka and Sansehra at her heels.

At a landing, she stopped before two large double doors. Azdava's study lay behind those doors. Where Azdava had taken her last agonized breath. Where the last part of Odessa's former self had died. Strapped on that table, pumped full of innocent blood.

"Someone should check that room. If anyone's in there, bring them down. We might need them," Odessa said as she began down the stairs again. Part of her had wanted to break the door down herself. Scour the incense-stinking room for any sign of Yakun or Tarik. But the depth of emotion that room stirred in her was too much for her to bear now. She could not afford to lose herself in such a place. Not when a god needed killing.

She raced down the same stairway Tarik had taken her down. Holding her hand as he took her to see the horrors that made Asha-Kalir's foundation. An entirely different Odessa leaped down the steps now. More devil than human.

The stairs terminated into a short hallway. Odessa did not stop in her headlong dash. She merely lowered her ironclad shoulder and charged down the hallway until she was crashing through the heavy bronze door. The door flew open, its lock bursting through the doorframe in an explosion of stone and dust. With the painful memory that was Azdava's study now at her back, she felt strong. She felt unstoppable.

The prison was as massive as she remembered. The cages filled with deformed and mutilated humans were stacked one upon another and lined in rows down the huge room's length. Odessa moved briskly down an aisle, looking not at the wretched beings in their cages but at the intricate network of tubes and pipes snaking along the ceiling not far from where she walked.

She found the cages in which the bleeders were kept. Their wide, lanky bodies stuck with needles from which dangled tubes that ran to the pipes above. The pipes would lead her to what she needed.

All the pipes twisting along the dingy, soot-stained ceiling led to the back of the room. Lined along the back wall was a row of giant cisterns. A network of pipes fed into these cisterns, and larger pipes cut through the ceiling to another level. To Khymanir and his horrific works.

Odessa stepped to the nearest cistern. Its bronze was tarnished and stained.

"What is this place?" Sansehra asked, halfway down the aisle Odessa had come through. "What are these things?"

"Khymanir's perversions," Remaka said. Then to Odessa, she called, "Have you found what you need?"

Odessa did not reply. Instead, she rammed her iron fist against the cistern, leaving a wide dent. Another strike and her fist punched through its side. Blood splashed around her arm as she thrust it to the shoulder inside the cistern.

Immediately, a current of intense power arced through her arm. She gritted her teeth as the blood's energy, concentrated in the cistern, moved through her like an unceasing bolt of lightning shooting through her arm and to her heart. It was pain and ecstasy in equal measures. It was power, old and stale but in such great supply its potency was immaterial.

Blood was steadily pouring down from the hole in the cistern and splashing into a pool around her boots. Her arm siphoned the blood's energy like a copper rod in a lightning storm, the power streaming into her. More and more every second. Until her every body part was filled with furious, unrelenting power. Until she thought she might rupture and burst. But still she held her arm inside the cistern. Taking as much as she could. A pulsing sensation battered the back of her eyes. An astounding pressure swelled against her temples. Her blood burned and her body screamed in ecstatic torment. Her fingers were trembling. The muscles in her neck pulled taut. Her chest heaved with her every quick, pained breath. But she could not stop. There was too much power to be drawn. And she needed it all. Every bit that could be had.

A terrible crash and rumble came from high above her head. Jarring her loose from her enraptured invigoration. She heard her name being called. Footsteps approaching behind her. With a reluctant snarl, she ripped her arm free. Iron grated against bronze. The blood, unstoppered, surged out onto the floor as she turned toward the sound of her name, flicking the blood from her arm. The channels along the iron arm glowed red and fiery. Sated and ready.

"Godsdamn, I thought we had lost you for a moment," Sansehra said, stepping forward. But Odessa's attention was focused beyond Sansehra. Coming up the aisle of cages was Khara. Tarik walked in front of her, his arm twisted behind his back. He stumbled ahead of her, his head lolling a bit. The bright red of a fresh bruise swelling on his face. A gash over his cheekbone had begun to trickle.

Odessa moved past Sansehra. Her arm was afire. The usual pulsing thrum was replaced with bright explosions of purest power. Flames roared in her chest. Her lungs a pair of bellows spurring the flames into a hellish conflagration. Her iron fingers ground together into a tight, straining fist. She walked briskly, nearly charging at Tarik.

"You son of a bitch," she said through bared teeth. Khara stopped Tarik where they stood at the end of the cages. Odessa charged to meet them, her arms pumping at her sides. Tarik looked up. Their eyes met. His eyes a deep, dark brown. Full of fear. Odessa wanted to take his head and crush it between her palms. Or pummel his sharp, handsome face until it was nothing but red, bone-flecked pulp. "Tarik, you son of a bitch. You fucking snake."

Tarik struggled against Khara as Odessa stepped close to him. His mouth opened to protest, but Odessa's iron hand gripped his throat before he could utter a sound. Her fingers trembled, aching to tighten. To rip through the soft skin of his neck and crush all that was underneath it. Blood pounded through every vein and capillary in her arm. The fire within it clamoring to burst free and envelope his head. Leave him screaming as the skin of his face peeled and his fat rendered to grease and sizzled down his chest. Just as she had killed his master, Azdava. Her mind was filled with alternating images. Tarik's soft, expectant expression in that frozen instant before they first kissed. Azdava's face as the fire gnawed the flesh away from her skull. Her popped eyes running in rivers of boiling sludge down her charred cheeks. The way her mouth had fallen open as the skin and muscle around her jaw peeled away. Mouth open as if screaming, but by then she could no longer make a noise.

Odessa squeezed his throat, leaning forward with bared teeth. "I should just fucking kill you right here." Then she released him, shoving him into Khara's solid frame. He leaned forward, his arm twisting further. He coughed and heaved and hacked up a gout of clear vomit.

Blood pounded in Odessa's ears. A roaring chorus telling her to kill Tarik.

She closed her eyes a moment and composed herself. Fortifying herself against the temptation that sang in the booming of her invigorated blood. "Stop that damned coughing," Odessa snapped. "You have work to do."

Tarik looked at her, his eyes wet. "I'm sorry." He leaned away from Khara's grip again and winced. "I didn't want to do what they did to you. But I didn't have a choice. You must believe me. I never wanted it to be like this."

A gust of hot air streamed through Odessa's nostrils as she stared down the sniveling Tarik. "I don't give a shit what you wanted. Just shut your mouth and do what I tell you."

Khara pushed him forward, and Odessa relayed to him in curt, pitiless orders what she required. He limped away and Khara followed closely, her eyes narrowed and her blade unsheathed. He found a length of tube and began his work.

Above them came another crash. And a loud roar began, steadily increasing in intensity.

"We cannot tarry long," Remaka said. "Sak-Tor could be killing Khymanir as we speak."

CHAPTER 42

When the maelstrom had reached its peak, it exploded in a rush of energy unlike anything Kunza had ever seen. The churning energy burst outward, knocking even Sak-Tor backward a few stumbling steps. Then there was a roar as the collected energy poured out along the path of the blood-filled channel and struck the fully lit vessel.

It was like a hurricane rushing into an endless tunnel. The roaring energy poured into the vessel for what seemed an eternity. The script work covering its entire body glowed with increasing intensity, becoming so bright, Kunza could feel the heat on his face even at a distance.

Then, without warning, the rush of energy stopped. Tapering off to nothing in an instant. In the absence of the roar, Kunza's ears buzzed. From the vessel radiated a powerful presence. It was like standing next to a massive fire. Waves of bone-chilling, stomach-churning power crashed over Kunza, and he fell to his knees. It was a familiar sensation but stronger than he had ever felt in his dealings with Talara.

Sak-Tor stood gazing with suspicion at the huge vessel. It was nearly double his height. His face was confused and enraged. Then as if he sensed it in the air like a terrible scent, realization dawned on him. Cold and dreadful realization.

"No. It can't be." Sak-Tor took a step backward, his weapons raised before him defensively. His sons, having destroyed the last of the Red Clay Warriors and Shadows, stared dumbly, their eyes shifting uneasily from their father and the vessel before them. "Khymanir, you bastard."

The vessel moved. First its fingers, then its hands. Its arms raised and fell. "It is strange having physical form again." Its voice was a low rumble. The clay giant looked with burning blue eyes at its hand and the intricate rune work glowing upon it. "It is cumbersome."

The giant's gaze drifted from its own hand to the devils crowded in the center of the room. "Son of Ogé, the Banished, why do you not kneel before your better?"

"Aséshassa, you bastard. You should have stayed where you belonged, far away from me." Sak-Tor raised a cyclone around him. He half-crouched, poised to strike. A malicious smile split his lips. "You and the others killed my father. Kinkiller, you would have been wise to not come within my reach."

Aséshassa's arm rose, the gems and bronze glittering in its hand. "Begone."

A blast of force erupted from the giant palm. Sak-Tor's sons were torn apart, their dismembered bodies and pieces of scale armor thrown across the room. Sak-Tor, with his magic, was not torn to pieces, only thrown onto his back near the shattered doorway.

"I will give you one more chance." Aséshassa took a step and left the blood-filled pool. His head grazed the high vaulted ceiling and dust rained down upon his shoulders. "Kneel before the Sage of Bronze and swear your fealty."

Sak-Tor had risen to his knees. His hands reached, found a club and a sword on the ground where they'd fallen from his grip, and picked them up. "You killed my father. I will swear nothing but my vengeance upon you." Sak-Tor rose to his feet. Blood trickled from scrapes all across his back and limbs.

"So be it," Aséshassa said, totally devoid of any emotion. He raised his hand again. Sak-Tor leaped forward, driven by the wind. His sword flashed through the air.

CHAPTER 43

With great reluctance, Odessa let Tarik flee relatively unscathed. Khara followed him for a while, her bladed hand on his shoulder, asking him where Yakun went. Odessa paid it no mind. She turned away from Tarik as he ran down the hallway at the top of the stair. The bronze drum strapped to her back sloshed as she turned, upsetting her balance a bit. A tube ran from the drum to a needle stuck through a gap in the iron gauntlet. Her bones thrummed with power like a struck tuning fork.

Khara came beside Odessa, her face hard. "I might know where he went."

"It doesn't matter," Odessa said. She was about to say more when a huge crash shook the palace.

"What was that?" Khara asked.

Remaka made her way to the head of the clustered Sisters. Their entehlos had been shut into a room full of mats and a tea set; she moved easily through the tight hallway. "Form up. We move now."

They were nearly to the end of the hall when the next crash came, louder and more explosive than the other, followed by the rumble and thud of falling rubble. The Sisters hurried down the hall toward the sound, boots ringing out on the tile.

They came to a large hallway of white stone with stained glass windows bearing the visage of gods on either side. A massive hole gaped in one of the walls and a pile of rubble was strewn across the hall. A trail of blood on white marble, drips and smears of it, led down the hall and around a corner into the palace's lobby. The Sisters followed it to the shattered remains of the front door.

Sak-Tor limped, bleeding from a number of gashes all over his body, supported by a few Torva warriors. They had almost reached the skull dominating the plaza. More warriors were filling the plaza. Odessa and the Sisters stood at the top of the palace steps, sudden indecision freezing them for an instant.

"Sak-Tor!" Remaka strode down the stairs, undaunted. Her long glaive held in a high stance, poised to strike, as quick as a viper, at any moment. "The Daughters of Ana Yuma will no longer abide your tyranny. You have persecuted and raped our kind for generations. Generations of women have suffered in your name." She reached the bottom of the stairs, the Sisters and Odessa, jarred from their stupor, followed close behind. "Your empire is built upon the backs of women and now you shall die by their hand."

Sak-Tor spun and roughly leaned against a warrior's shoulder. "Remaka, you treasonous bitch, now is not the time!"

The warriors around Sak-Tor massed around him and began to surround the Sisters as they descended the steps. All of them tensed and ready to charge. Eyes full of hate. The Sisters formed a tight wedge with Remaka at the tip. Odessa pushed to the front of the Sisters, blood sloshing on her back. She raised her hand and funneled the pounding energy that reverberated through her into the palm of her hand. Letting the pressure build for just a moment. At the first lunging step of the devils before her, she let the fire loose.

A gout of flame blossomed before her, swallowing up most of the devils before her. Red-hot heat filled the plaza, the concussive blast shattering windows and knocking to the ground those devils who were spared immolation. The Sisters charged into the plaza, leaping over charred bodies to kill those who remained.

For a moment, Odessa was light-headed. Suddenly drained. Then the blood pumping through the tube into her arm was pouring fiery vitality into her. The pounding thrum returned. The power arcing through her was steady and exhilarating.

Sak-Tor rose to his full height, pushing off the devil he had leaned upon. The wind around him began to churn. The stones beneath him cracked. Odessa reached out, feeling the overwhelming electricity in the air. His magic was like a swarm of locusts all around her. She raised her arm and funneled more throbbing heat into it, then released it in a blast like a long, drawn-out exhalation. Holding that release as the electric buzz around her dampened to a low, almost unrecognizable drone. She could feel something intangible inside her, straining painfully like a pulled muscle.

The Sisters charged Sak-Tor as his wind died. But he was unfazed by the impotence of his magic. A club in one hand and a sword in the other, he met them in the middle of the plaza. Remaka ducked beneath his swinging club and slashed at his ankle. But he was fast. One of his empty hands snapped forward to take her by the head and she was forced back before she could draw blood.

As Remaka fell back, Sansehra and Khara leaped forward. Sansehra slashed at his extended hand, slicing into his wrist before darting back. Khara slashed at his exposed ankle before leaping away from his club. But Sak-Tor's skin was hard. Their cuts had been shallow ones. But they had drawn blood nonetheless. The Sisters whooped and shouted, encouraged by the sight of the god's blood.

Odessa alternated between brief moments of lightheadedness and dimmed vision, and extended moments of heart-pounding, teeth-grinding euphoria. Her grasp on Sak-Tor's magic was a tenuous one. But she had it. She could hold it at bay. As long as there was blood in the drum, she could do it.

There came from behind her the sounds of footsteps and shouts of alarm. Odessa whipped around to see a slew of devils pouring down the steps toward her. Spears thrusting down at her. She released a nullifying exhalation and drew what power she could into her arm in the span of a second. A blast of fire consumed the devils charging down the stairs. Their burning bodies came tumbling down the steps. A few continued running until their legs collapsed beneath them.

In the plaza there were a great number of screams. Odessa turned to see Sisters torn apart by a blast of stone erupting from the plaza floor. More than half of the Sisters were thrown back, some bleeding and some missing limbs. Sansehra landed on her back, half of her face missing. Blood jetted from a gash in her neck. She was writhing and coughing blood. A mutilated hand reached to staunch the bleeding but there was little she could do.

Khara and Remaka had both retreated before the blast and only suffered a few scrapes. They and the other dozen or so Sisters still on their feet charged as Odessa took hold of Sak-Tor's magic and smothered it with prejudice. Choking it until there was nothing but a tiny buzz of residual static in the air. *You bastard.* She focused on his huge frame as he swung and hacked at the elusive Sisters. But at the corner of her eye, she could see Sansehra had stopped moving.

Down the road beneath the plaza, Odessa could hear nearby battle. Hooves and the crash of armored bodies. Lightheadedness swelled for a moment and she swayed before the fatigue ebbed and bright euphoria returned. If more devils were coming, they would need to finish this quickly.

Remaka was elusive, slashing and stabbing while dancing away from Sak-Tor's blows. But Khara was a wroth force to be reckoned with. She drew in close to Sak-Tor, beneath his swinging limbs, hacking a finger from an approaching hand before sidestepping and punching her blade into his side. Blood gushed from the wound, a river of bright scarlet. Sak-Tor screamed and swung his bleeding hand. Catching Khara in the side and throwing her across the plaza. She struck the ground hard and rolled limply across the cobblestone.

"Khara!" Odessa shouted, taking a step toward her prone form. But as she did, her hold on Sak-Tor's magic slipped. She froze and bore down on it again before it could rise above a distant drone. His wellspring of magic was seemingly infinite. Anything but her full, undivided attention would allow it to geyser out again. Her arm shook with impotent rage. She could not draw her eyes from Khara's motionless body. *You fucking bastard. I'll kill you myself, you son of a bitch.*

Sak-Tor's club pummeled a Sister to the ground, a gout of blood splashing from her open mouth. He grabbed at another as she stabbed into the meat of his calf. His hand around her head tightened. Her body convulsed for a moment then went limp before he threw her at Remaka. Remaka dodged the corpse and darted forward, ducking the swing of his club again and slashing a wide gash in his wrist before driving the blade of glaive into his chest. The blade sunk deep between his ribs. Sak-Tor gasped raggedly.

One of Sak-Tor's lower hands took hold of the glaive's shaft. Remaka immediately released it and leaped backwards. But Sak-Tor had expected that.

His sword swung in a blur. It caught Remaka in the side and cleaved her in two. Her two halves spun through the air and struck the ground across the plaza. Her body rolled a fair distance, her entrails spilling out and trailing behind her.

Odessa stood, helpless and in shock. Another wave of weakness came and this time she thought it was not at all physical. It was defeat. It was despair. *We've lost. Sak-Tor's going to kill them all.* But she held the magic at bay still. She had to.

The remaining Sisters charged Sak-Tor in unison, screaming their fury in an assault of curses. Sak-Tor was slowing, bleeding heavily and wheezing. But still he kept the Sisters at bay. He cut one Sister down at the knees and kicked another across the plaza.

In a matter of moments, more than a dozen were dead. Only a few remained standing. Faces grave and drawn in furious scowls. But there was defeat in their eyes. Resignation. All they could do was die fighting.

"Retreat!" Odessa shouted. "He's bleeding to death, just retreat!" Even speaking made her hold on the magic waver. But she had to save at least some of them. If she could not fight, she could do that.

The Sisters ignored her cries. Gods had a remarkable capacity for healing. They had to kill him now. End him this day or not at all.

Sak-Tor's club struck another Sister, her bones splintering before her body struck the plaza wall.

They're being slaughtered. They're being slaughtered and there's nothing I can do. Odessa's eyes misted and she hated herself for it. Hated her helplessness. If only she could hold the magic at bay and fight. How many might she have saved if she could do that?

Then came a brash horn blast from just outside the plaza walls. The sound reverberated throughout the plaza and Odessa's heart stood still. Her fiery, thrumming blood went cold in an instant. *The rest of his army. They're coming.*

From where she stood she could see nothing through the destroyed plaza gates. But as she looked, she did notice something. Khara slowly rising to her feet. A sheet of blood pouring down her face from one of her horns. She held a hand pressed to her side as she swayed on her feet.

Oh gods, they're going to tear her apart. Before Odessa could move or even shout, a cry came from beyond the walls: "Sisters! Incoming!"

The few Sisters still fighting immediately leaped away from Sak-Tor. From the gateway came a few Sisters carrying jars the size of melons. They threw the jars at Sak-Tor. He raised an arm to block his face, and a jar crashed into it, shattering and splashing thick, dark sludge all over his arm and face. Other jars struck his legs and the ground around him.

"Bitches!" Sak-Tor shouted. Odessa stopped him from saying any more. She dropped her hold on his magic and sent a gout of flame toward him in an instant. The flame was weak and a sickly red, but it crossed the plaza all the same. The sludge caught flame at the briefest touch of her fire.

Odessa dampened his magic at the same moment the sludge on his face blossomed in yellow tongues of furious fire. He slapped at the fire but it did him no good. It only spread the flames to his hands.

In seconds, fire consumed his whole body. Khara limped to Odessa's side as they watched him stumble back and forth, still trying to beat the flames away. His shin struck the skull's raised platform and he toppled, falling into the skull. Its domed brow gave beneath his weight and he crashed through it with a dry, brittle crash. His massive legs kicked pitifully. He screamed and raged, his voice becoming wetter and more guttural as his punctured lung filled with blood.

After a few moments, his sweeping legs slowed and then finally stilled. Odessa held her extended exhalation for a while, afraid to let it go. When she finally did, there was no geyser of magic. There was no static in the air. There was nothing. No magic. But there was something in the air. Something exquisite and enthralling.

Khara braced Odessa as she swayed from the strain. She relaxed in Khara's arms for a moment, letting the drum replenish her. The Sisters' reinforcements were pouring into the plaza. Taking defensive positions and planning their exfiltration.

"I'm fine," Odessa said after a moment, patting Khara's gauntleted hand. She stood straight, unassisted, the strength back in her limbs. A few steady steps and she plucked the needle from her arm and slipped the drum from her back. It struck the ground with a metallic thud.

Sak-Tor's corpse was still burning, but she had to get close to it. The dead god's life dissipating in the air was a heady intoxicant. Her arm burned with pleasure as she drew nearer.

Khara followed closely behind her. "Odessa?"

Odessa climbed onto the skull's platform. Shards of thick brain case littered the ground around Sak-Tor's collapsed corpse. Fire flickered from gobs of sludge. Her head throbbed. Her head filled entirely with the air so rife with the captivating sensation of a god's life. Some of Sak-Tor's life energy hovered around her arm, hanging like a condensing vapor. But she needed more.

Stepping around the burning corpse, she knelt beside his charred side. He had burned to the gristle and bone, and still he burned around his head, neck, and arms. She saw the wound Remaka had left between his ribs and punched her ironclad fist into it. The ribs bent and snapped as her fist plunged into his chest cavity. Divine blood filled the runic channels along her arm. Filled her with power so far removed from the impure blood she had pumped into her body.

It was like she had thrust her arm into the sun. Light burst in her vision and she felt an immense pressure build within her. Rising to the point of rupture in an instant. Stabbing pain arced through her entire body. Her muscles spasmed and convulsed, ravaged by sudden agony. She couldn't breathe. There was too much power flowing into her. Her body felt as if it were going to explode. Her very self about to fall apart.

She fell back, ripping her arm free. Aftershocks of pain lanced through her. Her skin itched and her blood was unbearably hot. But after the immediate pain receded, she felt strong. Stronger than she had ever felt in her entire life. Her muscles twitched now with overwhelming, unbridled power.

Khara rushed to her side. "Are you all right?"

Odessa nodded, still out of breath. "Yeah. I'm fine."

They were quiet for a bit. Khara looked at Sak-Tor's corpse and shook her head. "I cannot believe we did it. I can't believe he's really dead."

Odessa looked at Khara, then away. When she'd seen Khara be thrown, she was sure the Torva warrior had been dead. Now looking at Khara, a swell of relief and joy struck her like a punch in the chest. But that joy was short-lived. She remembered all that had been lost to get them here. "I'm sorry about Sansehra. And Remaka. And everyone. I'm sorry. I wished I could have done more."

Khara quieted her with a look and a gentle hand on her arm. "Now is not the time for mourning. That will come later." Khara took Odessa's hand and began to stand. "Now, we have an old man to catch."

Odessa was stunned, but she stood and followed Khara's lead. With her body vibrating with newfound might, she found there was nothing more she wanted in that moment than to get ahold of Yakun. Nothing else at all.

CHAPTER 44

Y ou are Talara's pet?" Aséshassa asked Kunza amid the destruction of the workroom.

Kunza, still kneeling as he had since Sak-Tor had been blown out of the room, bowed his head lower and said, "I am her Priest of Ashes, my Sage."

"Your title does not interest me," the god said. His every word shook in Kunza's bones. "What interests me is Talara's work. Why has she not incarnated as she had planned?"

Fear like that of a mouse in a lion's den grasped Kunza's heart and squeezed the strength from it. "I am afraid, my Sage, that neither of our potential vessels have reached maturity yet. But the one that we have the most hope for is useful in other ways."

"Slowing the Gray?"

Kunza nodded at the floor. "Yes, my Sage."

"A useless endeavor." The Sage of Bronze took an earth-shaking step. "Come with me, human. You will show me this Asha-Kalir." Another booming step. Kunza rose, still averting his gaze. "And we have Ogé's bastard spawn to be rid of as well. There is much to do and so very little time."

Kunza's heart sank as he followed the god within the clay giant host. He prayed to Talara for strength and realized he missed her cold embrace so very much.

CHAPTER 45

Ayana returned to Kalaro, weary and weak. She had spent weeks destroying hundreds of spore columns. She had not slept more than an hour or two in almost three weeks. Her body ached constantly. Her soaks in a shallow tub of blood did nothing to alleviate her pains. The bleeder they had brought to the camp outside Noyo had died four days ago and she had not been able to soak since. Her pains had only accumulated and compounded.

Even now, as she walked down the path toward the village, she could feel the Gray in her throat and nostrils. Whenever she coughed or sneezed, those fine white particles were in her snot. She had left Noyo days ago and still the Gray filth lingered.

She was tired and homesick. She had never felt more alone in her entire life. Her mute beastfolk followed close behind her as they always did, but they were not good company. Their presence served only to make her feel more alone.

When she reached the village, her people bowed and gave polite greeting, but that was all. Everything formal and in passing. She felt an alien in her own village.

The Elder's Lodge was quiet at midday. Many of the Elders had died, and those who still lived were busy in the temple. Inside the lodge it was cool. Ayana stood outside her mother's room a moment, her voice suddenly caught in her throat.

"Mama?" she said hoarsely.

There was no reply. She pushed past the curtain and stepped inside the room. Her emaciated mother lay on her rushes as she always did. Back to the door. Her chest rising and falling so slightly as to be nearly imperceptible.

"Mama? It's me. Ayana."

"Leave me," her mother croaked.

Ayana swallowed a lump trying to form in her throat. "Mama, I've been gone for weeks now. I just returned."

"You shouldn't have." Her mother's voice was dry and brittle. A constant, hissing whisper. "Should have stayed gone like your sister. The bad one."

"Mama, stop. Please." The lump returned to Ayana's throat.

"You and her. You should have been the ones who died. Not little Kimi. Kimi was always good. She never cried. She was always so good."

Ayana's eyes watered. "Mama, don't say that." She reached a hand out, desperate to touch her mother. Glean some semblance of motherly love from the woman who had once held her hand and kissed her before bed. As her fingers drew near, her mother recoiled, spinning around to face her.

"Don't touch me! Don't touch me with those hands. Those hands are death! They're surrounded in death!"

Ayana's vision was blurred by the rush of tears. "I-I just need you. I need you, Mama. Can't you just hold me? Please? I feel so alone and—"

"Get away from me! Go away! Leave me be! I don't want you! You're not my daughter anymore! You're his! You're not mine! Kimi was mine! You're not mine!" Her mother's voice rose to a high shriek. She pressed her knobby back against the wall, slamming the back of her head as she cried. "Go away! Go away!"

"Mama, stop!" Ayana grabbed her mother by the shoulders and pulled her from the wall, wrapping her in a tight embrace. "Mama, stop it. You have to stop this." Her mother was tense against her, pushing away. Shoving Ayana's chest. But Ayana held on. Hoping that her love would get through her mother's illness. Would rekindle something within her. And fix what had been broken by pain.

After a while, her mother sagged against her. All the fight leaving her.

Then Ayana smelled it. And felt it.

The stench of rot. Beneath the skin of her arms, her mother's flesh had begun to putrefy. Horrified, Ayana recoiled to find her mother's face and chest similarly rotted. The side of her mother's face that had been pressed to her chest was now tinged a foul green and black and a hunk of melted cheek had fallen off, clinging to Ayana's robe.

A scream unlike anything she had ever unleashed ripped through Ayana's throat. An inhuman scream of pure horror and revulsion. She screamed until her lungs were empty. Until her mother was a desiccated husk in her arms.

When the first people to hear her screams arrived, she was done crying. She had fallen silent. Her eyes glazed by tears and numb oblivion.

Townspeople milled about her. Asking her what happened. But she heard none of it.

She was truly and utterly alone.

ABOUT THE AUTHOR

Jeremy Knop is the author of All That Is Holy, a series that began on Royal Road as an experiment with serial fiction. He spent many years honing his craft, but it wasn't until after a yearlong battle with cancer that he truly pursued publication. Knop lives on a small farm in Michigan with his beautiful wife, Ashley, and their two dogs. Visit his website at www.jeremyknop.com.